D1527456

# THE FORSAKEN SON

## ARLA BAKER SERIES BOOK 8

**M.L. ROSE**

**THE FORSAKEN SON**

*Copyright © 2021 by M.L. Rose*

# Table of Contents

# CHAPTER 1

Susan was feeling drowsy. She only had two drinks, and that too her favourite white wine. Sancerre, 2014 vintage. Her head fell back on the car seat, and she stared out the window at the sky with dreamy eyes.

The promise of Easter was in the air. Signs of green life were appearing on the trees, and birdsong had returned in the early mornings. The snowy shackles of a silent winter were relaxing, melting into the wet earth. It was past sunset, and the mauve sky was deepening into shades of violet and blue. Looming darkened the approaching night, suffocating the last vestiges of light.

Susan didn't know where she was, but she trusted her companion. All the colours seemed to seep into one, the brown branches now bearing precious leaves, the yellow streetlights hesitantly flickering into life, and the maroon shadows of evening.

Susan blinked, and the scenery turned upside down, sky below, the ground above. She squeezed her eyes with the fingers and sat up straight. There, that was better. She turned to her companion.

"Where are we?" Her voice was thick, and it sounded unnatural even to her own ears.

Her companion didn't answer. The car took a left. The scenery looked familiar to Susan, but she wasn't sure of the location. Dense clumps of trees appeared on both sides, and they hung over each other on the road, creating an archway of foliage. It was visible because of the streetlights, and beyond the pale penumbra of lights, the inky night sky was clotted, faceless like a mask.

Susan's mouth was dry. "Can I have a drink?", She asked.

"There's none in the car," her companion said.

Susan said something, but she couldn't make out the sound of her own voice. Her head rolled back on the seat, and she stared out the windows again. Flashes of light passed overhead, interspersed by black shadows. Her eyes fluttered close, and all she could hear was the sound of her own breathing.

Her body gave a jolt, and she realised the car had stopped. She heard the door slam and her eyes opened. Then, a gust of fresh air as her door opened. She strained her eyes. There was a streetlight close to the car, and it shone down on the figure that had opened her door.

"Get out," her companion said in a gruff voice.

Susan was confused.

"Why? Where are we?"

Her companion stared at her for a few seconds. Then a hand reached out and grabbed her below the shoulders. She leaned against the car as the door slammed shut. Susan frowned.

"What's going on?" She asked.

She didn't get a response. The strong pair of arms supported her shoulders, and she leaned into her companion. There, that felt better. She could rest her head on the strong shoulder.

She inhaled the freshness of the open air, a touch of cold, mingling with the faintly acidic, lemony taste of the wine at the back of a throat. Strange, Susan thought to herself. She couldn't ever remember getting this drunk after two glasses. Admittedly, they were big glasses. And yes, she was intent on getting drunk. But this much?

Maybe she shouldn't have drunk so much wine after abstinence of three months. She was determined to lose weight, and alcohol had gone out of the window with her new diet. Maybe that's why she was feeling it so much. Well, the new diet had worked. She had lost 3 kg and dropped a dress size.

The shoes were crunching gravel, and soon she heard a different sound. It was the lapping of water. The smell of fresh, wet earth was strong now, infusing with the scent of flowers she couldn't identify. The air seemed cooler, and it made her eyes blink open. A row of yellow orbs glistened in the distance like a shimmering garland suspended mid-air. It seemed so far away. It took her some time to realise she was staring at streetlamps across the waters she was now facing.

Susan was confused. Once again, she turned to her companion and asked where they were. And again, she got no response. Her legs were heavy, and her head felt heavier. She could barely walk. She slid down the grassy verge as her companion got closer to the water.

Her feet squelched on wet ground, and she yelped when water splashed against her ankles. She was wearing jeans, and it turned soggy instantly, sticking to her legs. The water was freezing.

She straightened herself with an effort and resisted by pulling back. "Hey. I'm not going in there."

She stood her ground and breathed heavily. The evening breeze murmured softly over the black waters, and whispered in her ears. Her vision shook and moved, and she tried to make her legs move but found they were stuck in the mud.

Her companion had let her go and was watching her intently. Susan wanted to walk back to the car, but she had no strength. She forced herself to move, and with a gasp, she fell. Her bum landed with a splash on the water, and she was soaked immediately. She cried out, her hands digging into muddy waters.

She grabbed the hand that her companion offered, clutching it blindly. Then she felt both of her companion's hands on her arms, dragging her deeper into the water.

3

"No," Susan screamed, but her voice was weak. She felt water splashed against her chin, then rise up to her nose. Her companion was strong, relentless, pulling her deeper with consummate ease.

Susan coughed and spluttered as water went inside her mouth. The brackish, bitter taste filled her mouth. She was choking. She tried to speak, but her words were now submerged, as was most of her body. As Susan drowned, her last thought was that her companion would save her.

Then Susan couldn't think anymore, and the world turned black like the water.

# CHAPTER 2

Douglas Rand, known as Dougie to his friends, licked the white Rizla paper as he pinched, then rolled the corners expertly. He put the joint to his lips and lit the other end. He took a deep drag, held his breath for a few seconds then let it go. He felt the hit a few seconds later, a warm surge that rushed to his head, making him dizzy.

He loved the light-headedness that the first joint of the day provided. Not that he smoked that much. Dougie was busy with his electricals business, and it was flourishing. He only had time for a joint when he came out angling with his mate Sham.

The grass verge at the edges of the river was still damp, and they had bought their rubber mats and inflatable chairs. Sham, short for Ittesham, was busy fixing the baits to their fishing rods' hook ends. Dougie took a couple of drags and then handed it to Sham, who took it with a mumble of thanks.

Dougie stretched his arms over his head, then massaged his neck. Yes, mother nature was opening her arms again, and Dougie was most certainly up for a hug. It had been a long, hard winter. He was working like a dog, and today was his first day off. The sun was warm on his back, and although a light chill permeated the air, especially near the pond, it was tolerable.

Dougie had told his wife he was out on a job, and it wasn't a complete lie. He did work in the morning, but when Sham rang and asked him to come out angling, he couldn't resist. Dougie loved fishing. There was nothing quite like watching the waters, trying to guess what his scaly prey was doing underneath. Dougie was fascinated by fish. His proudest moment was catching a giant twelve-pound carp at the Coln River in

North London. For two years, that had stood as a record. The fish was so big it had actually dragged him into the water. It had taken two of them to pull the fish into the net.

Dougie grinned as Sham handed him a fishing rod. The Clapham ponds were not known for big fish. But they did have carp, and a three or four-pound fish was not unheard of. It also had trout and the red-striped fish called Sparks, which Dougie loved catching. He let them all go, of course, after photos had been taken.

He looked to the jetty, where their rowing boat was tied. They had been fishing for one hour now and not had much luck. During the winter, the fish stayed in the middle of the pond, where it was warmer. Perhaps that's why they weren't biting. Sooner or later, Dougie knew they would have to go out on the boat. He didn't feel like rowing today, and the cannabis had gone to his head. He wanted to relax and just watch the water for tell-tale bubbles. It was hypnotic at times, and he loved it. He really didn't feel like rowing and was hoping that Sham would do it.

Rod in hand, Dougie rose to his feet. "Would you mind rowing?" He looked at his friend hopefully.

Sham stood and stretched. He had less of the joint, so Dougie assumed he would have more energy. He was right. Sham agreed to row, and the two of them clambered onto the boat. They had cleaned the boat earlier. It was an old wooden thing, which stayed in the shed in Sham's garden shed most of the year. Sham was a carpenter, and he looked after the boat well.

Dougie watched the water as the rowing blades sunk into it. Green trees rose in the dark, knotted clumps all around the bank. This was a remote part of Clapham Common, and the ponds took up a big area. Three of the ponds were also interconnected, and it was possible to row from one to the other. The water got deeper as they rode out towards the middle. Sham stopped rowing, and they floated.

Dougie flipped a line into the water. It landed with a soft plop and disappeared beneath. He accepted the offered spliff from Sham with a murmur of thanks. Sham had one rolled spliff in each ear. He was well prepared. They also had a flask of water and biscuits in case they got the munchies.

Dougie's eyes were caught by a flicker of movement to his right. There was a pull on the line, and it stretched tautly. Dougie tensed. This was a big catch; he could tell by the tension on the line. He stretched backward, his spine jerking straight.

"Whoa bro, what the hell is this?" he exclaimed to Sham, who was also looking at the water.

"Give it some slack," Sham urged. "If it's a bigg'un, then you need to tire it out."

"But it's not playing, though. Just sitting there," Dougie's face was tight with exertion. The pressure on his arms was growing, and he knew this was a big carp, maybe one of those mythical ten-kilo beasts only seen in the big rivers.

"Reel it in, bro," Sham said. "Might be too big." He dipped his oar in the murky water, moving the boat to the left, so they faced the big catch.

Dougie pulled hard, his feet pushing against the woodwork, the butt of the fishing road firm between his legs. The line was bent to almost breaking point. Then suddenly, he felt the tension ease. He wheeled the reeler gleefully, bringing the mammoth catch up. He grinned. He could sell photos of this big kahuna in the angler magazines.

"Here we go," he shouted.

Both men stared at the near opaque water, waiting for the fish to splash up. Dougie narrowed his eyes as he saw something unusual floating on the water. It was a strand of seaweed, he thought, and the strands grew in number.

Surprised, he frowned. The tendrils of the seaweed floated into view. It was strange because weeds were not common in the deep waters out here. Weeds grew closer to the bank, but Dougie had never seen any so far out into the pond.

His mouth opened in surprise as he realised what he was looking at. Then a cold fear sank like a fist into the pits of the stomach. Nausea churned in his guts as bile rose in his throat.

It wasn't seaweed; it was human hair. The hair was splayed out like a halo around a bloated, floating figure. The face was puffy beyond recognition, and other parts of the body had also started to swell. Dougie heard a choking, guttural sound, and he looked up to see Sham's ashen face, staring at the corpse.

Before their terrified eyes, the corpse floated closer to the boat. Dougie could taste the bile at the back of his throat, and his heart was hammering like a piston. Now, he could also smell the putrid stench from the decomposing corpse.

"Move," he croaked, but Sham needed no encouragement. The paddles splashed noisily in the still water, taking the boat away from the floating corpse.

# CHAPTER 3

Detective Chief Inspector Arla Baker was staring fondly at her phone. On the screen, she could see her daughter, Nicole, playing with her mother-in-law Rita. Rita had taught Nicole a nursery rhyme, and as she sang the tune, Nicole pretended to lie down and fall asleep. Then she jumped up and started hopping as the song came to an end. Arla laughed and clapped her hand as Nicole took a bow, and the proud grandmother beamed.

"Well done, Darling." She blew kisses at the screen while Nicole studied her seriously, probably wondering why mummy was staring at her from a screen.

A knock on the door disturbed the happy family time. But Arla was at work, and she had to respond. She bid them a hurried goodbye and hung up. She sat back in the office armchair and asked whoever was knocking to come in.

The tall, wide-shouldered figure of Inspector Harry Mehta entered. He shut the door with a soft click and ambled over. Harry had recovered his dapper, suave ways now that Nicole was older, and he was getting more sleep.

His light coffee-coloured cheeks were smooth-shaven again, and he was back to dressing like the Eliot Ness of Clapham police station, as Arla liked to call him. Even the silk, Paisley pattern handkerchief on the right pocket of his blue suit was perfectly done. The tips of his black Oxford brogues gleamed. Harry perched himself on the edge of Arla's desk, and it dipped alarmingly. Harry stood, raising his eyebrows. Arla smirked at him.

"Getting fat, aren't you?"

"Does my butt look big in this suit?" Harry shot back, did a twirl, and stopped with his butt close to Arla's face. She reached out and slapped his arse, which pleased him immensely. Harry was always up for some hanky-panky in the office. The man was incorrigible.

He grinned like a mischievous schoolboy, his handsome face creasing up with laughter. His skin was smooth enough for flies to slip on, and she wanted to touch his cheeks, draw him closer. But she also knew the handsome devil was here for a reason.

He put his hands on his waist and gazed at her critically. "You enjoyed that, didn't you?"

Arla narrowed her eyes at him. "As your boss, I should be reporting you for sexual harassment."

Harry gaped at her. "You complain about me? Who slapped whose arse?" He came closer till he towered above her chair. Arla remained seated, looking up at him. He still made her quiver inside. She could smell his aftershave. Harry usually put on enough for five men, not one. He positively reeked for miles.

She could reach out and touch his legs but refrained. The thought of those muscular legs wrapped around hers sent a wave of heat pooling low in her belly, making her want to squeeze her thighs together. Their passionate lovemaking had returned, and Harry had made it clear he wanted another child. A boy, to be precise. She had to smile at that. Typical man, Harry was.

He bent at the waist, bringing his face close to hers. "All slap and no tickle, Detective Inspector Baker?" He whispered. He reached out a hand, trying to feel her breasts, and she feigned shock, slapping his hand away.

"You know where my fingers tickled you last night..."

Arla shot upright from her chair. She glared at him as a wave of crimson flared up from her neck.

10

"Shut up," she hissed, her eyes cutting to the door. It remained shut, luckily. And hopefully, none of her team was listening with the ear to the door. She shook her head and looked out the window, stepping away from Harry.

When she looked back at him, a lazy, satisfied grin was playing on his lips. She suppressed her own smile and looked back out the window again. The parking lot was full. Beyond the high boundary wall, she could see greenery slowly returning to the common. The sun was out, and there was that faint tremble in the air, the first flutter of sunlight after a dark and desolate winter.

Harry sighed, and she saw his features become serious. A sense of dread clutched at her heart. "What is it?"

Harry pursed his lips together. "Body discovered in Clapham Pond, seen by two anglers this afternoon. A couple of hours ago. Uniform has been there to check, and they have sealed the area. They've also taken statements from the two anglers."

Arla pursed her lips, then shook her head. The sun was out, and it seemed like the capital's crime spree was beginning. It never made any sense to her why violent crime rose in good weather and died down in the winter. Did sunlight encourage the dark minds of sick people? She would never know, but for her and her team, the busy period of the year was starting.

She asked, "Have you informed scene-of-crime and Dr Banerjee?" Dr Banerjee was the erstwhile Metropolitan police pathologist who had worked with Arla for the best part of two decades.

"Yes, they're on their way."

Arla grabbed her phone and the warrant card from her desktop. She smoothed down her suit coat and trousers. Then she looked up at Harry. "We might as well get moving then."

Beams of sunshine played hide and seek through the trees as Arla watched from the BMW passenger seat. Harry was driving. The three ponds lay at the south-eastern edge of the common, a particularly remote

11

part of the 6 acres of land that comprised the area. Beyond the ponds, the land sloped up in small hilly, wooded areas. There was no road access there, and Arla wondered about that. To her mind, getting to the ponds via the road would be far easier. Unless, of course, the victim had come down the hill and decided to go for a swim, maybe in a drunk or drugged state.

Arla realised she hadn't been to the ponds before. She knew about them, as there had been drownings there before. But there hadn't been a crime at the pond for more than a decade.

Harry drove past the green expanses of the common, with its banks of trees basking in the sun. Families were out frolicking on the green grass, and it brought a smile to her lips. She was looking forward to taking Nicole out over the weekend unless, of course, work intervened.

The road narrowed, then became a dirt track. The sounds of children and traffic from the roads faded. She wound her window down. There was nothing but the buzzing of bees and the smell of damp earth now. The humidity was strong, coming off from the water. She saw two uniformed police cars up ahead, and Scene of Crime's white van.

# CHAPTER 4

Arla stepped out of the car and stretched. She turned her face up to the warmth; it was nice having some light on her face. Unseen birds chirped in the trees above. A gentle breeze blew damp air to her face, and the scent of the pond mixed with something else. She crinkled her nose, dreading the source.

There was a bank of bushes before the ground sloped down to meet the water's edge. The water was beer-coloured. The pond was almost a lake as far as she was concerned. The opposite banks were hazy in a slight mist that clung to the slope of the hills.

There was a gap in the bush, and a well-worn path had been made by generations of anglers making their way down to the wooden jetty. To one side, a white tent had already been erected. It wasn't a crime scene yet, but the body had to be preserved, and samples were to be taken from their environment.

Arla greeted a few of the uniformed officers, saying hello to Andy Jackson, the uniformed inspector who was a veteran of the London Met. She and Harry signed their names on the clipboard handed to them by a uniformed constable. The ground was slippery as it sloped down to the pond.

Harry went first, and she held onto his elbow as they walked down. Before their jetty, space had been cleared, and for the first time, she saw the body. It was a bloated and macabre sight. From the hair and the genes, she could tell it was a female figure. The face was swollen hideously, and so was the abdomen.

The stench was unmistakable now, permeating in waves.

Inspector Jackson walked up to her and indicated two figures huddled on one side. "Those are the two anglers that found the body. We've got their statements, names, and addresses. Do you want to speak to them?"

Arla looked at Harry, who shrugged. He said, "I'll do it." He trudged off, and Arla squatted, observing the body closely. The skin was literally peeling off, which was a pity. She wanted to check for smudge marks on the neck. She observed the hands carefully, and the sight of lacerations on the knuckles interested her. This woman had resisted and put up a fight; or had her knuckles scraped on the ground?

The vest and cardigan she wore were partly decomposed. She couldn't make out any signs of struggle from them.

She heard footsteps behind her and half turned. She was pleased to see Dr Banerjee. As usual, he walked with a slouched gait, holding his black leather briefcase like a doctor's bag. His dark linen suit was crumpled, and the eyes invisible behind his glasses. He still had a shock of white hair, which he liked to say made him look younger than his years.

Arla rose from her crouching position and shook hands with Dr Banerjee. The older man smiled at her, his eyes crinkling at the corners. Arla was genuinely fond of him and treated him like a father figure. She had been to Banerjee's house and also attended both his daughters' weddings.

"How's Nicole doing?"

"She's learning dance routines to nursery rhymes," Arla responded with a grin.

"Aha," Banerjee adjusted his glasses and rubbed his hands together. "You know, despite my years, I still think back to when the girls were little. These memories you will carry forever, I can assure you. When they're cute, chubby, and little, they do unforgettable things. Enjoy this time; it doesn't come back."

A touch of sadness passed over Banerjee's features. He swallowed and looked away. Arla inclined her head.

"Everything okay with you, doc?"

14

"Yes, all fine," Banerjee said. But the tight line of his lips and the sudden firmness of his jaw spoke otherwise. Arla stared at him for a few seconds, then realised Banerjee couldn't speak with others in attendance.

Arla stepped closer to him and dropped a voice.

"Call me if you need to talk. You know I'm always here."

Banerjee had known about her sister's disappearance and had helped Arla immensely in those difficult days, when she had been a newly minted detective inspector. It was a long time ago, but she had never forgotten the pathologist's kindness. He was extremely knowledgeable about crime scenes and the minds of criminals. It wasn't an exaggeration to state that Arla had learned much about her job from Dr Banerjee.

He adjusted his glasses again and cleared his throat. "It's nothing, don't worry. Yes, let's meet up for a cup of tea and chat soon. It's been a while since I've seen little Nicole, anyway."

"I'm sure that can be arranged."

Banerjee glanced at the bloated corpse behind them, and for a few seconds, Arla thought how incredulous the whole scene was. Here she was, having a chitchat with Dr Banerjee, while the body of a young woman lay behind them in advanced decomposition. Then again, that was her job.

"As soon as the weather improves, the craziness starts," Banerjee said, his voice sombre.

"Yes," Arla said, falling into step beside Banerjee as they walked down the slope towards the body. "I know exactly what you mean."

Banerjee crouched by the body and put his mask and gloves on. A scene-of-crimes officer arrived, and he rose to put the gown on, helped by the officer. Arla watched as the pathologist examined the body from different angles. He took out a thermometer and inserted the probe inside the rectum with the help of two scene-of-crime officers. He jotted down the reading in his notebook.

Harry came back from questioning the two witnesses.

"Anything interesting?" Arla asked.

Harry shook his head. "They're both shocked. They seem a bit out of it, to be honest. I don't think they're capable of drowning someone and then turning up at the crime scene to gloat."

"Did scene-of-crime get their fingerprints and take DNA swabs?"

Harry nodded. "And I asked Lisa and Robert to check if there was anything on them on NPD." NPD stood for the National Police Database, an entire floor of computer servers in the Scotland yard building in central London.

"Well?" Arla asked.

Harry shook his head. "They don't have a criminal record. We'll wait to see what their fingerprints record show from identical ones. But I doubt we'll come up with anything."

Arla transferred her attention back to Banerjee. She wore a mask and crouched next to the pathologist.

"Talk to me, doc."

Banerjee sighed. "Young Caucasian female. I'd put her in the early 20s, from the lack of lines on what remains of the skin."

"Time of death?"

"Well, as you know, Arla, the human body loses temperature by 1° every hour. The average internal body temperature is 18°."

Banerjee looked around him. "Say the ground temperature is twelve to fifteen° now. The water temperature will be a lot less, about 4-5°. And if you go out to the middle of the pond, it can drop to near-zero."

"That low?"

"Yes. Unfortunately, water makes everything complicated. Time and cause of death become very hard to analyse."

He continued. "Do you know why the human body floats in water?"

"Enlighten me, doc."

"Because we have lungs full of air and a certain amount of gas in our intestines. But when a person drowns, what happens?"

"The lungs become full of water," Arla said. "And since water is heavier than air, it causes the body to sink?"

Banerjee smiled. "Well done. And once the body sinks, if the water is cold, then decomposition is slowed."

He took his glasses off, and his dark eyes blinked. He rubbed the corner of his eyes, and they flicked over sharply to Arla. The old glint in them was back.

"This body must have been in the water for five days at least, I would say. It's in an advanced state of decomposition. The gut microbes that have eaten their way through the intestine are proliferating inside the body. They're producing a whole load of gases; hence, the body is bloating. As the body puffs up with gas, it becomes light again and floats up to the surface."

"So, you're saying, this happened five days ago? The drowning, I mean."

Banerjee shrugged. "Five days or more. My best guess would be up to one week. It depends on the water temperature. It also depends on how deep her body was at the time of the drowning. If the water was cold, then say 5 to 7 days ago. If she drowned near the banks, where the water would be warmer, about three days."

Arla pointed to the hands. "Are those lacerations near the knuckles?"

Banerjee smiled. "Well spotted. Yes, they are indeed lacerations, like she's fought someone off with her fists or hit something repeatedly, like small stones." Banerjee shifted and beckoned Arla forward.

She came close to see that the pathologist had upturned the hand and was now showing Arla the palm. "Similar marks round the base of the palm.

17

That means she was dragged along the ground, and she was trying to stop. These scratch marks often result from rubbing against an abrasive surface like the road or dirt."

Arla looked up the path. Scene of Crime officers had marked areas on the ground with white circles. They were footprints, and she knew the photos would be sent to the footprint analyser. She hadn't observed the boot prints very closely herself; her attention was taken up by the body.

Banerjee stood, walked to the victim's feet, and circled to the left side. Arla followed him.

Banerjee pointed to a mark on the back of the left hand. Arla leaned over, squinting. The flesh had been indented in a circle, like a round, large apple core had been pressed on the flesh. The mark of a dollar sign was unmistakable.

"What's that?" Arla asked. Deep down, she suspected the answer already. And its significance made her shiver. This mark was not an accident. It was a premeditated sign. A sign that a seasoned killer was on the prowl, one who wanted to leave his mark on his prey.

"There are no other marks like this on the body from my preliminary inspection." Banerjee stretched a hand across the prone figure. "Of course, I've not looked at the underside properly, but I did have a quick look when we inserted the rectal thermometer."

Harry was observing from the other side, and he spoke up. "That mark is far too neat to be an accident." His eyes met Arla's, and she saw a grim determination in them. She knew exactly what he was thinking.

*Not again.*

# CHAPTER 5

Arla walked Banerjee back to his car. "I need a report on this soon, doc."

The pathologist stopped with one hand on the open door of his battered old Volkswagen. "How soon?"

"Tomorrow?"

Banerjee smiled, but it didn't touch his eyes. It was desultory and she saw the sadness in his face again.

"Got a couple of bodies in the morgue already. Not sure if I can get her ready for tomorrow."

"At least the samples for toxicology. They take a couple of days to come back, right?"

Banerjee nodded. "For blood, saliva, and vaginal fluids. OK, I will do." He held Arla's eyes for a second as if he wanted to say something. But then he thought better of it.

Arla stepped closer. "What is it, doc?"

The older man shook his head. "Nothing. Don't worry. I'll call you tomorrow."

With that, he slammed his door shut. Arla watched him reverse and drive off in a cloud of dust and gravel, an uneasy sensation coiling in her guts.

She turned and faced the bank. A row of almost waist-high bush and shrubbery covered the small ridge that led to the bank. The row was punctuated by regular gaps. The gap directly in front of her was used to drag this girl across, she assumed.

She walked up the path, then stepped on the plastic boards laid out by Scene of Crime.

At the top of the path, she turned and looked at the dirt road that led up to the ponds. Dense woodlands covered the dirt road on either side. The only clearing was near the banks. I'll look to the opposite bank of the pond, to the small hills, their slopes covered with greenery. It was far, and she wondered why these ponds were not called small lakes. Geography wasn't one of her skills, and she would have to sit down with an ordnance survey map to measure the distances properly.

Arla turned sharply around. The only way the victim could have been dragged here was through that dirt path. On the other end, the dirt path linked up to the road that snaked around the perimeter of the common. Someone had driven up that road… And then driven down the dirt track, or carry the victim across?

She sensed movement next to her, then saw Harry. "Penny for your thoughts?" Harry said.

"Make that a pound. How far are we from the edge of the common?"

Harry stretched along his hand, pointing to the left. "With our back to the water, about a couple of miles to the left, I'd say."

"And there are three ponds in total, right?"

"Correct. But this one is the biggest. It links up with the other two as well, but the links are narrow, barely wide enough for one boat to get through. Hence, they are classified as three different ponds."

"So, hypothetically, this girl could have been drowned in one of the other ponds and then just drifted across here?"

Harry pressed his lips together for a second, deep in thought. "Yes, possible. But that would depend on the time of death. If she was killed a week ago, then I can't see how the body would have drifted across this far. It's not a river, and there aren't any currents."

"Good point." Arla turned, so she was facing the river. Immediately she felt a cool breeze on her face. It rustled her hair and felt nice. "Why is this a pond? Look at how far the opposite bank is. Shouldn't this be a lake?"

Harry shrugged. "Not sure. Lake does sound better than a pond, though."

Arla stared across the waters. The breeze strengthened into a wind, and tugged at the corners of her jacket. Little grey ripples shivered across the pond.

"I'm just trying to figure out how the victim got here. There's no CCTV around, is there?"

"No. The only cameras are on the main roads."

Arla walked down the bank, pausing to check the ground carefully. The boot prints that scene-of-crime had circled with the white marker were big enough for a man's size. Harry was size eleven, and she guessed these to be size 9 or ten. The boot print analyst would have more to add.

As she stared at the grotesquely bloated corpse, Arla felt a surge of sorrow. That feeling soon turned into one of bitterness and anger. She didn't know how this woman had died. Suicide would be immensely tragic, but at this stage, she couldn't rule out foul play. And if there was foul play, why would a dollar sign be engraved on her skin. She knew that would have caused pain, and it was impossible that it was done while the woman was alive. She turned to Harry and asked him about the sign.

"I find it odd too. Psychopaths would leave a symbol, or something more cryptic."

"A gangland killing?" Arla mused. Money was often the factor in violent organised crime.

"Could be. Or it could be someone just trying to deceive us. That could be a dead end."

Arla nodded. It was known to happen. A clever killer would leave a symbol on their bodies just to plant doubt into the investigating team's minds: lead them down a blind alley and waste their time.

"She resisted, Harry," Arla said softly. "That's why she's got those lacerations on her knuckles. It's a shame we can't see any other signs of struggle on the body."

Arla knew that a drowned victim was a detective's nightmare. The water destroyed all visible clues on the body, and when decomposition set in, so did a process called skin slippage. Literally, the skin just fell away.

"Let's see what toxicology shows. Not to mention the DNA and dental records."

Carefully, Arla walked down to the edge of the water to avoid the white circle marks. She tested the wood on the jetty, then stepped on it. She was wearing gloves, as was Harry. The shoes were covered by sterile boot protectors. Harry held her elbow and told her to be careful on the jetty. She smiled at that. Always worried about her, was Harry.

"I'll be fine, Harish," she arched an eyebrow, smiling. Harish was Harry's original Indian name. She didn't move her arm away from his hold.

"Harry will do darling," he said, winking.

"That dollar sign and the lacerations on her knuckles are bothering me. I don't think this is a suicide," Arla murmured, almost to herself. Her sixth sense was ringing loudly, and it wasn't a pleasant sound.

The victim's skin wasn't wrinkled. The neck didn't have lines. The nails were well-manicured and looked after. This was a young woman, and some evil bastard had callously ended a promising life.

Arla thought of this poor woman's family, and she shuddered. Briefly, her own past screamed in her mind like a runaway train. She closed her eyes, dispelling the dark shadows of her memories.

Her jaws clamped tight, and a steely resolve began to take shape in her mind.

"We need a positive ID as soon as possible. Gather Major Incident Room 1. Ask uniform, traffic and media liaison to be present."

# CHAPTER 6

Major-incident room one, or MIR1 as it was commonly known, was full to the brim. It was the first time in many decades that a body had been discovered at the Clapham common ponds. All assembled officers, both uniformed and detectives, knew the news wouldn't be secret for too long. The two anglers who had found the body had probably already been offered money by the press for their story. By tomorrow or the day after, the news would be hitting the headlines of local papers.

Scene-of-crime had given Arla some of their photos of the victim, and Robert Pickering and Rosslyn May, two of Arla's trusted detective sergeants, were clipping the photos to the whiteboard. Lisa and Gita, the other two members of Arla's team, were busy coordinating the researchers, who were looking into recent police enquiries about missing people.

Arla stood and took her place next to the whiteboard, then faced the assembled officers. The hubbub of voices died down, and a hush fell across the room.

A fax machine beeped in one corner, receiving a transmission. Arla scanned the room and saw the usual array of faces: detective colleagues with their teams and uniformed officers. The sergeants from financial crime and the technical unit were also here, which pleased her. The door opened, and a woman dressed in a business suit slipped in, murmuring an apology. Arla smile at her. It was Mary Atkins, the forensic boot print analyser. Mary was in demand all across London, and it was good to have her present.

Arla cleared her throat and started. "I expect all of you know the Clapham Common pond-area reasonably well. It's a remote part of the common, at the southeast corner, with only one road access. I was surprised by how large the main pond was, where this body was discovered." Arla went on to describe the details of the case, then paused.

"So far, we have nothing from the fingerprints on IDENT-1. We are still waiting to see if there's a match on their DNA samples on the national database. What we need at this stage is a positive ID. Did scene-of-crime find anything about who she was? Credit card, or any other ID?"

Parmentier, the forty-something head of forensics, raised his hand. "No, but we did find a piece of jewellery by the water's edge. It was a gold necklace, and we only discovered it at the end of the day, after you left." Rob stepped forward, holding up a plastic bag.

"Thanks, Hank," he said, using Parmentier's first name.

Rob turned towards Arla and blinked an apology. "Sorry, guv, we just got this." Arla smile at him. Rob's chubby cheeks and his generous neck were spilling over his shirt collar. He was fond of his pork pies, but he was also a bloody good detective.

"Tell us all about it, Rob," Arla encouraged.

Rob pointed a finger at the necklace. "24 carat gold chain with a solid gold cross as the pendant. It looks expensive because it is. The latticed chain work is bespoke jewellery, and the rip over here shows where the chain was torn."

Parmentier raised his hand, and Arla pointed to him. "The break in the chain shows that force had been applied to remove it from the woman's neck. We couldn't find any obvious skin samples on the chain, but there could be skin fragments. We need to look at it under more powerful microscopes."

Arla said, "What's important is that the chain wasn't taken. The attacker, who, we can assume, was also the killer, had no interest in this fine piece of jewellery. We can rule out robbery as the motive. Did we find a mobile phone or purse? Or any other personal items?"

Parmentier shook his head. Arla looked at it, and at Jackson, a tall, handsome, square-shouldered Afro-Caribbean uniformed inspector. "Anything else, Andy?"

Andy shook his head. We had a team of ten who searched a 500 metre radius on the bank, guv. We found nothing."

"Get another team and search a 2-mile radius," Arla said. "Not just the bank, I want the woods searched, all the way up to the road. Don't forget the dirt track because the killer possibly used a car. I know we didn't find any tyre tracks, but those tracks are easy to conceal. I have a feeling the body was brought to the water's edge by car."

She shrugged, then pursed her lips. "I could be wrong, and the woman could have come down the hills on the opposite bank. But I noticed her dress wasn't torn anywhere. It was mostly intact, like the skin on her legs. If she was running from the killer through a forest, she would have lacerations on her legs and feet and also slashes on the dress."

Harry was standing to the far right with the rest of Arla's team. He said, "And the only lacerations we saw were on the victim's knuckles. Like she had been dragged along the dirt or tried to resist being attacked. With her hands."

"Exactly," Arla said. "My gut tells me that the victim didn't roll down that hill."

She turned towards Rosslyn and Gita. "Anything from the missing-persons database?"

Rosslyn stepped forward and read from the sheet of notes in her hand. "In the last five weeks, there have been seven missing people reported. Five of them are teenagers who have now returned home. The other two are young women who are still missing. Their names are Susan Remington and Emily Wright. Susan has been missing for over a week, longer than Emily was. Susan has fair hair, like the victim. Emily's hair is dark brown. The victim's height of 5 feet 7 inches also corresponds with Susan Remington.

Rosslyn looked at Gita, who was shuffling through screens on her iPad. Gita cleared her throat and stepped forward. She nodded to Arla, who grinned at her.

"Susan Remington is 25 years old and works for an accounting firm in the financial sector, called Clifford's. The firm is well known, one of the top 5 accountancy firms in the UK. They have several branches all over the country, but London is their main hub. She was reported missing by one of her work colleagues, Madelyn West. Thereafter, her mother also filed a report, just last night, that she had been unable to contact her daughter on the phone."

Arla asked, "The name Remington sounds familiar. Who is the mother?"

Arla saw Gita stare at her for a few seconds, and her heart sank.

"Sheila Remington is chairwoman of the Conservative party."

The collective groan across the room was loud. Arla sighed in disbelief. Why did it have to be the daughter of an influential politician? Now there would be pressure on her, not to mention additional media scrutiny.

Arla said, "Sheila Remington's been on the paper, hasn't she? Isn't she running in the party elections to become leader?"

Gita nodded. "She's one of three candidates, and she's got a lot of support from senior figures in the Conservative party."

"She must be blue-blooded like the rest of them, right? Did she make a fortune herself, or is it family wealth?"

"A combination of the two. She is the daughter of Sir Tony Remington, who ran a chain of furniture shops. He sold the chain to a US venture capitalist for an undisclosed sum, but our research indicates it would have been a couple of hundred million. His daughter has used the family funds to start her own interior decorations firm called Rosewood Interiors."

There was a murmur across the room. Arla nodded. "Yes, seen that name on the high street as well. They also advertise in digital and print media everywhere. Didn't know it was linked to the Remington family." She rubbed a hand across her forehead lightly. It had been a long day, and it was getting longer by the second.

"Good work, you two," Arla said briskly. "Rob, ring Dr Banerjee and give him the latest. We need those DNA samples as soon as we can. If she had a dentist, see if we can get hold of dental records. I would like to check her apartment out and get some samples. We need a match as soon as we can. Where did Susan Remington live?"

Gita said, "The family home is in the Chelsea embankment, but Susan had an apartment in Shoreditch, close to her office."

"We don't need a warrant, obviously, but it might be prudent to get one seeing who her family is." Arla knew how wealthy people liked to have their lawyers get in the way of police work. She didn't want to waste her time on cosmetic issues like illegally entering their victim's property.

"Inspector Mehta and I want to visit her residence first thing tomorrow morning. As soon as we have the DNA match, call the family for an ID. I doubt they'll be able to tell much given the decomposition, but it needs to be done."

# CHAPTER 7

*20 years ago.*

*London.*

Eleven-year-old Carlson looked at his stepmother in confusion. "Move? Move where?"

Shola, his mother, stirred the soup in her bowl, looking down at the table. "I don't know. But we have no money, and that's what the council said."

"But I have friends here. I got my school," Carlson said.

"I know that, son. And believe me, if there was a way, then I'd do it."

Carlson didn't know a great deal about the government, but he knew the city council paid for the flat they lived in and the bills as well. In fact, the huge apartment complex where they lived was all council flats. The buildings were tall, and there were hundreds of apartments, all cramped into tiny spaces. Carlson was lucky. It was only him and Shola. Some of his friends had families of four or even six living in two-bedroom apartments.

Carlson knew that Shola couldn't afford the rent in London. She worked as a cleaner, and a few times, he had gone with her to the hospital. They could eat in the canteen, and because his mother had a staff-pass, he liked to get seconds or even thirds. He loved the hot custard with apple tart, and one of the serving ladies was Ade, another Nigerian woman like Shola. Ade made sure Carlson's plate was always heaped full.

Carlson munched on a chip and studied Shola. "How long do we have?"

"I don't know. I got the letter this morning that in the near future we would have to move. These apartments need to be renovated. I know what they mean." Shola rose and started to stack plates in the kitchen sink. "Have you seen the damp on the walls? And the paint peeling everywhere? There's mould in the corners of the roof. Not nice, living like this."

"But I don't want to move," Carlson whined. He scratched his curly black hair. He wanted to get braids done, but Shola forbade him. She had wagged a finger in front of his face.

"That's what those bad boys in the street do. That's not your future."

"Not all of them are bad boys," Carlson had protested. "Anton is my friend."

Shola had put both hands on Carlson's shoulders and pressed down gently like she was trying to stop him from rising like a balloon.

"Anton is a lot older than you, Carlson. I don't want you mixing with that lot. If I see you, you're going to be in trouble. Do you hear?"

Carlson shrugged, and Shola grabbed his right ear. She bent it till it hurt. "Ow," Carlson squirmed.

"Did you hear what I said?"

"Yes."

Shola let go of him and squatted in front. "You're going to school to get an education. Then you're going to have a proper job one day. Be a good man."

"Okay, mum."

Shola had smiled and hugged Carlson.

Shola had been the only person who loved Carlson. And he wanted to help his mother. He knew she did two jobs. She also worked in the evenings and weekends at private homes in the neighbourhood. He knew she didn't earn much, only £4-5 an hour as a cleaner. He overheard her speaking to Esse, the Sudanese woman who lived in the next block. Shola was away for work a lot, leaving Carlson with plenty of free time on his hands. He made his mind up. He would use that time to earn money.

Then maybe one day, they could get out of this crappy estate and rent a lovely private flat. Carlson daydreamed as he helped Shola clean up the kitchen. He could have a TV in his room. They could do with a bigger kitchen and a nice dining table, not one that moved every time he put his elbows on it. And a garden? Carlson smiled to himself. Yes, a garden in the summer would be so nice. He could bring his mates around, and they could play while Shola had tea with her friends.

Shola kissed his forehead as she tucked him into bed that night. Carlson grabbed her hand as she was leaving.

"Mummy?"

"Yes darling."

"Everything will be alright. Trust me."

Shola grinned and squeezed his hand. "Okay darling. Now go to sleep. You have school tomorrow."

# CHAPTER 8

A rla shut the door, then crouched in the hallway. She spread out her arms, and a giggling Nicole ran towards her. Arla gripped her three-year-old daughter tightly and kissed her cheeks.

"Yay, mummy!" Nicole said, grabbing Arla's neck tightly. Rita, Harry's mother, came out of the kitchen. She put a hand on her waist and watched mother and daughter.

"I'm convinced," Rita said, "she knows it's you by the sound of the key on the door. She even told me it's mummy, then ran for the door before I could stop her."

Nicole said, "I ate chicken and rice. It was yummy."

Arla put Nicole on the floor as she took off her coat. "What else did you do?"

Nicole was soon back in her mother's arms. Arla's heart melted at the tight grip her daughter had around her neck.

"I did some colouring with crayons, and then I had cheesecake, then I watched Peppa Pig."

Arla put Nicole on the kitchen counter while she reached for a glass of water. The kitchen smelled of a sumptuous lamb biryani. Pangs of hunger contracted in her belly. She had skipped lunch, and it was almost 7 PM.

Nicole asked, "Have you heard the Peppa Pig song?"

Arla thought for a while, then shook her head. Nicole's eyes brightened. "If I sing to you, then maybe we can do it together?"

"It's a deal."

Nicole stared at her mother. "What's a deal?"

Arla kissed her daughter's fluffy, light coffee-brown cheeks. Little Nicole was a replica of her dad. She had huge chestnut brown eyes and dark hair. Unlike most babies, Arla's daughter was born with a whole head of spiky hair, and Harry had given Nicole the affectionate nickname of the hedgehog.

"It means I'll sing it with you."

"Yea. Yay." Nicole clapped her hands. "If you put me down, I'll get the iPad now."

Arla marvelled at how technologically adept her three-year-old was. When she was a child, using a TV remote was the pinnacle of her abilities. Now Nicole had her own iPad, bought for her by her doting grandmother. Arla smiled as Rita handed her a cup of steaming tea.

"Thank you. And also for the cooking. It smells heavenly."

Arla lifted the lid of the big pot on the gas hob. Yellow and white spiced and saffron flavoured rice, mixed with chunks of tender cooked lamb, met her eyes. She inhaled. Rita had also prepared the cucumber and yoghurt accompaniment, raita and the lentil dish, dal. She noticed the oven was on. "What's in there?"

In response, Rita asked her to move, then took out an oven tray. "Grilled peppers, red onions, and courgette."

"Looks yummy. How did you make it?'

Rita shrugged. "Very easy, you chop the veggies, then mix it with olive oil and some Harissa powder. That powder is my extra, but you can just use olive oil and seasoning."

Arla took out a fork and tried one of the peppers. The spice was mild, and the taste was stunning. The vegetable had retained its firmness, and she didn't waste time in having a few more straight from the tray.

33

Nicole came back with her iPad and held it up to her mother. Shall we watch it now?"

Rita said, "Let Mummy eat something first. Why don't you show us your colourings while she eats?"

As Nicole went back into the lounge, Rita said, "Bring her to the dining table, and I'll lay out a plate for you."

Arla glanced at her watch. "It's getting late. You've been here the whole day. Shouldn't you be getting home?"

She knew home was an empty place for Rita. Her husband had died, and Harry's sister didn't live with her.

"What time is Harry back?" Rita asked, taking out a plate from the cupboard and putting some biryani on it.

"Hopefully, an hour," Arla said. She knew Rita would like to say hello to Harry before she left.

She looked over Nicole's drawings. And the little girl explained in great detail what each shape meant. This continued while Arla ate her food at the kitchen table. Nicole sat on Rita's lap and even took a few mouthfuls of the vegetables from her mother.

After Harry arrived, Rita said her goodbyes and left. Harry took his daughter upstairs to get ready for bed-time. He would tell her stories, then read one of the books that she had chosen. It was their father and daughter evening ritual. Just before sleep, Arla would join them and tuck Nicole into bed.

Once Nicole was asleep, Arla joined Harry in the lounge. Harry had changed into a T-shirt and jeans, and his long frame was sprawled out on the sofa. A glass of red wine was on the coffee table next to him. Arla took a sip from his glass, then snuggled up to him. She settled comfortably against Harry, and he spooned her as they watched the TV. It was the news, and Arla was thankful there was no mention as yet of the body found in Clapham common.

Harry raised himself to reach for the glass. He drank some, then gave the rest to Arla. His hand moved over her belly, then lowered down to her waist. She murmured softly as he nuzzled the back of her neck. She pressed her buttocks against him and felt his manhood stiffen. A low heat gathered between her legs, and she squeezed her thighs together. Harry's lips found hers, and his tongue flicked the corners of her mouth. Arla raised herself as she still had the wine glass in her hand.

She put the glass back on the table and then lay back with a sigh. Harry stretched, then yawned.

Arla asked, "Did Dr Banerjee get back to you?"

"Not yet. But he did mention the DNA samples. It's being sent to the labs. I did find out more about the Remingtons, though."

"I got hold of Madelyn West, the victim's friend who reported her missing."

"What did she say?"

"Sounded distraught. I didn't give her any details, obviously. Just told her it's part of an ongoing investigation. She pressed me, though. I told her we would call her back tomorrow."

"Did she have any concerns about Susan before she disappeared?"

Harry paused, and she sensed he was gathering his thoughts. "Well, she was kind of hesitant. I got the feeling she knows more than she's letting on. She denied knowing anything specific."

"Is she lying?"

"Maybe. She knows the mother well. Has been to the family home several times. The Chelsea home, as well as their pad in the country. Nothing short of a country manor with grounds near Chichester. Said she went horse riding there with Susan and her mother."

"Land owning gentry," Arla snorted. "Definitely blue-blooded."

35

"I asked her if we could see her tomorrow. She said she was away first thing on a business trip. She worked with Susan at the same office."

"Is she really going or just avoiding us?"

Harry kissed Arla's shoulder. "Who knows the machinations of the complex female psyche."

"I want to see her," Arla murmured, sighing with pleasure as Harry's lips moved down her arm. "This is getting interesting."

Harry lowered Arla's pyjamas, and his long fingers explored the apex of her thighs, moving to the centre.

"Definitely interesting," he whispered.

# CHAPTER 9

Arla was up before Harry. She checked on Nicole, who was still asleep. Her thumb was in her mouth as she slept peacefully. Arla observed her daughter to her heart's content. There was nothing more peaceful than watching your own child sleep, she thought.

She dared not touch her because Nicole had awakened once overnight already, and she had to give her one and a half bottles of milk before she went back to sleep. She didn't want to encourage that pattern; Nicole needed to sleep through the night. It wasn't a problem anymore, and to be honest, Nicole had been very good as night sleep was concerned. Six months from her birth, she was sleeping all the way through. Arla blew her a kiss and went to get ready.

She and Harry alternated the morning baby duties. One of them stayed back to get Nicole ready and take her to either the childminder or to Rita's. Today was Rita's rest day. Arla would finish early, as she did often now, so she could pick Nicole up at 5 PM. It meant she had to bring some of her work home, but she could catch up on reports and direct most of a team from home. Occasionally, she did the night visit as long as Harry was back home.

Harry was shaving by the time she had finished breakfast. She kissed him goodbye and took the tube from Tooting Broadway to Clapham common. It was 7:30 in the morning, and rays of sun filtered through the trees, playing hide and seek with her eyes. There was a quickness in the air, more grass on the ground, more chatter on the streets.

London was warming up, and there was a buzz. Arla turned her face up to the sun and walked with a carefree step. She took the route through the common, heading for the police station. It took almost half an hour, but she needed the exercise.

She could only go for a run once a week now; the rest of it was yoga and exercise at home. She had to watch how much booze she drank. Both Harry and she were fond of a tipple, and it was customary to hit the pub after a long day at work.

She avoided that now, and motherhood was a convenient excuse. But hard-drinking was part of the Metropolitan police culture. It was the same up and down the country. She had lost count of the detective inspectors who had lost their careers to booze. She knew she wouldn't be one of those, and neither would Harry.

The job could be overwhelming. But she had Nicole to think about now and their future. Harry still went to the pub after work, and she suspected he also had a couple of cigarettes while he was there. He dared not smoke at home, as she had now given up completely, but she had to admit, her lungs did itch for a cigarette every now and then. She avoided it by consuming more coffee.

The station was more or less empty when she entered. At work, the uniform sergeant inclined his head in greeting and pressed the buzzer to open the bullet-proof double doors for her. Arla walked down the familiar green lino corridor, the noticeboards on the sides festooned with mugshots of criminals and charts of daily and monthly criminal activities across London.

The detective's open-plan office had two people present, and they both raised their hands in greeting. It was Lisa Moran and Rob Pickering, two of Arla's oldest associates. Lisa asked her about Nicole. Lisa was in a same-sex relationship with her long-term partner, Clarissa. They had adopted a boy, and Matthew was now seven years old.

"Shall I get you a coffee, guv?" Lisa asked.

"That would be very nice of you, thank you," Arla said.

Rob was gathering up a sheaf of papers on his desk. He looked at Arla expectantly. She smiled at her experienced detective sergeant. Both Lisa and Rob were now inspector grade material, and she would happily sign off their recommendation forms. But they would not find jobs in the Clapham station and would be posted elsewhere in London, or maybe even outside. She wasn't keen on losing the team she had worked hard to gather around her. At the same time, sooner or later, she would have to let them go.

"Give me five minutes, Rob," she said.

Her office faced the back parking lot, and the rows of cars glistened in the morning sun. Behind that, the greenery of the common undulated in a breeze. At least it wasn't cold, Arla thought to herself as she logged into her computer.

She set the photo of her sister Nicole straight so that it was facing her. As was customary, she spent a few seconds remembering her lost sister. Lost, but never forgotten. Every day her heart ached. No, it did not get better with time. Yes, it was like a cloak that would be draped around her shoulders forever. Life was like that for some people.

She checked her emails quickly and sighed with relief that she didn't have any from her boss, commander Johnson, or any of the top brass. Her intray had a few papers in it, and she would deal with them in time. She wasn't the duty senior investigating officer for the week, thank goodness. There was a knock on the door, and Lisa entered with a steaming cup of coffee and biscuits.

Arla arose and took the cup from Lisa.

She eyed the blonde woman as she sat down. Lisa was in her early 30s, and she was chubby but with a pretty face and freckles over her nose and upper cheeks. She struggled to keep her weight in check, and Arla suspected she drank more than she should. It was part of the Met culture, but that was no excuse.

Arla lowered her voice. "Everything okay at home?"

"Yes," Lisa said. Just the usual pressures of life, you know."

"Anything bothering you?"

Lisa smiled and shook her head. "No."

Arla knew how it was. Their jobs were pressured and result oriented. They weren't paid a lot, and the situations they dealt with often left them with nightmares. But they still did it for the love of the work and despite the cliché – to get justice for their victims.

She touched Lisa on the shoulder and then gave her a pat on the back.

"You can always talk to me, right? About anything at all. Clarissa, Matthew, or anyone."

Lisa grinned. "Thanks, boss."

Rob entered, and the three of them settled down.

# CHAPTER 10

A rla sipped her coffee. "Harry and I will visit Susan's apartment now to get DNA samples. If we get a positive result, we will secure the place and send in SOC. What about dental?"

"Still awaiting to hear from the lab," Rob said.

Arla sighed in impatience. She knew that it was too early to get the results, but sometimes the system could work miraculously fast. "I'll call up the lab as soon as they open." She checked her watch. It was 8:15, and the lab should be open in fifteen minutes.

Rob said, "But we have got pictures of her from her employer's website, and some from Google images."

Arla took the sheaf of papers that Rob had prepared. One of them was a CV, with a photo at the end. The rest of the A4 papers were also photos of Susan Remington at social gatherings and one with what looked like her family.

Arla looked at Susan's photos with interest. She was a beautiful young woman with shoulder-length blonde hair, grey eyes, and tanned skin. She was smiling at the camera, a confident person who was clearly used to flashing light bulbs. Her eyes fell to the V-neck of the pink floral dress she was wearing. A gold cross pendant adorned her chest, and the necklace matched the one recovered near the body.

"Same chain," Arla murmured to herself, "same necklace, again."

She paid close attention to the rest of the face. Susan obviously took pride in her appearance. The forehead was smooth, and she was a young woman, but Arla couldn't rule out Botox. The shape of her nose was pristine. The upper lip certainly had dermal filler on them – that pout was unmistakable.

She flicked to the next page. It showed full-length photos of a laughing Susan with a group of female friends outside a nightclub in London. There was also a photo of her with a man dressed in a suit. An expensive suit, Arla noted, and the man had a regal air about him. She put the photo to one side.

A photo with an older couple and a younger man who were probably her family. When she asked Rob and Lisa, they concurred.

Lisa said, "That older woman is definitely Sheila Remington. We checked with other photos online."

Mother and daughter certainly looked alike, Arla thought. Sheila Remington had looked after herself. She was supposed to be in her late 50s or early 60s but looked young for her age. She was slim, nicely attired in a charcoal grey dress that covered her chest and fell to her knees, exposing toned, athletic legs. Her husband was taller, thin, with sparse white hair and glasses. The younger man looked a bit like an older Harry Potter, and she couldn't quite see the family resemblance.

"What's the son's name?" Arla asked.

"Rupert," Lisa said. Arla smiled at that. Rupert Remington, the name had an upper-class ring to it.

Arla judged Susan's height to be about 5 feet 7 inches, which would correspond with the victims'. She flipped open her laptop and followed Rob's instructions to the right webpage. When she found Susan's images online, she used a magnifier app installed on her desktop to look closely at Susan's fingers.

The nails were perfectly manicured. The knuckles were free of lacerations, but the image was getting pixelated. She zoomed out and stared at the photo of the smiling, pleasant young woman. Susan liked to pose, judging by the hand on her hips and the position of her chin. As the daughter of an illustrious mother, she was clearly aware of her pedigree.

Lisa said, "Sheila Remington has been courting the press of late. Before the Tory party leadership elections, she's been bolstering her support for social causes. The Remington foundation has donated a lot of money to inner-city youths training projects."

Rob picked up from where Lisa stopped. "She's projecting a softer image than her rivals. I think she knows London is largely a Labour voting region."

Arla smiled. "Yes".

Most of London's voters live in council-owned flats or private rented accommodation. The majority didn't have much sympathy for the moneyed class that was responsible for funding the Conservative party. It was a paradox she never got used to. London's financial sector produced most of the country's wealth, but most of London's voters were left-wing. The millions stuck inside hopeless council estates; their lives dependent on state aid.

"Anything else?" She asked. "Does she have a work mobile number? Are we looking for the call data?"

"We've sent emails to her workplace but have not had a response. She does have a work mobile, but it's going to voicemail. And no, we still haven't found a phone at the crime scene."

Arla turned to the photo of the man who she thought looked like Susan's boyfriend. It clearly wasn't her brother, and the way they held each other was obvious.

"Find out this guy's name. Do a photo ID search," she showed the image to Lisa and Rob. She looked under metadata and discovered the photo was more than five years old.

"Already done it, guv," Rob said with a smile. "His name is David Braithwaite. Lord Braithwaite, to be precise. "They were an item back then. But recently, she's been seen with other men, if you can believe the gossip columns." He glanced at Lisa.

Arla raised her eyebrows. "You read the gossip?"

Lisa intervened. "That was my input, guv. My trawl through the internet revealed she was not with Lord Braithwaite anymore. But no new names were mentioned."

Arla was impressed. "What time did you go home last night?"

Lisa shrugged. "So much can be done from home, guv. I have access to the NPD and HOLMES." She grinned. "Not to mention *Hello* magazine."

HOLMES stood for Home Office Large Major Enquiry System – the supercomputer that stored all major crime and murder inquiries in the UK. In less than five seconds, HOLMES could crunch through data, photos, and sound bites that would take an entire CID team weeks to trawl through.

Arla tapped the photo of David Braithwaite. Something about the man's face bothered her. He had a beard and was tall, handsome. He and Susan made a good couple. While Susan was smiling in the photo, David had a slight smirk that didn't touch his eyes. There was something curious and vacant about his look that Arla couldn't understand. It bothered her.

"Any news on Lord Braithwaite?"

Rob said, "Nothing apart from the fact his father sits in the House of Lords. Jeremy Braithwaite has important connections to senior figures in the Conservative party. He is known to have a string of offshore companies, all of which invest in real estate in the UK and abroad."

"What's the source of the offshore funds?"

Rob and Lisa shrugged. Arla smiled to herself. The source of a family's wealth often wasn't revealed. It had been handed down the generations.

"So, two wealthy political families decide to tie the knot. Seems like a marriage made in heaven. I wonder how far they got. And more importantly, what caused the breakup."

She glanced at her watch. It was 8:45. "I'm going to make some calls to the lab to get hold of the DNA results. Then Inspector Mehta and I will visit Susan's workplace, and then her home. I want you guys to dig up all the data on Lord Braithwaite, his family, and anything you can get your hands on. The uniforms team will continue their search this morning, right?"

Lisa nodded. "Andy Jackson is meant to be at the site already, with his team. Inspector Stevenson will follow, and I will catch up with them later in the afternoon."

"Excellent. I really hope we find some more material evidence at the crime scene." The victim's body was so badly decomposed due to the water immersion, she didn't have much hope with what Dr Banerjee would find, for once.

Arla spoke to the head of the London Metropolitan's biological lab, as she had previously worked with him. A personal chat always helped, and she was promised the DNA result within half an hour.

At 9:10, there was a knock on her door, and Harry entered.

"Nicole's fine. Had her breakfast and with Agatha now," Harry said, referring to the childminder. Harry came forward and pecked her on the lips. Arla filled him with information Rob and Lisa had gathered.

Harry stroked his chin, frowning. "Was Susan engaged to this Braithwaite guy?"

"Lord Braithwaite," Arla corrected. Harry rolled his eyes.

"I don't know, and that's what we need to find out. These families like to announce their engagements in the Sunday papers, don't they? Might as well look for that." Her notebook was open, and she scribbled a reminder for herself.

There was a knock on the door, and Rosslyn May poked her head in. Rosslyn and Gita, the two new detective sergeants, had rapidly become key members of Arla's team. They were junior to Lisa and Rob, but as her two senior sergeants looked to become inspectors, Arla was confident Rosslyn and Gita would easily take up the slack.

Rosslyn was 5 feet 8, with short dark hair and a trim figure. "I got in touch with Sheila Remington's secretary. Sheila will meet you at the Chelsea townhouse today at twelve in the afternoon. Is that okay?"

Arla grinned. It was great having a competent team. "More than okay. It's great. Did you get hold of anyone else?"

"Yes, Gita spoke to her workplace last night, and I understand Inspector Mehta," she indicated to Harry, who was half turned in his seat, "spoke to Madelyn West, the victim's friend."

Harry said, "Indeed I did, but thanks for speaking to her workplace as well. We're on our way to her office now." He shifted his focus to Arla. "Maybe from her office desk we can get some DNA samples. We should get the statements from her office before we visit her home."

"That's our morning sorted," Arla said, rising. "See you in the afternoon," she waved at Ross, who waved back and shut the door.

# CHAPTER 11

*20 years ago*

The school canteen was rowdy and noisy as usual. Boys pushed each other in the lines for food. The girls were quieter; they stood in groups of three or four, chatting in hushed tones and glancing at the boys. Carlson got his tray and looked for his friend Anton. He saw Anton wave from a corner, and sat down next to him. He was best friends with Anton, who came round to his apartment a lot.

"Hey, Fam," Anton greeted Carlson as he sat down. Fam stood for family, and it was a traditional greeting.

Carlson said hello to him and sat down. "I've been thinking," Carlson said, between mouthfuls of his fish and chips.

Anton rolled his eyes. "You and your ideas. Honestly. Just give up while you're ahead."

"Seriously, bruv. We got to make some peas. Help out our mothers."

Anton's mother was also a cleaner at a different London hospital. He frowned at Carlson as he chewed on his food. "How are we going to make them peas?" Peas was the standard slang for money.

"We got to think about what people want. Look around you. What's man them and gal them using?"

Surreptitiously, Anton swung his head left and right. Then he shrugged. Carlson clucked his tongue against his cheek. "I mean, what do they really want? They all use phones, right? And they wear trainers."

Anton gaped at his friend. "So you're going to sell them phones and trainers?"

"No, stupid. That's just an example. You get me? See what people want. Then try and sell it to them. That's the way you make some peas."

Anton looked dubious. He dipped a chip in some gravy and took a bite. Carlson said, "I got this idea, right? I'm good at maths, and you're good at English." Carlson was in the top third for maths in his whole year. He liked maths. Numbers didn't lie, and he found them easy.

Anton looked at him guardedly. "Yes?" He said slowly.

Carlson dropped his voice to a conspiratorial whisper. "We know the boys who are shit at maths and English, right? What if we help them out with homework and ask them for money?"

"No," Anton's eyes were wide open. "No way, fam. If the teachers find out, you're going to be in serious trouble, bruv."

Carlson considered this. He had got into trouble last year when he had shouted at a boy during exam time. The boy was needling him in the back, asking Carlson to help him cheat the exam. They almost got into a fight, and both were kept after school.

Luckily, Carlson aced the exam. But he remembered that event. His mother was called to the school. He didn't want that to happen again. If he got kicked out of school, then Shola's problems would be much worse.

He nodded, staring at Anton. "Good point, bruv. We got to be careful."

They ate their food in silence. Then Carlson had a lightbulb moment. He stared down at his fish and chips. "I got it. Your mum taught you how to make burgers, right?"

Anton narrowed his eyes at him. "Yeah, so?"

"We could buy some mincemeat, add the spices and make the burgers at home. Then we sell the burgers at the school gates."

They stared at each other for a few seconds. Carlson said, "You got any money saved up?"

"About a fiver from my lunch money."

"I got about ten. Let's hit the supermarket. We can buy all the supplies and spend Sunday making some burgers. Come to mine. My mom is going to be at work the whole day. Monday morning, we start selling them at the school gates."

"How much for?"

Carlson pursed his lips in thought. "If we spend £15, most of our money will be on the meat. Let's see how many burgers we make. I'd like to make 30 burgers and price them at 1 pound each. That way, we spend £15 but make 30 back. We doubled our money. 100% return."

Anton grinned and inclined his head. "Now that sounds like a plan, fam."

*****

School was over, and there was a stream of children coming out of the main entrance and the courtyard. The gates had throngs of children chatting and laughing and some parents waiting. Carlson had a spring in his step as he walked out. He had just got an A in maths, and his teacher, Mrs Pearson, had lavished him with praise. Mrs Pearson had red hair and blue eyes, and Carlson thought she was very pretty. She really liked Carlson. She had patted him on the back as she gave him the report card.

"You're a very clever child. You have a bright future ahead of you. Make sure you show this to your mother."

Carlson grinned at her. "I will Miss, thank you."

Anton caught up with him, and the two friends discussed going shopping straight out of school. It was Friday, and they might as well buy their supplies now, Carlson said, and cook a small batch because they might not get it right the first time.

They walked past groups of boys, and a bunch of older guys looked at them as they walked past.

"Light-skinned son of a bitch."

"White man did his mother and left her..."

The comments were said loud enough to float over to Carlson's ears. His spine jerked straight as his jaws clamped together. A blind, dark rage filled his soul. Carlson was black, but like many Afro-Caribbean children, his skin was lighter than others. He had talked to Shola about this, and she had explained to him how the colour came out differently in different generations.

It was not uncommon for two black parents to have a light-skinned child. She had also told him how cruel kids could be in the playground. Black people often taunted the lighter-skinned members of their own race. Carlson had ignored the snide remarks about his colour for long enough. He couldn't stand anymore—his fists became stiff as he came to a halt and turned around.

Anton grabbed his arm. "They're idiots, man. Just let it go."

"No."

Carlson marched up to the boys, who are easily a couple of years older than him, and taller. They all had hoodies on, hair done up in braids. And a couple even had spliffs in their ear—a safe place to keep them and also to show off.

Carlson raised his voice. "Which one of you idiots said that?"

"Oh, look who it is. Mr light-skinned clever clod. You're just a wannabe black boy, aren't you?"

"Yeah," another one of them laughed. "*Choc ice*, that's what you are."

Anger roiling inside Carlson's heart burst at the seams. *Choc ice* was a particularly derogatory remark. It meant people who were black on the outside but white on the inside.

Carlson gnashed his teeth, yelled, and launched himself at the boy. The taller boy held him off easily and threw Carlson to the floor. Anton grabbed him and whispered in his ears fiercely.

"There's two teachers outside. You want to get detention?"

Carlson's chest heaved, a veil of red rage still clouding his senses. He glared at the boys, who pointed at him and laughed. Anton spun him around and held his head in both his hands. "Look at me, bruv."

Carlson held the deep brown eyes of his friend. Anton said, "You're better than them. Don't lower yourself to their standards. How we going to sell burgers at the school gates if we get into trouble now?"

Carlson blinked as Anton's words seeped into his consciousness. He swallowed hard, then exhaled. "Yes, I get that." He stood and rubbed his forehead. "Come on, let's go."

# CHAPTER 12

Harry and Arla decided to take the tube. They got off at Shoreditch, a hip and trendy part of east London that had been regenerated in the last decade. The East End of London had been the dominion of the working classes and newly arrived immigrants. Historically, the East London docks received the ships that bought exotic spices, tea, gold, and silk from far-off India and other colonies.

After the industrial age, the huge docks of East London sat forlorn and unused, gathering rust. As the 20th century dragged on, they became hulking eyesores on the banks of the Thames. Space was at a premium in this city of ten million citizens, and private developers were swift to voice their interests to the government.

As Arla walked next to Harry, she looked at the old warehouse buildings that had preserved their original brick and stone architecture but had trendy modernised interiors. Some were apartment complexes, and others were bars or furniture shops for the affluent city workers who dwelled here.

Harry stopped in front of an art gallery and pointed at a shirtless, muscled young man's photo in front of a window. "That guy is a spitting image of me," he exclaimed.

"Keep dreaming, Harry," Arla rolled her eyes, then tugged at his sleeve.

She smiled at the injured look on his face. Harry's ego was like an inflatable balloon. So easily punctured. He grabbed her hand as they walked, then gave it a squeeze. It was nice coming out for a walk outside of their regular area. She didn't mind holding hands here, where no one knew them. They stopped in front of a warehouse that had been converted into apartments. There was an underground garage, and the iron gates were shut.

Harry squinted at the number for deliveries and rang it. He explained who he was, and the gates slid open. A podgy man in dark overalls stepped out of the caretaker's office on the side.

Arla showed the man her warrant card. He was expecting them. He took them up to the elevators, and they rose up to the third floor. The landing was nicely carpeted, with art posters on the wall. It was discreetly lit, with views of the muddy brown Thames from the rear-facing windows. The caretaker stopped in front of the apartment, numbered 406. He made Arla sign a release statement before he opened the door. They stepped inside.

The interior was all minimalistic, post-modernist glitz. Digital pads had replaced light switches, and they could also be activated by voice.

Original framed modern art hung on the walls. In the lounge, there was a flatscreen TV recessed into the wall, below a traditional gas fire which contrasted with the modern fixtures.

Sheepskin and Persian rugs had replaced the carpet, and Arla's heels clicked on the varnished hardwood floor. The door in the lounge led to the balcony, which faced the river. The caretaker left them alone.

They put on gloves, and Arla went into the bathroom. She put Susan's toothbrush and her tweezers, shaving razors into separate specimen bags for DNA samples. She also took swabs from the sink and the bath. Then she joined Harry in the master bedroom. The four-poster bed was impressive, harking back to a bygone era. She marvelled at the cobalt blue patterned canopy on top of the four-poster.

"I'd love a bed like that," she thought aloud.

"Yeah," Harry smirked. "I could tie your hands to the posters, and you'd…" She smacked him on the arm and glared at him.

She took off the duvet and had a look at the bed sheets. The bed was disturbed, with a depression on either side. That was interesting. A couple had lain on this bed. She took more swabs from the white sheets, which had some stains on them.

Harry looked under the bed and then in the dresser. It was stacked with dresses and shoes. From the collection of clothes and their labels, Arla knew Susan was a devoted member of the temple of *haute couture.*

She joined Harry in the second smaller bedroom. The bed here was undisturbed. Harry pressed his lips together." Whoever she was sleeping with wasn't living here. There are no boxer shorts and no toothbrush in the bathroom. All the personal items belong to her."

Arla nodded. "For all we know, she had a one-night stand." She met Harry's eyes, aware he was on the same train of thought. "We need to know who this guy was."

"CCTV on the street, and also inside the complex. Let's check with the caretaker."

Harry scribbled stuff in her notebook and picked up the specimen bags. Arla spent some time in the lounge, noting the books, which were a collection of romance novels and finance textbooks.

She stepped out onto the balcony. The fresh breeze coming off the river was cool and smelled of dampness with a hint of sewage, mingled with exhaust from the streets. She looked at the corners of the small balcony and behind the small round table with two chairs.

She found an ashtray with two stubbed-out cigarettes. She took out the specimen bags and took the samples of both the cigarettes. Excitement was building in her guts. Had Susan been smoking the cigarettes with her new partner? She wondered what they would find from the DNA samples on the cigarette stubs.

Harry knocked on the caretaker's door and waited for him. Arla noticed how empty the apartment complex was. She hadn't seen a single soul inside, and no cars had entered or left. She decided to ask the caretaker.

The man scratched his head. He spoke with an Eastern European accent, and his name badge said Avalowski.

"Most of the apartments are empty. Some of them go on short-term lets in the summer."

Arla asked, "Are they mainly investment flats, bought for rent?"

Avalowski shrugged. Harry asked him about the CCTV, and they walked into an adjoining room where there were four CCTV monitors working. Avalowski asked about the dates.

They discovered the body on 25 March, and Susan had been reported missing on 18 March. That was a couple of days after her disappearance. She asked for CCTV footage from the eleventh till 18 March.

It took some time for the caretaker to go through the images. It helped as they were all digital and easily downloaded. He could search for the dates in question. Harry and Arla sat on either side of him as the images played on the four screens. They focused on the landing of her floor. Arla recognised Susan's figure on an image from 14th March, a Tuesday. Susan stepped out of the elevator, and there was a man with her.

"Freeze that image," she instructed.

"Zoom in."

As the couple passed under the cameras, the man's face became visible. He was Afro-Caribbean, with a nearly shaven head, and he was strikingly handsome. He wasn't much taller than Susan, and she guessed him to be less than 6 feet. But he was well built, thick around the shoulders, and his tight T-shirt showed off his large biceps.

"I want these tapes," she said briskly. "Harry, please send them to Lisa and ask her to check on HOLMES for photo identification of this man. If we find a match, I want a name and current location by this afternoon."

She memorised the face, staring at it intently. She had to keep an open mind as it was early in the investigation. But she knew this man would be important in the case.

# CHAPTER 13

Arla called switchboard-control to dispatch a uniform team to pick them up. The DNA samples they had gathered from Susan's apartment were time-sensitive, as the lab was waiting to do the DNA match with the body. Arla wondered what she would do if the samples didn't match. She needed the result before she could visit Sheila Remington. When the squad car arrived, Arla gave them the samples, and they took off, sirens blaring.

Her phone rang as she went back inside the caretaker's office. It was Gita. She sounded excited.

"Guv, we got hold of her dentist. She had one in Shoreditch. I just rang up several local to her. We got hold of her dental records."

"Excellent! Have you sent them to Dr Banerjee?"

"Yes, just waiting to hear from him."

"Good. Keep me posted."

She went back inside, where Harry was going over the images with the caretaker. She gave him the news, and he nodded, looking relieved.

"To be honest, I was kind of dreading going to see Sheila Remington without a positive ID. Let's hope it comes through. But what if it doesn't?"

"Then we keep looking."

Arla thanked the caretaker, and they left. Harry didn't find any more useful images, and they had a copy of the files now. They started walking towards the tube station.

"She's got the same necklace as the victim. Hair colour is a match, and if we allow up to a week for the body to surface from the water, the time of disappearance also makes sense. I'm pretty sure it's her."

She raised a hand. "But you're right. We should head back to the nick and make sure we have either the DNA or dental records to match."

Arla didn't have to wait that long. The call came through while they were on the train. Gita informed her the dental records were a match. Arla thanked her and removed the phone slowly from her ear. She nodded to Harry and mouthed a yes.

*****

Chelsea Embankment runs along the Thames. Its magnificent red-brick mansion terraces line the road facing the river and give way to detached houses in the side streets. Opulence takes on a different level here, as London's wealthiest financiers commissioned the best Victorian architects who built these sumptuous homes. Not much has changed in that respect, Arla thought to herself wryly.

The wide tree-lined avenue was a pleasure to walk down. The grand residences on each side were well maintained, but she wondered how many of them were actually occupied. As they approached their destination, she noticed Harry check his tie and flick an imaginary speck of dirt from his sleeve. She suppressed a grin.

Number 57 had a driver at the front, unlike the other houses. There was a blue uniformed security guard. She showed her warrant card and was shown up to the front door. The tall double-doored portcullis didn't open. Instead, there was a peep hole on the door, which slid apart, and a pair of eyes observed them. A smaller door opened to their right. Harry had to lower his head to enter, and Arla wondered if this was the normal entry route to the house.

It took her eyes a few seconds to adjust to the relative dimness inside. An elderly woman had let them in. Arla showed her warrant card again, and the woman, whom Arla assumed to be the caretaker, excused herself. Arla looked around her.

The vault of the reception area was so big that she felt she was in the nave of a church. The ceiling was impossibly high, and she could just about make out the frescoes in the wall. It all seemed very Vatican-esque to her. The ceiling looked like a cheap imitation of the Sistine Chapel.

She glanced at Harry, whose long neck was still craned upwards.

"Wow," Harry murmured.

"Easily impressed, aren't you?"

He glanced down at her. "I was looking at the nude figures. They've got nothing on Your naked curves......"

She kicked his leg hard, right where the bone sticks out in the ankle. Harry grunted and swore under his breath. He hopped on one leg.

Arla looked up as footsteps sounded down the gigantic hallway. Double doors had opened, and the elderly woman was being led by another woman who walked swiftly. She was in her sixties, Arla guessed as she drew closer. She was wearing a dark green jacket and matching skirt. Her shoulder-length hair was expertly groomed and she wore just enough make-up for work. Only her eyes gave away the torment that must be eating away inside her.

"Hi, I'm Sheila Remington," the woman said, her voice clear and steady. Arla and Harry shook hands with her.

"Thank you," Sheila said. "Would you like to come this way?" She led them down the hallway, but before the larger set of double doors, they turned right into a lounge room with statues, busts, and large framed oil paintings of men and women whom Arla judged to be of the Remington clan.

Chandeliers punctuated the ceiling, and they were all huge and glittered. The floor was hardwood, parquet tiled. Beyond the wood and glass doors to her right, she could see green lawns.

"Would you like some tea or coffee?" She asked. The elderly woman was still hovering behind her.

"I'll have a glass of water, thank you," Arla said. Harry declined anything.

They sat down in front of the large fireplace, and Arla wondered if it was still functional. It was big enough to roast a hog inside.

She took her time to study Sheila. The red rim around her eyes and the bags underneath them spoke of sleepless nights. Her face was pale and drawn, the cheekbones jutting out, her jaw clamped tight. Arla knew she was suffering, and in her experience, parents wanted closure at this point. They needed to know.

Sheila spoke before she could. Her hands were clasped on her lap, and her spine was ramrod straight as she stared at Arla.

"Well, please tell me. Have you found her? Have you found Susan?"

"Yes, I believe we have." Arla described how the body was discovered, the gold chain on the neck, and the dental records.

"Dental records are unique to every individual. We should have the DNA sample match by later this afternoon. But it is clear already that we have found Susan." She paused. "I'm very sorry."

Sheila stared at her for a few more seconds, then her head dropped. She might be a hard-nosed politician and a canny businesswoman, but she was also a mother. She couldn't hold the tears back. Arla walked over to her and knelt by her feet. She didn't touch Sheila but spoke in a soft voice.

"I know words will never take away your loss. But I can promise you one thing. We will find out exactly what happened to Susan. We will not rest till we find out the truth."

Sheila took out a handkerchief and dabbed at the red tip of her nose and her eyes.

"She's got her own life." Sheila stopped speaking and screwed her eyes shut again. "Sorry, she *had* her own life. But it was unusual not to have any contact for this long."

Arla went back to her chair. Harry had his notepad out already, and she did the same. Harry asked, "I know this must be very difficult for you. But can you remember when you last saw her?"

Sheila thought for a while, then frowned. "Well, her friend Madelyn called on the 18th of March, I think. I remember that day as we had a defence select committee meeting in Parliament that I had to attend. My son Rupert sent me a text asking if I had seen her. I said no."

"So, when did you last see her?" Harry pressed.

Sheila looked at Harry, her eyes dull and vacant. Almost like he wasn't there. Arla felt heartbroken for the woman, but she also knew Harry was doing the right thing. They needed her statement and also her alibi if she had one.

"Maybe the weekend before 18 March," Sheila's eyes flickered down to the ornate rug. "Yes, I think that's right. She came home for Sunday dinner."

"So you mean Sunday the 13th? That was the weekend before the 18th of March."

Sheila nodded. Harry asked, "Who else was at home at that time? Did you have Sunday lunch as a family?"

"My husband and my son." She didn't elaborate any further.

Harry said, "We will need to speak to both of them if you don't mind. It might be easier to speak to them here at home, then…" Harry broke off and glanced at Arla. She took over.

"It would be easier if we could speak to your husband and son while we're here. I'm sure they don't want to come down to the station, do they?"

Sheila's sighed. "My husband is abroad on business. He comes back from France tomorrow. You can certainly speak to him then. I believe Rupert is upstairs."

"Does he live here?"

"Yes, he does." Sheila looked at Arla, and her gaze was direct and steely.

Arla kept her voice neutral. "Then we would like to speak to Rupert, please, if you don't mind. He is aware of what's going on?"

Sheila nodded. Harry said, "It's best if we speak to him alone."

"I shall see if that can be arranged," Sheila said. Her accent was very posh, Arla noted. She was certainly aristocratic, and although her regal bearing was now diminished under the burden of her grief, her accent remained close to royalty.

# CHAPTER 14

Arla and Harry remained seated while Sheila left the room.

The vases inside old-fashioned wooden glass cabinets looked expensive. Arla didn't know a thing about Chinese vases, apart from the fact that they looked beautiful. As her eyes swivelled around, she caught Harry looking at her.

"Normal response, right?"

She knew he was referring to Sheila's grief-stricken reaction. Not overblown, quite appropriate, as she would expect. She felt Sheila's distress was genuine.

Arla had known grief like that once, and she didn't want to experience it again. She studied the intricate patterns on the rug, then the oil paintings of nameless aristocrats on the wall. She lived her life by suppressing memories. But cases like these served as triggers, and Arla had spent enough time with councillors to know she needed to distract herself.

The elderly woman, whose name she still didn't know, walked into the room. She announced, "Rupert Remington."

Harry glanced at her, and she could see the half-smile on his lips. She couldn't remember the last time she was in a house where the host had to be announced.

The young man who walked in had the appearance of a high nerd. Thick-rimmed brown glasses sat awkwardly on the bridge of his nose. His head seemed larger on his thin neck and narrow, sloping shoulders. Arla got the impression if she went up to him and pushed him, the head might snap right off the neck.

Rupert had sunk in cheekbones, and he folded his hands in front and stood there, watching them. He wore a full sleeve vest over a T-shirt and brown slacks, with black shoes. His eyes flitted nervously from Arla to Harry, like he was a schoolboy waiting for punishment.

Rupert sat down facing them.

Arla decided to open proceedings. She explained what had happened and waited for his reaction. Rupert took his glasses off, frowned, then massaged his eyes. His head sunk down on his chest, and he remained like that for a while, as if trying to gather his thoughts. Arla gave him time.

She could see the anguish on his face as he looked up. With the glasses off, his dark eyes were intense, probing. The heavy frown didn't leave his forehead.

"I can't believe this. I really cannot."

Arla kept her voice soft, gentle. "When did you last see Susan?"

"Rupert pursed his lips as he thought about what to say. It pleased Arla that Rupert didn't have anything prepared. In a murder enquiry, when the relatives blurted their responses too quickly, it was always suspicious. Like they had been expecting those questions.

Rupert used the handkerchief to dab at the corners of his eyes. The tip of his nose was red, and his upper lip trembled before he spoke. "She came for Sunday dinner a couple of weeks ago. Middle of March, I think."

"The 13th?"

"Yes, I think so."

"And you didn't see her after that?"

Rupert shrugged. "I have University, and she has work. She lived alone, as you know. We didn't see each other that often."

"On average, how regularly did she visit?"

"Maybe once a month? I'm not sure. I know that when she didn't come here, she stayed in touch with mummy."

"Were you close to her?" Arla kept her voice low and tone neutral. Rupert had put his glasses on, but he maintained eye contact with her, which she liked. His hands were still, and his facial muscles were unmoving. Liars also often contracted their neck muscles, which was a giveaway. So far, she hadn't seen any indication that Rupert might be lying. He seemed calm, relaxed, while obviously sad.

His shoulders rose slightly, then fell. "We were different people, you know? I was always the bookworm, and she was the popular girl in school. We went to different schools. I was at a boarding school for boys."

Arla nodded. "Thank you. So you weren't close to her?"

"Not like when we were children. I mean, we had different lives. But she was my sister, and this is terrible, just awful." His forehead creased again, and he took his glasses off. He put an elbow on his tie and massaged his temples.

Harry glanced at Arla, then inclined his head. She could see that Harry was also comfortable with the statement. Harry was a good detective, and she knew his instincts would be buzzing if he sensed something wrong. So far, their antennas remained silent.

Harry spoke, his voice as low as Arla's. "Thank you, Rupert. So you saw Susan last at lunch on Sunday 13th March and then did not hear from her again. Is that correct?"

"Yes." Rupert put his glasses back on and looked at Harry.

"You sent your mother a text on 18th March to tell her Susan was missing. Is that correct?" Harry asked.

"Yes. Her friend Maddie sent me a text because Susan hadn't turned up at work for three days."

"How well did you know Maddie?" Arla asked.

"She's been Susan's friend for a long time and used to come to our house. Again, I have not seen her for a while, but she had my number, I guess."

"Thank you," Harry said.

He shut his notebook, and Arla did the same.

Arla said, "I would like to see your mother once more, please."

Rupert stood. "Thank you." He got up and walked out, and after a few minutes, Sheila came back in. She took her seat opposite Arla and Harry, but not in the armchair Rupert had just vacated. She sat down at one corner of a three-seater sofa and crossed her legs. She looked pointedly at Arla. "Anything else I can assist you with, Inspector Baker?"

Arla noted a touch of impatience in her voice. It annoyed her, but she suppressed it. She kept her tone civil. "From Sunday 13th March till 18th March, when you got the text from Madelyn via your son, did you not have any contact with Susan?"

Sheila shook her head. "No, I didn't. I don't know if she contacted Rupert or my husband, but I wasn't in touch with her. She was busy with her job and me with mine."

Arla asked, "Can you think of a reason why she would do anything like this?"

Sheila upturned her lower lip, and a frown creased her face. "Do what exactly, Inspector Baker? Do you mean, not turn up for work for several days, and then..."

"That's precisely what I mean. Did she have any troubles that stopped her from going to work? Or anything she was trying to get away from?"

Sheila shrugged. "No personal or financial reason, as far as I know." She splayed her hands. "I don't think she was in any financial distress, or she would have told us. As for her personal life, I'm afraid I didn't know a great deal. I'm not sure if Rupert can help, but maybe her close friends like Madelyn will be your best bet."

Arla nodded. She scribbled Madelyn's name, circled it, and then wrote down 13th till the 25th and put a big question mark next to it. She shut her notebook and stood.

"Thank you very much for assisting us. Once again, I am sincerely sorry for your loss. We shall not leave any stone unturned in getting justice for Susan."

Harry murmured his deposition as well, and the three of them shook hands. The elderly woman came forward and showed them out.

# CHAPTER 15

*20 years ago*

Carlson wished he was taller. He squared his shoulders, puffed out his chest. He held out a burger inside its wrapper and shouted at the top of his voice.

"One for a pound. One for a pound cheaper than the canteen. And much more meat. We got plain burgers, cheeseburgers, and quarter pounds. Chili sauce, no extra."

Anton stood to one side, keeping an eye on the large Tiffin box full of burgers. Over the weekend, they got 8 pounds of meat and made more than 40 burgers with their £15. Carlson was excited. He had sold two burgers already, and he had no doubt that within a week, he would have sold them all. It was lunchtime at school, and there was the usual crowd of children milling around in the courtyard and outside the gates. Anton said it made more sense to sell their stuff outside the gate and Carlson had agreed. He didn't want to get into trouble.

A girl called Shania strolled up with her friends. She had long black hair, and her chocolate brown skin was perfect. She had beautiful, large eyes, and Carlson thought he was in love with her. Her friends were all pretty too, but Shania stood out. Carlson had his heart in his mouth as Shania stared directly at him.

"Hi Carlson," she whispered. God, Carlson thought, even her voice was attractive.

He swallowed hard. "What's up, Shania?"

She cocked her head to one side and indicated the burger he was holding. "You selling burgers?"

"Not just any burger. These are homemade, with special sauce. We got sweet and chili and pickle sauce as well." He glanced behind at Anton, who nodded vigorously. Carlson turned his attention back to Shania quickly. "What do you want?"

Shania put a fingernail to her lips. It had red nail polish, and Carlson looked at it with interest. It was the first time he had seen nail polish this close up. His mother rarely wore it.

Two of Shania's friends appeared to behind her. Anton straightened her and brushed imaginary specks of dust off his coat. "Hello girls," he said. Carlson still had his eyes fixed on Shania.

"You want to try one?"

Shania smiled at him, and Carlson couldn't help but grin. She nodded. "Yeah, sure."

Carlson thought quickly, then lowered his voice. "Okay, listen up. If you buy three burgers for you and your friends, I'll give you three for the price of two. So, three burgers for two pounds."

Shania turned to her friends, who shrugged. Carlson did a mental high-five with Anton. "Great," Carlson enthused. Anton opened the box and handed three fresh burgers to Carlson.

"See you around," Shania said, her eyes lingering on Carlson.

"Yeah, sure," Carlson said, stepping forward to say goodbye. God, did that just happen? He stared at Shania as she walked off with her friends, chattering.

By Wednesday, day three of their new venture, the boys had sold a total of eleven burgers. They had made their money back, and turned a profit. Carlson was giddy with excitement.

"Yeah, bruv." He did an elaborate high-five with Anton. "This is just the beginning. We should start making chips and sell that as well. Maybe put in some jerk sauce with the chips; man-dem will love that."

Anton did a small dance, shuffling his feet on the pavement. "I'm feeling that, cousin. This is wicked."

He opened his mouth to say something more but then froze, his eyes fixed behind Carlson. Carlson whirled around in alarm. A male teacher was standing behind him, his arms folded across his chest. It was Mr Gunter, an English teacher in year six. He was known to be strict, and all the children were scared of him. Mr Gunter had his navy blue blazer on, and he adjusted his glasses as he stared at the boys.

"I've been observing you for the last three days. Are you aware that selling anything outside the school gates is not allowed?"

Carlson stared back at the teacher with his mouth open. Mr Gunter said, "Did you ask anyone's permission before you started?"

Carlson felt a cold fear sink into his abdomen. He shook his head and looked to the ground. Mr Gunter's voice was stern. "If the headmaster hears of this, both of you will be in detention. You will also get pink slips sent to your homes."

The fear was spreading inside Carlson's body, numbering his fingers and toes. Pink slips were bad news. Very bad. After three pink slips, boys were told to stay at home, and some of them even had to go to special schools after that. He was in deep trouble.

Carlson's Adam Apple bobbed up and down as he swallowed with difficulty. "It's only burgers, sir. And people like it. They taste nice. Here, would you like to try one?"

Mr Gunter bent at the waist and brought his face close to Carlson's. Behind the teacher, Carlson could see a ring of children, who had gathered to watch the ordeal with interest.

"Are you trying to bribe me, boy? Well, it's not going to work." He stood straight, and his eyes flicked over to Anton. "Give me that box. I'm going

69

to put it into storage, and you can collect it when you go home. And if I see this again," he narrowed his eyes and pointed at the two boys. "Both of you will be in detention for the rest of the year. Not to mention a meeting with the headmaster."

# CHAPTER 16

As they walked out of the Remington mansion, Harry took out his phone. He made a call to Clifford & Sons, the accountancy office where Susan worked. Madelyn West was still out for the day, and she was indeed on a business trip. The receptionist told Harry she was due back in the office tomorrow morning.

Arla said, "Have we tried Madelyn's own number? You've already spoken to her, right?"

Harry nodded. "Yes, I got the number from the switchboard." He dialled Madelyn's number as they walked down the leafy avenue. It was a lovely street, the pavement wide, the buildings a combination of semi-detached and detached mansions.

She suspected each one would be in the tens of millions. A four-bedroom family house was a million-plus now in London, she knew because she had been searching.

It struck her as strange that two streets down were the tall council building complexes - free accommodation paid for by the tax payer.

She wondered what the inhabitants of these council estates thought when they looked down upon these grand mansions. London was inexplicable at times, pockets of extreme wealth, surrounded by glaring poverty.

Harry hung up his phone and turned to her. "Not answering. Left a message for her to call back."

By the time they got back to Clapham station, it was almost 2 PM. They picked up lunch and an order of five coffees from Alessandro's, the Italian café near the station. Harry put down the coffees and bagels on

Rob's desk. Rob's eyes brightened as he wiped the sweat from his forehead and reached for a bagel. Arla spread the sandwiches on the table.

"For all your hard work." She said, opening the box of tuna salad she had. Rosslyn, Lisa, and Gita pulled up chairs, and Arla discussed her morning's findings with them.

After listening to them, Arla said, "Susan's apartment is very chic. I forgot to ask Sheila if Susan actually owns it. But the most important findings were the two cigarette butts and the condition of her mattress. She had clearly slept there with someone, and I think it was a man. Any news when the DNA swabs will be back?"

Rob gulped down a bite of his egg and bacon sandwich, then spoke. He had finished eating his bagel already. "The DNA match is back. The samples from her flat match DNA from the body."

Arla nodded. She had expected as much. "And the DNA from the cigarette butts or her bed?"

"Nothing as yet."

Harry said, "I also took swabs from the bath, and shower area, just in case the person she had been with used it."

"Yes, we have to wait till the samples find a match."

"Fingers crossed," Arla murmured. She didn't hold out much hope.

Arla took a generous sip of her coffee and felt better. She needed that. "What about the man on the CCTV image? Who walked down with Susan on her hallway on fifteenth March?"

Harry said, "That was at 6 PM, two days after she had Sunday lunch with her family."

"Correct," Arla said. "It was late enough for her to have finished work and come home with this guy. HOLMES can find us a photo ID." She looked at Harry, who dug into his pocket and came out with the disk drive which contained the CCTV images. He offered it to Lisa, who accepted it with a murmur of thanks.

Rosslyn said, "Banerjee called. He wants you to see him at the morgue."

Harry smirked. "Great news, just after our lunch."

Arla rolled her eyes. "Don't be such a drama queen." She turned her attention to her team. "Have we got the social media profiles of everyone involved?"

Gita spoke up. "Yes, we have. Susan's Facebook page is interesting. She's also got a Twitter and Instagram account. She clearly liked travelling and partying. She also posted photos of her work do's."

Arla took the phone from Gita's hand. She flicked through the Instagram photos, and one showed Susan in a polka dot bikini, posing with a cocktail glass in her hand. She was alone, on a tropical sea beach. The sand was white, and it reached up to her ankles, the water behind sparkling blue. There were several photos from the same resort but a few others from other exotic locations.

Arla noted the dates of the photos. Some went as far back as 2018. She scrolled upwards and found photos of her with David Braithwaite. They did make a nice couple, she noted. She saw photos of them on board in a yacht, possibly in the Mediterranean or Turkey. David had an athletic and toned body, and he was holding his girlfriend close. Susan liked her figure and flaunted it. Arla supposed that the photos of her sunbathing were taken by David.

She went through her Facebook feed and found similar photos. Susan liked animal charities and children's welfare groups. She had posted their images. Arla was looking for the man she had seen on the CCTV. So far, she had found nothing.

She turned to her team . "What about the rest? WhatsApp and Tiktok?" She grinned. Speaking of Tiktok made her feel old. She didn't even have an Instagram account.

Gita and Rosslyn exchanged a glance and leaned forward. "It's interesting you say that, guv. We looked through her friends' lists and checked their photos as well. We did this for the top ten friends with whom she communicated with regularly."

Rosslyn carried on. "We found one Instagram account which has photos of Susan that are, well, dodgy."

Arla frowned. "What do you mean dodgy?"

"Like nude photos," Rosslyn said, dropping her voice. She took out a phone. Here, I saved some."

Harry leaned close to Arla to have a look. Their shoulders were touching, and she could smell his aftershave. She didn't mind anymore. After Nicole arrived, her relationship with Harry had become common news.

Arla murmured, "Several photos have been deleted from Susan's Instagram account. But some are still present on this account." She shook her head. The nude photos of Susan were taken on board the same yacht she had just seen. There were a couple in the hotel room and another on the beach, with the light fading. She imagined whoever Susan had been with suggested that they wait till the beach was deserted before they took the photo. Susan was pouting and posing with her well-shaped bum sticking out.

Arla said, "This account is called 'Red Devil'." The profile photo of the account was a monster's face, with two black horns sticking out from a red face. All of the nude photos came from that account. She read the caption below several photos.

*"I've got more like this, want to see?"*

*"This one is my favourite. How would it look like on a billboard?"*

*"Or maybe on TV?"*

Harry sat back and folded his hands behind his head. "This looks like revenge porn to me."

Rob asked, "More importantly, how did the Red Devil get hold of her nude photos?"

Harry coughed into his fist. "We have to suspect David Braithwaite first. Then any friends she had, during that period. What's the date on the photos?"

Gita said, "the Red Devil account is still open but not used. The last message was four weeks ago. It was sent to Susan's account."

Arla scrolled to check. "Yes, that's right. Susan deleted that message, so we don't know what it showed."

She pressed her lips together, a sense of disquiet spreading in her mind. It seemed as if Susan was the target of a concerted campaign. But what for? What did this Red Devil hope to achieve?"

Harry voiced her thoughts. "Did the Red Devil want money? Or just to discredit her? Or to cause her stress."

Rob said, "Well, she had plenty of money. Imagine if these photos were made public, and the national tabloids picked them up. It would make her and her family look like a fool, right?"

Arla shrugged. "It would definitely cause her mother a great deal of embarrassment. Don't think it would do her much harm politically. But politics is perception, and if these images were to become public, the Remington family name suffers."

She looked up at Rosslyn and Gita. "Good work, you two." She smiled at them. "Can you ask the Tech lab to see if they can locate this account ?"

Arla knew it was notoriously difficult to find out the physical location of the IP address that was posting social media messages. If the IP address kept changing, they had no hope.

Rosslyn nodded, "I'll ask them."

Arla said, "And keep trying to get the DNA matches. That guy who went to her apartment-- I want an ID if possible." She turned to Harry. "Hope your pretty stomach's now settled, Inspector Mehta. We have to visit the morgue. By the way, do we know when the family is going to see the body?"

Lisa said, "This afternoon. She glanced at their tablet in her hand. "It says 3 PM."

Arla glanced at her watch. It was 3:15. "Let's go now, and we might be able to catch the family. Let's see if they have anything further to add."

# CHAPTER 17

Arla stared out the window as Harry drove. He had rolled the window down, and his right elbow was sticking out as he drove with one hand.

The sun had dipped under a bank of clouds, making it cooler. Traffic was humming its busy hour tunes: it was close to school break time. As always, Arla wondered what Nicole was doing. She couldn't wait to see her daughter.

She forced her mind back on the case. "Was someone trying to discredit Susan or her mother? With that revenge porn, I mean."

"Could be both. But I think it's Susan who would bear the brunt of it. Imagine the stress she must have been under, fearing those photos were made public."

Arla took her eyes off the streets and grinned at Harry. She lifted a hand and stroked his smooth, light brown cheeks. "Getting in touch with your feminine side, Harry?"

"I'm just saying. You don't see a lot of revenge porn against men, do you? It's women who are mainly affected. And targeted."

"Of course." Arla sighed. "As if being judged for how you look, what you wear, and even what you eat isn't bad enough." She clamped down on her jaws. Her temper flared as she thought of the idiot who had made Susan's life a living hell.

"God knows what that poor girl had to go through." She clicked her fingers. "Was there any mention of depression or anxiety in her doctor's notes? This is the type of confidential thing a patient would discuss with their GP."

Harry shook his head. "Not that I can recall. But you're right; it might be worth another check. Especially if she changed her doctor recently. When she moved into a new flat, did she get a local doctor?"

Arla sat up in her seat. "Good thinking, Harry. She probably had a family doctor when she lived with her parents and a new one now. We need to get hold of her medical records."

Harry parked the car at the hospital's parking lot, and they took the elevator down to the basement floor. Going to the morgue always gave Arla the creeps. It was funny because she was used to dead bodies. She had seen her fair share of gruesome murders. But the location of the morgue, deep down below ground level, in an empty corridor with no signs of life is what she didn't like. And although she would never admit it to Harry, she was glad he was there with her.

Their footsteps echoed in the wide, empty hallway. Arla was glad to reach the doors of the morgue and pressed on the bell. Lorna, Dr Banerjee's assistant, opened the door for them. They got changed into surgical gowns and stepped inside the morgue space. Dr Banerjee had his back to them, working on a body on a gurney. He turned when he heard Arla approaching.

"Aha, there you are. I was wondering if you got lost on the way."

"Yeah, Harry's driving can be erratic at times."

She winked at Dr Banerjee, and Harry frowned at both of them.

Arla looked around her. "Have the family gone?"

"Yes, you just missed them. Sheila Remington and her son attended. The husband is still away on a business trip, she told me."

Arla nodded. Dr Banerjee said, "She's a stoic woman. She took it well. So did the son. Not easy to see this." His chin pointed to the covered corpse on the gurney.

78

Without further ado, Dr Banerjee took the covers off Susan's corpse. Arla noticed the bloating had gone down. Presumably, as Dr Banerjee had dissected into the abdominal cavity, a lot of gas had been released. She was glad that she was wearing her mask.

"Water really is the devil when it comes to forensics," the pathologist said ruefully. "I'm afraid there isn't a great deal I can add from the outside. Starting from the top, the hair and scalp look intact. I found something interesting in the teeth. Actually, it's the forensic odontology dude who found it."

"Who?" Arla frowned.

"The dentist who works here. I call him when I need an opinion on victims of dentition."

"What did you find?" Harry asked.

"The enamel on her teeth is almost all worn out. The enamel on all of the teeth is mostly worn out. It's quite strange, and it's only seen in particular cases."

"Such as?" Harry asked.

Dr Banerjee raised his eyebrows. "Well, acid corrosion is the main cause. Mainly acid from vomiting. Or from gastric reflux."

"Are you saying Susan vomited a lot?"

The pathologist glanced at both of them. "Both of you are detectives. What do you think?"

Arla thought about it for a while, and she didn't like it. "A woman who vomits a lot means one thing, doc. She was trying to bring her food up. Are you saying she had an eating disorder? Like bulimia?"

A look of sadness passed across the elderly man's eyes. He blinked a couple of times.

"That's exactly what I'm saying. The destruction of enamel in her teeth is so pervasive, and it could only be caused by very frequent vomiting.

79

It probably happened many years ago as well, maybe when she was a teenager. Unfortunately, we see this sometimes."

Arla said, "Especially in a family like hers. Maybe her mother was a perfectionist."

Dr Banerjee nodded. "Yes, that is possible. Eating disorders are more common in families with high achieving parents. Girls suffer from body dysmorphia, which means they hate what they see in the mirror. Very sad."

This might explain why Susan was thin, but she was also filled out in the right places, Arla thought. Judging by her recent photos on social media, she certainly didn't have an eating disorder. Hence, this had to be from a long time ago. She glanced at Harry. "We really need to get all of her medical records."

Dr Banerjee looked up at them. "Haven't you got her medical records already? I'm pretty sure I have, as they follow as a matter of routine after a positive ID. I become the responsible Doctor at this point, as you know."

Arla brightened. "Great. Have you had a chance to look through them?"

"No. I can certainly send them to you, and your team can go through them."

Arla nodded, and Banerjee continued with his examination. "The skin on the neck is almost all gone, but the trachea or windpipe, as you know, is a very superficial organ. It didn't take long to find out that it was ruptured."

"Meaning broken?"

"Yes, unfortunately. Someone strangled her. I can't say when. By the way, there's plenty of alcohol in her toxicology report. And something else too. The lab found cocaine in her bloodstream."

Arla digested this in silence. Banerjee said, "Due to the alcohol and cocaine, she was clearly in an altered state of mind. There are no signs of struggle in her body. And I have a feeling she was strangled after she was drowned."

Arla raised her eyebrows. "Why drown her first, then strangle her?"

"Susan's killer dragged her into the water, and she probably swallowed a great deal. When she stopped struggling, he just pressed on her neck, popping the trachea easily. That's why she didn't struggle."

"How do you know she didn't struggle?"

"There is no bruising in the adjoining muscles. No cuts or lacerations either."

Harry shifted on his feet, then rolled his shoulders. "That's strange. Why break the trachea this way? Did he want to leave his mark on the body?"

Banerjee shrugged. Arla stared at him, and then her eyes fell on the exposed neck. She shivered, a sudden fear clutching at her own throat. If a killer left a sign like this, it meant they had a fetish about the neck. She remembered how the necklace had remained with the body. It was separated but close enough to be retrieved. The killer did not take the necklace.

Aloud she said, "The person who broke her trachea had to be strong, right?"

The pathologist nodded. "Yes, this was a swift and clean rupture. So quite possibly by a man or a very strong woman."

Harry said, "This points to a man, Doc." Arla nodded her agreement. Her brain was on fire, exploring different angles. Susan's life was slowly dawning upon her mind, small patches at a time, like an unfinished jigsaw.

Dr Banerjee shook his mop of silvery hair and continued. "There are no signs of sexual activity. No semen in the vagina. None in the anal cavity either." Dr Banerjee moved down to the legs. "Can't find a great deal in the legs. As you had noticed before, no lacerations on the shins or ankles means she probably didn't run through a forest." He moved his attention from back of the body to the hands.

"The fingernails have traces of nicotine, which means she was a smoker. And this sign on her left hand," Dr Banerjee pointed to the dollar-mark, "It was probably done with a sharp knife. It's a rough approximation, as you can see. The person who did this wasn't very skilled, but again, they wanted to leave a mark.

Arla said, "It's the mark that I find puzzling. Using a dollar sign is very unusual, even for a psychopath."

Harry touched her arm. "Who knows what goes inside those insane minds. But don't forget it could be a fake sign."

Arla nodded, then stared at the sad remains of what had once been a vibrant, young woman. Susan Remington was a complex person, and it would take time to peel through the layers of her personality.

She asked Dr Banerjee, "When did she die, Doc?"

"Very difficult to say," Dr Banerjee moved his head sideways. He peeled off his gloves and chucked them in the bin. He walked back towards his desk, and Arla and Harry followed. "When was she last seen?"

"As far as we know, Tuesday 15th March. We are still looking for witnesses. We found the body on 25th March."

"I was going to say she was submerged for about a week. That's when you start to get the skin slippage and the advanced stage of bloating we found. To be honest, we're lucky that the fishhook snagged on her. Otherwise, she might still be drifting in the centre, near the bottom of the pond."

"If you're saying seven days, that means the 18th March? Is that correct?"

Dr Banerjee blew out his cheeks, then exhaled. "This is a problem with water, I'm afraid. Very hard to give you a more precise time of death, other than a range. Definitely five days, but no more than ten, I would say."

# CHAPTER 18

Arla glanced at her watch. She was getting late. Thankfully, Rita had volunteered to pick Nicole up from the childminders. But Rita was going out to see her friends later that night. Arla had to be back home soon.

She addressed her team and spoke rapidly. "We know that Susan probably had an eating disorder. I want details of that and all of her medical history from when she was a child."

Arla had already sent Lisa the medical notes Banerjee had emailed to her.

"We need to build a picture of her final days. We need to know her routine. From when she woke up and went to work, what she did at work, who she was friends with, who hated her, all of it."

She glanced at Rosslyn and Gita. "Any sign of the IP address of the Red Devil?"

Gita shook her head. "The Tech Lab is still looking into it. But it doesn't seem like one IP address. And the ones that have seen so far had their GPS location turned off."

Arla looked towards the ceiling. She had made some progress into the casc, but she was still in the dark about how Susan died.

Rob said, "The revenge porn photos were recent, guv. The stress of that could have played on her mind?"

Rosslyn said, "Is that why she was drinking and taking cocaine? To cope with the stress of her photos being leaked to the media?"

Gita said, "Or to her parents?"

Arla raked her tongue across the top of her lips. It was possible, especially given the mental illness that Susan had lightly suffered earlier in life. She didn't know much about eating disorders, but it was logical to assume Susan would be prone to feelings of insecurity and anxiety. Did the Red Devil know about her eating disorder? If he did, then he was a total gutter snipe, Arla thought in disgust.

"Maybe," she conceded. "But given her recent way of life, I doubt she was depressed. And maybe she took cocaine recreationally, as so many young people do."

She shook her head. "Okay team, I have to go. Inspector Mehta will take over from me." She glanced at Harry. "Did we get hold of the telephone number and her call log?"

Rob said, "We've got a telephone number and are waiting for the call log. I'll have it on your desk by tomorrow morning, guv."

Arla stood, then leaned against the table with her legs crossed. "The actual phone was never found, right? Or her purse?"

The team shook their collective head, and Lisa spoke. "Nothing near the body, guv. Who knows if it's in the pond."

Arla narrowed her eyes, pondering. Could Susan have gone out without her phone and purse? No, that was unlikely. She couldn't think of a reason why. Unless....

Her chain of thought was broken by the phone ringing. With a sigh of impatience, she snatched it up.

"DCI Baker."

"It's me," said the withering, growling voice of her boss, Commander Johnson. Arla's heart sank.

"Come up to my office, right now."

# CHAPTER 19

Commander Johnson was built like a grizzly bear. He was standing by his desk when Arla knocked and entered his room on the fourth floor. Despite his height and width, Wayne Johnson had thin, sallow cheeks and narrow, darting eyes. He focused those blue eyes on Arla as she sat down on a chair without being asked to. He gave her a nod, the strained expression on his face not changing. Arla returned his acknowledgement with silence.

"Why wasn't I told about Susan Remington's case?" He said in his habitual gravelly voice.

"We only found the body yesterday, sir, and it's been one thing after another."

"You went to Susan Remington's house. I trust you know who she is." It was a statement, not a question.

"Oh, I did some research before I went," Arla said, not bothering to hide her sarcastic grin.

It had the desired effect. Johnson puffed out his chest, and the knuckles on his fists went white. "Do you know who called me this morning?" His voice boomed out.

The windowpanes might have rattled, but Arla didn't move a muscle on her face. She was used to Johnson's histrionics.

"I'm not psychic, sir. Maybe you should tell me?"

Johnson's bushy eyebrows, which looked peculiar over his small eyes, lowered till they were almost touching his nose. He waggled a finger at her. "Don't get smart with me, DCI Baker." He used her full title when he was upset. Most of the time, he addressed Arla by her first name.

" I don't have much time, sir. I have to get back to pick up my daughter."

Johnson's features softened somewhat. The tension went out of his jaw, and his spine relaxed slightly. He squeezed his eyes shut, then exhaled a long breath. "The justice minister Lord Braithwaite, that's who. Apparently, he's good friends with Susan Remington."

Arla narrowed her eyes, her mind churning. "Lord Braithwaite?" There had to be a link to David Braithwaite.

But it wasn't his father, that much she knew. An uncle, maybe? She was annoyed that she didn't know. Her team was brilliant, but they should have dug this out. Of course, it could be a coincidence, with no family connection. Arla explained her thoughts to Johnson. His mouth fell open.

"I can't believe it. If the justice minister is a relative, and this is a murder enquiry, then this certainly is political hot soup."

Johnson sat down heavily on his chair, making it shake. He looked at Arla with a weary expression on his face. For once, she empathised with him. She too, was tired of pressure on the Department.

"Have you told the media liaison?"

"Yes, I sent them an email. My team is aware of keeping it closely under wraps. The rest of the staff don't know the family connections."

Johnson said, "We need to make sure this doesn't leak to the media, Arla." His blue eyes became flints, throwing daggers at her. "If it does, I'm going to hold you responsible."

Arla bristled, and her nostrils flared. "Well, as assistant deputy commissioner in charge of southwest London, it's actually you who's going to be held responsible, sir. With all due respect, my team is working flat out, and I can vouch for them. If some other staff speaks to the press, there's nothing I can do about it."

Johnson's jaws flexed, and his gaze hardened. Then he blinked. Arla knew Johnson couldn't intimidate her. They had worked together for far too long, and she had stared him down many times. She was right. Johnson softened his voice.

"Okay, let's see what happens. Do we have any suspects?"

"At this stage, sir, everyone is a suspect. But I don't think it's her near family. The ex-boyfriend, DB, is. But so is the man she was caught on CCTV with, in her apartment. And number 3, the Red Devil, who was targeting her with revenge porn."

"Why is DB a suspect?"

"He might be upset that she broke up with him. He could also have targeted her with revenge porn."

Johnson pursed his lips together, and Arla sighed. "I know it's not great. A breakup shouldn't lead to murder. The CPS might laugh at it. But I'm trying, sir."

She continued. "Maybe more happened between them. I suspect that, sir. This whole revenge porn thing is strange. What if it is DB, faking an Instagram account as the Red Devil? After all, he was best placed to take nude photos of her."

"Have you interviewed any of the suspects?"

"Well, the only one we know is DB. The other two we're still looking for."

Johnson tapped a finger on the desk, frowning. "Find out the link between the Justice Minister and DB. If there is one, and he is our number one suspect, we are in deep waters." He stretched out a hand and pointed to Arla. She didn't like it. Her jaws clamped tight as she glared at him.

"Do not interview DB without my permission. Is that understood, DCI Baker?"

Arla gave him a withering look. It infuriated her that despite her seniority, Johnson took that tone with her.

"Yes," she said coldly, then slammed the door shut on her way out.

# CHAPTER 20

*20 years ago*

Carlson bounced the football on the ground as him and Anton walked home after practice. He was sweating and dying for a drink. The summer sun blazed above them, and the heat was turning leaves from green to yellow. In the Winstanley estate of Battersea, where they lived, there weren't that many trees. But those that did were wilting in the blazing sun.

"Bruv, we really got to make some peas," Carlson said.

They stopped outside a cornershop, letting people come out before they went in. Carlson had thought about stealing magazines from the cornershop, but it was too risky, and the payoff wasn't good. He'd be lucky to make a pound from each magazine he nicked and sold later. The burgers had been his best business venture so far, and he was still in shock that it was shut down so quickly.

He learnt later that to open a burger stall anywhere, he either had to get a licence from the council or open up a shop. And as the councils didn't give licences for street hawkers in London, his dreams of making money from selling burgers were now a distant hope. In any case, as the lady at the council had told him kindly, he was far too young to be earning a living. He should be at school studying.

*You sound like my mother*, Carlson had grumbled to himself as he walked off after thanking the woman.

What was he going to do?

Shola had now lost her job in the hospital, and they had no money. Whatever little they got from the council just covered their food bill. Carlson was now eleven and a half, and he was a little taller than before. But annoyingly, Anton had shot up, despite only being three months older than him. In fact, most of the boys aged between eleven and twelve were taller than Carlson. He hated that.

"You keep talking about making peas, fam. Why don't you just give it a rest?"

"You won't understand, bruv. We ain't got no money."

"Neither do we."

Both of them lapsed into silence. They came from single-parent homes, and their poor, hard-working mothers did the best they could to add to their menial jobs. Anton knew that Shola now had immigration problems and that she'd been made redundant. He wanted to help his friend but didn't know how to.

The streets of London could be cruel. It was grey, dismal, and damp, and the skeleton paths of their estate in south London reeked of poverty, drugs, graffiti, and guns. The world they saw on the TV screens seemed like fantasy, where people lived in nice homes with gardens, got college degrees, nice jobs and mortgages. Both boys suspected already that it would not be their life. Unless a miracle happened, their lives would be shaped by the only reality they knew – the reality around them.

"I'm going to steal a dog, bruv," Carlson announced.

Anton gaped at him. "Say what? What for?"

Carlson frowned at his best friend. "You really are stupid; you know that? Do you know how much a pit bull terrier of good pedigree costs? Up to 500 quid, bruv."

Anton raised his eyebrows. "For real?"

Carlson shook his head. "Just follow my lead, bruv. Okay?"

They got their drinks and were walking along the pavement. One of their friends was walking past them. Carlson asked him if he would put the football into the grounds of their estate, and the boy nodded. It wasn't Carlson's football. Balls often lay around in their estate, and whoever picked them up was their owner. Carlson walked along, Anton following reluctantly.

"Yo. Where we going, man?"

Carlson didn't reply. They were on a street with single-family homes, with gardens in the front. They were council homes, and people were very lucky to get them. There was a severe shortage of single-family council homes in the London area, and most families were cooped up in the tiny apartments where the boys lived.

Carlson stopped under the shade of a tree and watched a house opposite. A pit bull puppy was playing in the front garden. The dog's owner was giving himself a suntan. He was old, with rolls of fat in his midline bulging over the shorts he was wearing. His face and arms were slowly turning red, but he didn't seem to care. He was fast asleep.

Carlson said, "There you go. I've been watching that house every time we walk down here. The puppy won't do anything if we grab him."

Anton whispered, "But what about the owner?"

"Look at him. He's fat and old. We can easily outrun him. And only his wife lives with him, and she's also fat and old. Don't worry; I've thought this through."

"Have you really?" Anton muttered, shaking his head.

They waited for a few minutes, keeping an eye up and down the road. It remained quiet, most people relaxing indoors in the hot summer afternoon. The man rose from his sunbathing, probably aware that he was now too hot and getting sunburned. He went inside but left the front door ajar. Carlson knew this was his chance.

He streaked across the road and jumped over the short fence. He scooped up the puppy in his hands. The dog squirmed, then barked a couple of times.

*Shit,* Carlson thought. He ran back over the fence, but the front door had already opened, and the fat owner appeared, his bulk filling up the doorway.

"You! Stop!" He screamed.

Carlson had taken off the street already, pumping his legs as fast as he could. He didn't know where Anton was. He heard more shouts behind him.

Damn, the man was following him. He kept running and took a left. If he went straight and took a left again, he would end up at the gates of their estate. But the next left turn proved to be a dead end. Carlson could have climbed over one of the fences and gone into a house, but it was difficult to climb up a tall fence with the puppy in his arms.

But he had no other option. He had to try. He thrust the squirming puppy inside his coat and pulled up the zip. He could hear running footsteps at the mouth of the alley. He ran up to the fence and leapt higher. His fingers closed over the top of the fence. He heaved himself up, straining at the shoulders.

The puppy barked and wriggled inside his coat. Sweat poured down Carlson's face, blinding his eyes. He managed to pull himself up till he was astride the fence. But before he could jump to the other side, a large hand grabbed his foot. A hand pulled him down, and although Carlson resisted, he wasn't strong enough. He toppled back down and hurt his chest and shoulder as he thrashed down on the pavement.

The man began to curse and used the word that Carlson had heard before. He didn't like it, but there wasn't much he could do. He had brought this upon himself. He fought against the man, trying to escape. But the bloke was strong, and he pinned Carlson down to the ground.

His face was grazing the pavement, and he could smell the dust. More footsteps sounded, and he was hauled to his feet. Three men looked down at him, and they were all white. Carlson's heart sank.

"Take him to the police station," the dog's owner snarled. "Sick and tired of pests like you."

# CHAPTER 21

T he BMW's window was down, and Arla poked her head out, staring at the giant needle stacks of glass and metal buildings. They rose to dizzying heights, tall enough to puncture the bubble of lazy white clouds in the blue sky. Not that she could see much of the blue sky, most of it was obscured by the dense canopy of this urban jungle. Men and women in sharp suits hurried along the pavement. Minimalist Japanese sushi bars gleamed next to traditional British pubs.

Harry manoeuvred the car expertly through the traffic, then turned into the underground parking lot of the global accountancy firm headquarters where Susan worked. Arla checked her phone quickly before she lost her signal. Nothing new from her team. But Rosslyn and Gita had uncovered the crucial link between David Braithwaite and the justice minister who shared the same last name.

It was indeed his uncle, brother to his peer father. Arla marvelled at that. Three men in the same family, all in the House of Lords, and one of them the justice minister. The whole situation gave her a headache, and she knew the fallout from this case would be far-reaching, no matter how much containment Johnson and the commissioners in the London Metropolitan tried to do.

They showed their warrant cards at reception and went up to the fifth floor, escorted by a guard.

Madelyn West was waiting for them. She was a vivacious brunette in her mid-30s. She looked after herself, Arla noted with a twinge of envy. Definitely a size 8. Madelyn wore a figure-hugging navy blue dress that came down to her knees. It was full-sleeved and covered her chest. Her hair was tied back in a ponytail, and although her lipstick was a dark red, and her makeup was not excessive, Arla could see this was a woman who liked dressing up. Her high-heeled blue felt shoes were definitely Bond Street, not the high street.

They shook hands and were shown into a private office at the end of the open-plan office space, where numerous accountants sat at their desks.

A jar of coffee was brought for them, with three cups.

Arla got straight to the point. "Thank you for seeing us. You reported Susan Remington missing on 18 March, is that correct?"

Madelyn West had light brown eyes with grey flecks in them. It went with her hair. Her eyes were large and expressive, and Arla noticed that more than once, she flicked those eyes to Harry, then smiled at him.

"Yes, I did. Susan hadn't been to work for three days, and I sent her brother a text that morning. I believe Rupert passed it to Sheila, her mother. Neither of them knew anything, which I thought was odd. I started getting concerned."

"Had Susan been under any work-related or personal stress, as far as you know?"

"Not that I know of," Madelyn said, pressing her lips together. She studied the glass desktop. "We often travel with our work, and we have to finish projects within tight deadlines sometimes. The big corporates often throw us information at the last minute before we complete their accounts. It can be stressful."

Arla said, "But presumably Susan was used to that stress?"

Madelyn nodded. "Yes, she was. She was also punctual at work. I thought it was out of character."

"When she didn't turn up, at what point did you contact her?"

"On the second day. I rang her phone a couple of times, left her a message, and then sent her emails. None of them were answered. That's why on the third day, I got in touch with her family."

"Thank you. When did you last see Susan Remington?"

"I was out of office on Monday 14th March. But we exchanged texts, I'm sure. We normally do. I saw her on Tuesday, and we had lunch. That was the last time I saw her."

Madelyn frowned, and she appeared lost in thought. Arla picked up on it.

"Were you going to say something?" She prodded. Madelyn glanced at Arla, then at Harry. She shook her head.

"How long have you known Susan for?"

"For a long time," Madelyn said, a tinge of sadness creeping into her voice. "We became friends during A-levels. We went to different universities, but then started working here and…

"And?" Arla could sense something behind Madelyn's words, a weight that the woman was pushing away, shielding from view.

Madelyn shrugged. "And we rekindled our friendship."

Harry asked, "Were you close friends?"

Madelyn looked at Harry and smiled again. A small flame of irritation flickered to life inside Arla, and she tried to ignore it.

"Depending what you mean by close," Madelyn arched an eyebrow, and her voice was low, throaty. Okay, this was flirt mode. Arla decided to put her foot down.

"Close enough to tell you if she was in fear of her life?" She demanded.

The sudden change of tone distracted Madelyn. She snapped her head back towards Arla, frowning.

"What do you mean by fear of life? Was Susan in some sort of danger?"

"I cannot comment on an open investigation. Could you please answer the question?"

Madelyn upturned her lips, grimacing. "Nothing quite so dramatic, no." She said in a colder tone, staring back at Arla. "Just the usual troubles, you know."

Arla asked, "Did she have a man in her life?"

Madelyn shook her head. Her response was very quick, Arla noted. Too quick for her liking. She cocked her head to the left and held Madelyn's eyes.

"So, you were good friends from a young age. You said you were close. And she didn't tell you about any of her relationships?"

"If she had a man in her life, then perhaps she would tell me about it, yes. But she didn't, and hence I have no reason to think that she did."

Arla lowered her tone, realising Madelyn was becoming confrontational. She knew from experience that she had to be friendly and supportive in order to get information out.

"I'm sure she would have confided in you," Arla said in a soothing voice. "This is a tragedy, as you can imagine. We want justice for Susan, and her family wants closure."

The tension dissipated from Madelyn's face, and the corners of her shoulders dropped. "I know. I can't believe this has happened," she whispered. She gulped. "So where was her body found? And how?"

Arla glanced at Harry, who nodded. The family knew, and presumably, they would speak to Madelyn. Harry said, "She was found drowned in one of the Clapham Common ponds."

He didn't elaborate any further. Madelyn's jaws dropped, and she slumped back in her chair, her hand going to her open mouth. Her complexion paled as blood drained from her face. Arla observed her reaction. This was genuine shock and disbelief unless Madelyn was a great actress.

"Please think carefully about your last few meetings with her," Arla said softly. "It would make a great deal of difference."

Madelyn squeezed her eyes shut and rubbed the corners of her eyebrows. Arla and Harry exchanged a glance. From the glint in Harry's eyes, she knew he suspected Madelyn.

They gave her some time, and Madelyn finally opened her eyes. With a tissue, she dabbed at the corners of her red-rimmed eyes. "Susan was… a complex person."

They waited. Madelyn sniffed and composed herself. "She had problems with eating and her body shape. This was when she was younger, as a teenager."

"Go on," Arla encouraged her.

"Even now, she was prone to spells of anxiety. Sometimes, she would stay indoors and not come out."

"Was there any time when she didn't attend work?"

Madelyn shook her head. "It wasn't like that. She was a very bright and engaging person on the outside, a social butterfly. But when she was alone, she was very different. She could be insecure, and…" Madelyn bent her head to study the carpet.

"And?"

"She just hated herself a lot. Wondered about what others said about her. What they thought about the way she dressed and looked."

Arla was listening intently. "Was she ever on antidepressants?"

Madelyn looked up, her eyes wide. She glanced from Arla to Harry. Arla said, "Anything you tell us will be treated in total confidence. You will not be held responsible for any information you give us, and it will not be used against you in a court of law. You are not a suspect; you are only giving a statement."

Madelyn gulped, then took a deep breath. "Okay. Even her own GP didn't know about this. But she used to see a private psychiatrist in Harley Street. Yes, she was on antidepressants."

# CHAPTER 22

Arla stared at Madelyn silently for a few seconds. Madelyn licked her lips, then pressed them together. Her hands were on her lap, and Arla could see them moving.

Harry kept his voice low and friendly. "Why did she not want her GP to know?"

Madelyn shrugged. Harry asked, "Is it because she didn't want her family or her employer to know?"

Madelyn glanced at Harry, then to Arla. She seemed to be weighing up things on her mind.

Arla decided to make it easier for her. "Both. Right?"

Madelyn appeared relieved. She nodded in agreement.

Arla asked, "What was the doctor's name?"

Madelyn hesitated. Harry said, "Madelyn, you won't get into trouble for this. We promise."

"That's right," Arla confirmed. "You're not breaching any confidentiality laws here. You're actually helping a police investigation."

The woman sighed and took out her phone. She searched for a while.

"Donald Worthington, consultant psychiatrist. You can look him up online."

Arla had seen her fair share of psychiatrists and counsellors while dealing with her own issues. They were in the past, but that didn't mean they had gone away. With an effort, she forced her mind to the task at hand.

"Madelyn, what was Susan's relationship with her mother like?"

Madelyn studied her nails before answering. "When we were teenagers, it wasn't great. I guess all teenagers have a difficult time with their parents, don't they?"

She shrugged. "But when she got older, I'm sure she was on better terms with her parents. She didn't talk about it a great deal. "

Arla knew it was an evasive answer. She pressed gently. "But how close was she to Sheila Remington? Or to her father?"

"It's hard for me to say. Yes, I was friends with her at school. At the time when she had all her eating problems. I think Sheila could be a strict mother. But then, so was mine."

"What about her father?"

"I think she was close to her father. They got on well."

"But she didn't get on so well with her mother?" Arla persisted, but Madelyn was reluctant to say more.

"Look, I really don't know. First of all, it was a long time ago, and we were young. Secondly, it's not like I am a relative, and I never lived with her."

For the first time, doubts were rising in Arla's mind about Sheila's relationship with her daughter. She had to investigate the family dynamics in more detail.

Harry changed track. "Did you know David Braithwaite? Or do you know him, still?"

Madelyn upturned her lips. "Not very well. Madelyn spoke about him, of course. But that was after she broke up with him. It was during her university days, and by the time she started working here, David was in her past."

"What did she say about him?"

Madelyn relaxed back in her chair. The tips of her shoulders rose briefly. "Not a great deal. They were together for a while, and she didn't speak much about him recently."

"Did she tell you about any man she had met now?" Arla repeated her question from before. She watched Madelyn's reaction closely. If Madelyn was close to Susan, how could she not know about the man in her apartment?"

Again, Madelyn appeared hesitant. As the interview had progressed, Arla could see that she had relaxed. She was easier with them, and that was a good sign.

"Like I said, she was a social butterfly in public. I guess many of us are like that." She smiled at Arla, who did the same, just to encourage her.

"So, she liked meeting men?"

Madelyn nodded." She worked hard and played hard. I obviously don't know about everything she did. She had her own life. And no, she hadn't mentioned any man in particular."

"But if she was casually dating a number of different men, did she not tell you about any of them?"

Madelyn's eyebrows rose. Her voice hardened, becoming defensive. "I'm not sure what you mean about casual dating. …

Arla put a hand up. "I'm sorry. I didn't mean to imply that she was sleeping around. I just want to know if she had mentioned any names."

Madelyn shook her head.

Arla folded her hands on the desk. "Do you think there is a chance Susan might have committed suicide?"

Madelyn blinked at her, then frowned. The frown didn't leave her face, and her head sank down on her chest. From that position, she nodded.

Islay asked, "Is that a yes?"

Madelyn breathed in deeply, then exhaled. "I guess so."

Harry glanced at Arla. Then he spoke in a soft, non-judgemental voice. "But you said she didn't seem down or depressed. That's when you last met her on 14 March. Is that correct?"

"No, she didn't, but she was good at hiding her emotions. Like a lot of us, I guess."

Arla frowned at that last statement. What was Madelyn trying to say? She wouldn't maintain eye contact with them and stared at her own lap.

A few seconds passed, and it was clear that there would not be any more information from Madelyn. Arla slid a card across the table. Harry did the same.

"Thank you for speaking to us. We might need to talk to you again. If you can think about anything that Susan said or did in the last few days, please let us know. It might seem insignificant, but it could make all the difference."

Madelyn looked up at them, her face blank. Then she nodded.

Arla did not speak till they were inside the BMW. Harry drove out on the road, and Arla put the window down. The sun was blazing.

She pondered over the interview.

"She's hiding something, I'm sure of that," she murmured, thinking aloud.

Harry tapped a finger on the steering wheel as he turned it. "I agree. She wasn't going to reveal anything but then told us about that private doctor. We should see him, right?"

"Yes, certainly. But she gave us the doctor's name because she knew we would find out when we looked through Susan's laptop. There would be some emails or even letters to her address."

The scene-of-crime team was still going through Susan's flat. Their job was far from over.

"A suspect?" Harry turned to look at her as he stopped at a red light.

Arla nodded. "Definitely."

# CHAPTER 23

*20 years ago*

Carlson sat in the car with his head bowed. The two policemen sat ahead, and the car sped off. Carlson sank lower in the seat so his face couldn't be seen from outside. He knew the streets well. These poisoned networks where hope died and crime thrived. The only streets he had ever known.

He stared down at his hands and touched the bleeding knuckles. His face felt swollen and bruised, and when he touched his chin, it came back damp and red. His face had been pressed into the road. Hot tears stung the back of his eyes, and he brushed them off with his sleeve.

He had tried to stay out of trouble, but he knew he had done something wrong today. He'd been stupid. But he was more than twelve years old now, and like many other children, he should be helping his mother financially. Shola had no one else. Thinking about his mother only made the tears flow faster. A deep sorrow shrouded his heart, and the shroud became a fester, wounding him inside.

What had he done? Was there any way out of this?

The car stopped at Battersea police station, and he was marched out of the car and up the steps. The uniformed policeman, the men, and women in suits, the desks all of it were a blur to Carlson. He was told to take a seat in the plastic chair, and he was aware other people were staring at him. He glanced at them surreptitiously. He was the only child in the room. He noticed a group of three men in the corner. One of them had a shaven head, large eyes, and a flat, broad nose. His skin was the colour of chocolate, and he was staring at Carlson intently.

Carlson looked away because he recognised the man. Some of the older boys in the estate hung around with that lot. He had seen them around. The guy's name was Kamali, and it was an open secret that he was a gangster.

A police officer approached him. Carlson looked up as the woman spoke to him.

"My name is Constable Fisher." The woman had brown hair and a kind face. She lowered her voice and asked in a concerned tone, "Let's get your cuts and grazes looked at. Would you like some water?"

Carlson didn't know what to say. He looked to the ground, then nodded.

"Come with me," Constable Fisher said. Carlson followed her. When he looked towards Kamali, the man had gone.

The policewoman pressed her ID badge to the side of the door, and it opened. They went inside, and she handed Carlson over to a nurse. The nurse applied some first aid to Carlson's cuts and put her bandage on his left knuckle. Then the policewoman came back, and the nurse left.

Constable Fisher said, "Would you like to tell me what happened?"

Again, Carlson didn't know what to say.

"Start with your name. Then I want to know your address and who you live with."

Carlson knew he had no choice. He didn't know how to get out of this mess, and he couldn't exactly bluff his way out. He could have given Anton's name, but he would only tell his mother. So he had to give Shola's name.

Constable Fisher listened to him carefully and took notes. Then she put the pen down. "Look at me." Carlson did.

He didn't know how old Fisher was, but he guessed the same age as his mother. There was something about the woman he liked. Her white uniform with black-and-white tie was the same as many police officers. But she seemed different. She was nice.

"You don't have a police record, Carlson. I know life can be tough, but what you were doing today isn't right, is it?"

Carlson stared at her. Easy for you to say, he thought. You probably have a loving family, home, and friends. I've only got my mother, and nothing else.

"If you had a dog, and someone tried to steal it, how would you feel?"

Carlson shrugged, and the policewoman repeated her question. He answered, "Bad."

"Exactly. So why did you do it?"

Carlson held her eyes. "The council is forcing us to move. We have no money. I want to help my mother because she is going to lose her job."

Constable Fisher's face softened, and the corners of her eyes crinkled. "You're a good boy. But this is not the way. Someday, when you're old enough, you will realise that."

Carlson nodded and looked down. There was a loud knock on the door, and then a policeman poked his head in. He had a whispered conversation with Constable Fisher, and then the door opened wider. Shola stepped in. Her eyes were wide with horror, and she was clutching the strap of her frayed old handbag tightly.

She came forward and looked down at Carlson. He was so ashamed he couldn't look at her. Her voice was hard as steel.

"What have you done, boy?"

Carlson didn't reply. The policewoman took his mother to one side, and they had a conversation. Then Shola signed some forms. Constable

Fisher said, "As he is a minor, he won't be charged. But he needs to stay off the streets. Next time he won't be so fortunate."

*****

Six months passed by. Carlson was taller now, and he was catching up with Anton. He also had newfound respect within his friendship circle because he had seen the inside of a police station. He didn't realise that counted as a badge of honour amongst his peer group.

There was a guy in their estate who forged student identity cards. A couple of his mates had fake ID cards, which showed they were sixteen years old.

That allowed them to get jobs in factories. Carlson joined a stocking warehouse where his job was to unwrap pallets full of food products and stack them on shelves. It was hard work. He went after school in the evenings when he knew Shola would be working on her second job. They both returned home around ten o'clock, and Carlson pretended he had been with his friends.

But working in the evenings meant he wasn't doing his homework, and he was tired at school. His grades began to fall, even at maths. Soon, he had slipped to the middle third of maths, when he had once been the top five students in his whole year. Mrs Pearson, the teacher who liked him, took him to one side after everyone else had left the classroom.

"Is everything okay at home?" Mrs Pearson asked, her concerned eyes hovering over his face.

"Yes, fine."

"And you're happy?"

"Yes."

From the look on her face, he knew she didn't believe him. "I'm worried about your grades, Carlson."

"I'll work harder, Miss. I've been a bit lazy, I'm sorry."

Mrs Pearson looked far from convinced as she stared at him. Carlson left the classroom as quickly as he could because he was late for his shift at the factory. He hated the factory work. The pay was bad, and he earned less than Shola did, which wasn't much anyway. After three months of backbreaking work, he had saved up less than a thousand pounds.

One day, he clutched the money in his pocket and strolled into an estate agent's office on Battersea High Street. A man wearing a suit looked up at him as he entered. The surprise was evident on his face. He stared at Carlson for a few seconds, like he was an alien creature from an unknown planet.

"Can I help you?" The man's tone was unfriendly, and Carlson took an immediate dislike to him. Well, he would show this idiot.

"Yes," he said as he slid into the seat opposite the man. He squared his shoulders and lifted up his chin, trying to act confident. "I wish to rent a two-bedroom apartment close to the train station."

"Indeed. And what's your budget?" An ironic smile tugged at the corners of the man's face, and Carlson hated the smug expression.

"Why don't you show me what you've got?"

The man smiled wider. "Okay." He clicked on his keypad and searched his screen.

"Two-bedroom flats within a ten-minute walking distance to the train station start at £1,000 per month. Depending on the spec of the property, they go up to £2,000 per month. You will have to pay two months full rent as a deposit and also submit references from your workplace." He raised his eyebrows. "Do you work?"

"Yes," Carlson said, staring back at the man. But his heart was sinking. He had no idea renting was *this* expensive. Where would he find the money for the deposit?

"I need to see your payslips," the man continued in a haughty tone, but the look on his face was one of amusement. "You need to show that you can afford not just the rent, but the bills and council tax."

"How much would the bills be?"

"For an average two-bedroom flat, you're looking at £200-£300 a month, plus council tax, which will be another £100."

Great, Carlson thought to himself. He needed £1500 a month, and he knew his mother earned less than half of that. He would need to be almost full-time at his factory job to make that sort of money. Which meant he would have to give up school. A black weight was pressing against his throat. He had misjudged this badly. He needed a lot more money.

His Adam's apple bobbed up and down. "Thank you very much. Could you please provide me with the details of some properties? I shall inspect them and then be in touch."

The man shook his head slightly, the glint of amusement not leaving his eyes. He printed out the details of a few properties and handed A4 sheets of paper to Carlson. He stuffed them in his pocket and left the estate agents office. He squeezed his eyes shut as he walked on the road. He had never felt so demoralised in his life.

# CHAPTER 24

David Braithwaite had agreed to be interviewed at his office. It was past mid-morning, and the traffic was building up. Mr Braithwaite had his office in Knightsbridge, a stone's throw away from the Royal Albert Hall and Hyde Park Corner. It was perhaps the nicest residential address in the whole of England.

Arla feasted her eyes on the elegant mansion terraces of Prince Albert Road as they broke free from the traffic. Many of these huge buildings were now foreign embassies, with their country's respective flags hanging from the awnings. She knew that the rear of each house opened up to a common large square garden, as well maintained as the front of the buildings. Harry parked on a side street, behind a Lamborghini Diablo. He gripped the steering wheel, and his mouth was open as he stared at the car.

"You're drooling, Harry," Arla said with disapproval. "Put your tongue back in. You'll never be able to afford that."

He grinned at her. "No, but I can rent it. If you wore a skimpy bikini and rode shotgun with me on the passenger seat? I bet we would turn heads everywhere."

She shook her head in disgust and got out of the car. Supercars were scattered round on both sides of the road. She had no time for them but was forced to wait for Harry, who inspected the bright green Lamborghini. She walked up to him.

"Come on; we have work to do. Why does a grown man have gape at a car?"

Harry rolled his eyes and put his thumb on his forehead. "Tired of being under the thumb," Harry grumbled. He trudged behind her, looking dejected with his puppy dog eyes.

The concierge at the desk of the marble-floored lobby took their names and asked them to take a seat. Arla looked at the wooden beams on the ceiling and the long cathedral-type glass windows. They weren't stained, but the latticework on them was intricate. She felt transported in time to a Victorian age where she half expected a butler in a long tailcoat to approach them. The concierge, who was indeed wearing a uniform, reappeared a bit later. They followed him into a hallway and to the elevators. They were taken up to the fifth floor, and the concierge guy knocked on a door, then poked his head in.

Arla and Harry were shown into an office that looked like an Oxford don's study. There was a big leather-topped desk in the middle, with thousands of books on the shelves on either side. The bookshelves ran from the floor to the high ceiling, and there was a shelf ladder.

The figure perched on the shelf ladder was a tall, slim man who came down and shook their hands. He had a thin face, with a long nose and large, attentive dark eyes. His black hair was oiled and side-parted, making him look like an academic. He wore thin-rimmed, round spectacles that intensified his professorial look.

It wasn't what Arla had expected. This man did not look like the fashionable cad she had seen in the photos. And the photos were only a few years old. She could see the resemblance, of course. It was the same man, but she found it astonishing he had changed his looks to this extent.

"Inspector Arla Baker, pleased to meet you." The words rolled off David Braithwaite's tongue in a pure Etonian accent, all the syllables perfectly enunciated. "Please have a seat. Would you like some refreshments? Tea or coffee, perhaps?"

Arla and Harry murmured their dissent. David walked across a table and sat down in a high-backed, dark brown leather armchair worn with use.

He steepled his fingers and regarded them with an interest that a zoologist reserved for new specimens of life.

Arla cleared her throat. "I think you know what we are here for."

David blinked a couple of times, and his expression changed. He sighed. "Yes, it's a horrible thing. A total, utter tragedy. She was such a sweet girl. I can't believe this has happened."

"Have you been in contact with Susan Remington recently?"

"No, I can't say that I have. As you know, our relationship came to an end almost three years ago."

"When did you hear about her death?"

A look of surprise dawned on his smoothly shaven face. "When the switchboard of the police station called, of course. I believe I spoke to a detective sergeant called Lisa Moran. She informed me and asked if I would meet with you."

Arla nodded. "So you didn't know about what happened before that?"

David's forehead crinkled for an instant, then vanished. "No, of course not. As I have explained, I wasn't in contact with Susan nor her family."

Arla opened up her notebook. "Could you please confirm where you were from the 13th till the 18th of March?"

David blinked again, and his eyebrows rose a fraction. "That's six days. Do you want me to recount where I was for each one of those days?"

"I'm sorry. We don't have a definite date in mind, but if you could please give us an idea of what you were doing in that time period."

"I was here, working." David shrugged. "Sometimes I have to leave the country on business, but I'm always back within a couple of days. But for the whole of March, I've been in London."

"What about the evenings? What do you do after work?"

David took a moment to answer. Arla picked up on the hesitation. He cleared his throat before continuing. "After work, I will probably go to the club or do some exercise at the gym. After that, I either go home or stay back at the club for a few drinks with my friends."

"Are you single?"

David nodded. Arla didn't see a ring on his left hand. "Do you live alone?"

David nodded again without speaking. Arla said, "Can anyone prove that you were at the club or at home?"

David's expression didn't change. His eyes flicked over to Harry, then back to Arla. "I don't go to the club every evening. It's a members club called Annabel's. Some evenings I am home on my own. I'm afraid that for those evenings, there's no one who can corroborate my story."

"Where do you live?"

"On the other side of Hyde Park, at Holland Park Gardens, as it happens. I walk back home through the park. It's rather invigorating." David smiled, then relapsed into seriousness. Arla could see that he was relaxed. She glanced at Harry briefly, and he took over.

"Could you please tell us the circumstances involving your breakup with Susan?" Harry demanded, raising his voice slightly. It got David's attention.

"Why does any couple break up, Inspector Mehta?" David said, and Harry was impressed that he remembered his name. "We just wanted different things, I'm afraid."

"Such as what?"

"I wanted a family, children, and she wanted a career. And as you know, she worked for a global accountancy firm, which would mean she would travel a great deal. Our lives and our wishes were just not compatible."

Harry leaned forward. "Do you mean a difference in personality? Or your lifestyle?"

For the first time, Arla saw David hesitate. His pronounced Adam's apple bobbed up and down in his long neck. The tip of the long nose quivered, and the professorial mask slipped a fraction. But he recovered quickly.

"I'm quite a simple person, Inspector. I get up in the morning, come to work, go to the gym after work, and then stay at home."

Harry raised his eyebrows. "And Susan wasn't like that, is that what you mean?"

David cocked his head to the left, and his shoulders rose. "You could say that. She had lots of friends, and she liked parties. I'm not really a party person, if you know what I mean. I prefer the quieter life."

"Would it be fair to say you parted on bad terms?"

The look of gentle tolerance fell from David's face. His jaws clenched, and his lips pressed together in a tight, almost white line. His eyebrows met in the middle, and his voice hardened. "Now, why would you assume that? What are you trying to imply, inspector Mehta?"

Harry shrugged. "Nothing. It seems so far what you've said points to a relationship that wasn't very happy."

"That doesn't mean we left on bad terms," David snapped. Then he relaxed his back into his chair and took a deep breath. He took his glasses off, polished them, then put them back on. And just like that, the smooth, suave mask returned. He smiled at them.

"We sat down and talked about it. She was happy to let me go, and so was I. Our families brought us together, as we were acquaintances. But in the end, it wasn't to be. We left on good terms."

"But you didn't remain friends?"

"As I've already explained, we did different things. We don't have the same friends. Hence, we didn't stay in touch."

David glanced at his watch. "I have to be in another meeting in five minutes. Is there anything else you'd like to discuss?"

Harry looked at Arla, who said nothing. They rose, and David extended his hand. "I'm available if you have any questions for me later. Please don't hesitate to give either my secretary or myself a call."

Once they were back in the car, Arla strapped her seat belt on, thinking about the interview. It ended abruptly as if David was in a rush.

"Touchy, wasn't he?" Harry said, reversing the car.

"Especially when you asked him about the breakup," Arla mused. She knew Harry had been goading David, and he became defensive. What was the reason?

"I think there is more to Lord Braithwaite than meets the eye," Harry said.

"Which Lord Braithwaite do you mean?" Arla smirked. "There's three of them."

Dark clouds were scuttling the far corners of the blue sky, and it seemed like an omen. If the Justice Minister's nephew were a suspect in a murder enquiry, the media would have a field day. She desperately hoped this remained under wraps. She also knew it was a forlorn hope.

Sooner or later, the media vultures would get wind of it. Probably pay off some copper to get the latest gossip, she thought in disgust. It was known to happen. Eager journalists were also known to falsify ID cards and approach witnesses and suspects in a case.

"Shall we bring him in?" Harry remarked. "He could be the man behind the revenge porn. Maybe she embarrassed him, and he was angry after the breakup. He might not have an alibi for the night she was murdered."

Arla tapped a fingernail on the door handle. "He had motive, means, and opportunity."

"Is that a yes? You know that Johnson will be breathing down your neck for a suspect, right?"

"Not for this one, Harry. We can't bring him in unless we're absolutely sure."

*****

David Braithwaite watched from the window in his office as the black BMW reversed and then drove slowly down the road. His hand shook as he pressed the corners of his eyes, then massaged his forehead. He had expected this, but the question from the male police inspector had thrown him. Was he a suspect already? What else did they know about his relationship with Susan?

The police must've interviewed Susan's family. And also her friends. He thought for a few seconds, then took out his phone. This was a burner phone, which was encrypted and had been given to him by a MI5 officer. David rang Sheila Remington's number. She picked up on the first ring as if she'd been expecting him.

He didn't waste time on pleasantries. "The police came today. An Inspector Arla Baker and Harry Mehta."

"Yes," Sheila said. They came to see me as well."

"Did they ask you about Susan and me?"

"No. Don't worry. I don't think they'll be targeting you."

David gripped the phone harder, and his voice rose. "You don't know that! They just asked me if our breakup was a bad one. Why ask that if they don't suspect me?"

Sheila's tone was low. "You need to stay calm. Panicking at this time is going to be detrimental to all of us. If the police think you're hiding something, they'll keep coming back. Do you understand?"

David breathed for a few seconds, thoughts churning in his head. He had never liked Sheila Remington, and her daughter was even worse. He cursed himself for getting involved with them.

Sheila spoke again, her voice was firm this time, "You know what's at stake here. We've come this far. You can't let us down now. "

David didn't say anything. His jaws clamped tight as hatred for everyone, including himself, bubbled up in the dark corners of his heart. He wished he had never listened to his uncle. He had so many regrets, and now he had given dangerous people like Sheila Remington the keys to his life. Sheila would always blackmail him.

He gritted his teeth. "I know. Just make sure you don't say anything to the police if they ask you about me. Got it?"

"Don't worry about me," Sheila replied in the same detached tone. Then she hung up.

David thrust the phone back into his pocket and walked to his office. Then he took out his phone again and dialled the second number on the phone. It rang several times, then went to voicemail. He left a message.

"Madelyn, call me back as soon as you get this. I think the police are on to me."

# CHAPTER 25

*15 years ago*

Fifteen-year-old Carlson listened with his ear to the door. The man was speaking, and his mother was silent. Carlson didn't know what it was about, but the man and woman who turned up uninvited this morning wore suits and seemed like trouble. He had never seen smartly dressed people come to their council block flat.

When they arrived, Carlson was in his room, checking messages from his buddy Yemi. Yemi was two years older but shorter than Carlson. Yemi was now a junior member of the neighbourhood gang and had just got the latest iPhone.

Carlson didn't hear the couple introduce themselves, but he ran to the front door, in case it was one of his friends. From his mother's serious expression, he knew the couple wasn't welcome, but his mother, Shola, had no choice but to let them in.

Carlson pressed his ear closer to the door, so hard that it creaked. The voices inside were muffled.

"… You came into the country without a visa. Isn't that true?" The man's voice said.

Carlson heard his mother reply, but he couldn't make out the words. Then the woman said something as well. Carlson could only hear the man's voice.

"… Cannot stay in the UK; you will be deported."

Shola raised her voice, and Carlson heard her clearly this time. "But I live here with my son. We have a life here. I can't go back to Nigeria. I have no one there. No family."

"I'm afraid you should have thought of that before you came into the country illegally."

Carlson heard heavy breathing, then Shola spoke again. "Like I said, they promised everything was legal. I even asked them if I should apply for asylum. They said I didn't need to. I just had to give them the money."

The woman said, "These are well-known criminal gangs who traffic vulnerable individuals. Why did you give them your money?"

Carlson heard a smacking sound, which he thought was his mother slapping her legs. Her voice rose several decibels. "Because they seemed so respectable! They were at the government office. They looked like the real deal. Please believe me."

The man said, "Unfortunately, some overseas governments are working with organised crime. The criminals bribed government officials with big money. I'm afraid that happened in your case."

"So you can see it's not my fault." After a pause, Shola spoke again. "You do believe me, don't you?"

There was silence for a while, and Carlson heard nothing but his own breathing. Then the woman spoke, her voice soft. "Unfortunately, you have broken the law. Therefore, there is now a deportation order against you. You have forty-five days to leave the country."

"Forty-five days?" Shola wailed. "You guys told the hospital, and they took my job away. Now you're kicking me out of the country?"

"Like I said, Miss Adeyemi, the matter is out of our hands now. We shall be telling the council of our decision."

Carlson heard the people inside the room stand up. He ran from the door and into his room. He peeped through his bedroom door and saw his mother slam the door shut and then lean against it. He came out.

119

"Who are they, mum?"

Shola straightened herself and passed a hand over her weary face.

"Just some people. Don't worry. Have you had dinner?"

"I'm not hungry. Tell me who they were."

Shola walked past her son into the kitchen. She got busy with washing up in the sink, but she was staring out the big windows. It was the same depressing view from everywhere – the pastel and grey coloured blocks apartment blocks, with numerous small windows engraved on them at regular intervals—a prison by any other name.

Carlson lifted himself up on the kitchen counter and sat there dangling his legs. Shola glanced at her son. "Don't you have any homework to do?"

"Done them all."

Mother and son were silent for a while. Shola took out the frying pan and looked inside the fridge. Carlson asked, "We don't have any money, do we?"

Shola didn't answer. She wasn't young and pretty anymore. She didn't have any skills either and the domestic cleaning job in the hospital was all she could do. Now she had lost that too. Carlson knew his mother wouldn't answer, so he continued.

"I'm going to get a job, mum. We are going to be all right."

Shola shoved the frying pan away. Her eyebrows were raised, and her lips quivered. She raised a finger and wagged it in front of Carlson's face. "You won't do anything like that. You're meant to be at school, and that's all you're going to do."

Carlson frowned and spread his arms. "But we don't have any money. I know you borrowed money from the old woman next door. Don't lie."

Shola leaned against the counter and touched her forehead. Her eyes were shut. Carlson said, "I know things, mum. Believe me; I can make some money."

Shola knelt on the ground. "Come here."

Carlson went forward and hugged his mother. It was nice hugging her. She smelled of fried onions and yams with rice, which they had for dinner last night. It was a nice, comforting smell, and he loved his mother. He had no one in the whole world apart from Shola. And he would do anything to help her out. He hugged her tightly and felt her do the same.

Shola kissed him on the forehead and then ran a hand through his curly hair. "You need to get an education and then get a proper job when you're grown-up." She put a finger on his lip as he started to speak. "I won't hear of it. Do you want to be like me when you're older? No. You need to work hard at school now so that you have lots of money when you're grown-up."

Carlson watched his mother in silence.

# CHAPTER 26

*14 years ago*

Carlson picked up the stiff brown envelope that had just arrived in the post. It had Her Majesty's Home Office stamped in the top right corner, and he knew what that meant. He had come to regard the two words Home Office with dread. Despite having spent most of her adult life in this country, Shola was now being regarded as an illegal immigrant. The letters from the Home Office were continuous, one arriving every few weeks.

Carlson had watched Shola lose weight. Her cheeks had become hollow, and bags appeared around her eyes. To his mind, his mother looked sick. He didn't know what to do. He was getting close to his GCSE exams. He was still working at the factory, but he had worked hard, and his grades had picked up, especially in maths. He had chosen his GCSE subjects and even what he wanted to do at university. He wanted to study mathematics and get himself a job in the city. It was a distant dream because he had no idea who would pay for his life at university. Maybe he could take student loans.

Carlson tore into the envelope and looked at the letter. His heart rate accelerated a notch, and his mouth went dry as he read the red letters in bold at the top. "Deportation order – do not ignore."

He skimmed through the rest of the letter. Once again, the Home Office was giving them 45 days to leave. Within two weeks of this letter, an immigration enforcement team would visit their flat. It was the same as the last few letters—incessant warnings about their deportation.

Carlson flopped down on the kitchen table chair. It was a Saturday, and his mother had gone to work. He had a factory shift starting in a couple of hours, not that he wanted to go. He hated the job. He had to pull heavy boxes and stack them on long steel shelves, and his shoulders and arms ached every evening. He was finding it exhausting to concentrate at school, but he had no option.

He also saw Yemi, the boy who had joined the local gang, driving around in new sports car. Yemi was friends with Anton, and he loved showing off. He had just bought an £8000 Rolex Daytona watch. Yemi was 18, though, and legally he was an adult. But Carlson wanted to know what they did to earn so much money.

 He boiled water for some tea and looked out over the never-ending landscape of high-rises and clumps of trees. In the distance, he could see the gleaming towers of Canary Wharf, the temples of finance, where billions of pounds were made every day. He wondered where all the money went. Could some of it not trickle down to people like him and his mother? Or maybe it already did. And this is all they got – this shoebox-like apartment, the suffocating prison where his life seemed to grow shorter by the day, where every single morning, a new dream died.

As he drank his tea, his eyes fell on the Home Office letter again. He shook his head. His only life had been in England. Would he really be forced to move to some foreign country? It all seemed quite ridiculous.

The front door opened and he looked up in surprise. Shola walked in, looking shattered. She really had lost weight. Her clothes looked large on her, and as she took her jacket off and then her cardigan, Carlson noticed how thin his mother's arms were.

"I thought you were at work?" He asked. Shola had her back to him, making herself a coffee. She didn't reply as she sat down at the table with the drink.

Her once clear eyes now looked dull, the whites yellowish. The bags under her eyes had hollowed further and turned darker. Her rich brown skin colour had turned rusty. Her hand shook as she picked the cup to take a sip.

Carlson frowned. "Mum, what's going on with you? You barely eat food anymore. Is it just the stress from the Home Office, or is there something else going on?"

In response, Shola squeezed her eyes tightly shut. Her chin sank to her chest, and she remained like that for several seconds. Then she spoke. "There's something I need to tell you."

Carlson waited, a sense of dread chipping away at the corners of his soul.

"Last month, I found a lump in my breast." His mother didn't look at him. Her words were halting, slow. Like she was looking for the right words and couldn't find them.

"I went to the doctor, and he referred me for a scan called a mammogram. After the scan, they took a biopsy. Which means they put a needle inside and took a sample." Shola's chest heaved. "It came back showing cancer." Her eyes flicked to her sons, and this time she held his eyes. "I've got cancer of the breast."

Carlson's mouth fell open. A black weight had moved from his throat down to his chest and was clearly consuming his whole body. He felt numb. He didn't know what to think.

Cancer? Did his mother really have cancer?

"But... How? And why?"

Shola shook her head. "I don't know. Even the doctors don't know. I rang my family back home. Your grandmother had breast cancer. But my sisters are okay."

"So, what does this mean? What's going to happen to you?"

"I'm going to have more tests. Then I'll be seen at a hospital called the Royal Marsden. I have an appointment already. I will have more tests there, and then the doctors will decide what to do."

Carlson couldn't speak. Words had died inside his brain, frozen like icicles.

Shola said, "I might need to have surgery. Or even other treatments. Like taking different tablets. They call it chemotherapy. They might also give me radiotherapy. We don't know at this stage."

It was like a foreign language to Carlson. He didn't know what to make of it. Shola leaned forward and grabbed both of his hands.

"I want you to know that I'm here for you. I'm always going to be here for you." Tears trickled out of her eyes, but her facial expression did not change. She didn't break down. She didn't lower her head. Her eyes never left Carlson's. She wiped the tears without breaking contact.

"Just trust me. It's going to be okay." She smiled, but Carlson could see the desperate sadness clouding her face. His heart was breaking, and he felt a growing pressure behind his eyes. He couldn't take it anymore. He went over and hugged his mother, kneeling on the floor. He gave way to the burning hot tears. They cascaded down, wetting Shola's skirt. She covered him like a comforting blanket, holding him tight.

They stayed like that for a long time, not moving.

# CHAPTER 27

Rain clouds hung down ponderously low, their gunmetal grey bellies almost brushing the skyscrapers of Canary Wharf in the distance. A whispering rain had already started, dragging a veil across the city, smudging the red traffic lights, the people, and endless cars into the same shade of nondescript grey.

Harry parked the BMW in Harley Street, England's epicentre of medical excellence. He upturned the collars of his grey suit and retrieved an umbrella from the boot. He held it over the passenger door as Arla got out, and then she took the umbrella from him.

"Thank you, Harry," she said, kissing him with her eyes. He grinned, and together, they crossed the road, heading for one of the red-bricked, beautiful buildings that lined this exclusive corner of London. The traffic and bustle of Oxford Circus, less than a block away, seem to fade away. Arla had already spoken to Prof Donald Worthington, who ran his private clinic from this building. He had agreed to speak to them at short notice.

They were asked to meet in a reception area that was different from the doctor's chambers. The leather sofas were dark and comfortable, and lots of potted plants gave the place a warm feeling. Prof Worthington, an elderly man with receding white hair, came out to greet them himself. He smelled of tobacco smoke, and his spine was slightly stooped, but his dark eyes were sharp and attentive. He smiled cordially as he shook hands with them.

"Do come in," the professor said as they opened the large mahogany door to his office. There was a pall of sweet tobacco smoke inside, despite the open window in one corner. The desktop was littered with magazines

126

and books. Prof Worthington stacked things in one corner, apologising for the mess.

He sat down and gazed at them meditatively.

"I'm very sorry to hear this. I last had contact with Susan about a month ago."

Arla had her notebook out already. "Can you remember the date?"

Prof Worthington looked at his desktop and clicked on the keyboard. "Ninth of February. She came here, as usual. She was a troubled young woman, as you know."

"Can you elaborate?"

"She suffered from bulimia when she was doing her A-levels. I think she had to take a year out and do her A-levels again because she suppressed the condition for a while."

"Did she see you then?"

The elderly man shook his head. "No, I'm not an eating disorder specialist. But in more recent years, she suffered from spells of anxiety. And low mood. I would say anxiety was the main feature."

"Did you know much about her personal life?"

The professor's eyes held Arla's. "Like many people who suffer from anxiety, she tried her best to hide it. As you know, mental illness is not something people talk about, and when they do, it is often treated as a weakness or stigma, which is completely inappropriate."

"Did her family not support her?"

The professor shook his head slowly. "No. I think she was closer to her father than she was to her mother. I got the impression, in fact, that her mother didn't help her at all. Especially during her traumatic divorce."

Arla frowned. "Do you mean she was married to David Braithwaite?"

The Prof looked surprised. "Yes, didn't you know that?"

Arla and Harry glanced at each other. A sense of unease spread through Arla's mind. "I knew they had been together but didn't realise they were actually married."

"Possibly the families suppressed everything after what happened."

Harry asked, "What do you mean?"

Prof Worthington settled back in his chair, and his attention swivelled to Harry. "She always had her misgivings about David Braithwaite. I think he managed to charm her initially, but she wasn't sure about the marriage. However, her parents were very keen, and she gave in. She regretted it later."

"Why?"

The professor steepled his fingers and brought them close to his face. "I'm breaching doctor-patient confidentiality now. I know you are conducting an investigation, but I'd be grateful if you kept this to yourself."

Arla nodded solemnly. "Everything you tell us is confidential."

The professor let out a breath. "They argued often. David had a jealous streak in him, and he didn't like Susan's friends. From what she told me, he had problems with her staying in contact with any man. I'm afraid sometimes their arguments became violent."

"How do you mean?"

"She told me he slapped her once. He also locked her in her room, and she had to climb out the window."

Arla was aghast. "And she didn't report him?"

Prof Worthington spread his hands. "His uncle was the justice minister, and his father worked for the MI5. She was scared of repercussions, especially for her family. It was a complex situation."

The professor dipped his head and stared up at them from under bushy eyebrows. He seemed to be contemplating his next words. "And then she got pregnant."

Arla felt a coldness sweep through her body. "By her husband I presume,"

"Yes, by David. She didn't want the pregnancy. He did, and so did both their families." The Prof said and shook his head slowly. "She chose to have an abortion. You can imagine how that went down."

Arla's mouth opened in shock. "Do you know when this happened?"

"I believe they were married for three years, so this would have been roughly three years ago."

"David went mad, according to Susan. She saw me regularly during this period. Apart from me, she also saw a counsellor. Her family stopped giving her money, and although she had a job, she was on maternity leave that wasn't generous by any means."

Harry asked, "And this led to the divorce?"

"She had made her mind up about the divorce before she got pregnant. I guess the pregnancy was the final straw. She told me there was no way she would carry his child. Then she would be totally under his control. Her life had always been a prison, and it was getting worse every day."

Arla's ears pricked up. "What you mean by always?"

"She had a difficult relationship with her parents. Especially her mother. She once told me how she couldn't wait to go to university and leave the family home behind."

Arla digested this avalanche of secrets in silence. Harry cleared his throat after a pause. "What happened after the abortion?"

"Susan moved out of the marital home. At first, she didn't have anywhere to live. So she moved in with her friend. Madelyn, I think her name was."

"Madelyn West, her colleague at work who also knew her from when she was young."

Prof Worthington clicked his fingers. "Yes, that's right. They went to the same school, and then also started working together. Madelyn was a big help for her at that time. She also threw herself into work and managed to save up enough for a deposit for the flat. Her parents didn't help her at all. Things went from bad to worse after the divorce."

"In what way?"

Prof Worthington was silent for a while. Then he spoke slowly. "The threatening messages started. She got hate mail, and she also saw tortured animals left by her front door."

"Tortured animals?" Arla said, her heart sinking.

"Yes. Dead birds with their wings torn off. A dead rabbit that had been skinned and its head chopped off. She saw it as she opened the door on her way to work. That was particularly traumatic for her."

Arla grimaced, and her Adam's apple bobbed up and down. The coldness had claimed every part of her body now. She felt rigid with shock.

Harry said, "Did you know about the revenge porn?"

"Sadly, yes, I do. She felt all of it came from David."

# CHAPTER 28

Arla wrote down David Braithwaite's name in her notebook and circled it. She added arrows radiating out of the circuit. She wrote down the names of Sheila Remington, then David's father and uncle.

She narrowed her eyes as she gazed at Prof Worthington, who had lapsed into silence.

"How did she know it was David leaving the dead animals and doing the revenge porn?"

The Prof took a sip of water. As before, he gazed at Arla for a few seconds before replying.

"I don't think you appreciate fully the extent of the abuse Susan suffered. David had employed a private investigator to track her every move. This was while she was his wife. It carried on after she moved out."

He continued. "Susan wasn't paranoid when she mentioned her phone being tapped. Every time she picked up the receiver, there was a series of clicks and other sounds. Her mobile phone would also become very hot for no reason. The battery was being used up by an app hidden on her phone. She took her phone to a security expert, who diagnosed the problem. She had a spyware running in the background, which was installed on her phone by someone she knew." The professor spread his hands. "This happened while she was living with David. Before she got pregnant. Who was the best person to install that app?"

Arla went to speak, but Prof Worthington raised his hand.

"I am a psychiatrist. I know very well what the symptoms of paranoid schizophrenia are. Susan wasn't paranoid. She was definitely being followed and watched. She did see the same person around her house and outside the tube station of her workplace. She once took photos and showed them to me."

Harry leaned forward." Did she take the photos on her own phone?"

"Yes."

Harry looked at Arla. They didn't know where Susan's phone was, and it seemed as if the killer had either taken it or it was lost. Which would be mighty convenient because it would contain a treasure trove of their evidence that Prof Worthington was referring to.

Harry asked, "Do you know the name of the security professional Susan went to see?"

The professor shook his head. "No. But I do know the cumulative effect of all of this was a breakdown in her mental health. Her anxiety levels spiked, and then she fell into depression. That's when I decided to start her on antidepressants. She took a tablet called mirtazapine."

There was silence for a while, and both Arla and Harry were busy scribbling in their notebooks. Arla looked up as a professor got up and went to the window. He lifted it higher, and a breath of fresh air came into the room. He took a pipe out of his pocket, and the tobacco pouch then stuffed the pipe with some tobacco. Standing by the window, he lit it, then took a puff. He glanced back at them and raised his eyebrows. "Hope you don't mind if I smoke."

Arla had to smile. Prof Worthington fit the bill of an eccentric academic and not a fake one like David Braithwaite. The smile left her face. She was beginning to realise what she was up against.

"Do you know what David Braithwaite's father did for the MI5?"

"Susan said he was a spy. He often had to travel abroad for his business, and it is well known that the MI5 uses such people to spy on foreign governments. Lord Braithwaite struck deals with foreign companies, which gave him valuable insights into how they worked. It also got him in touch with government officials who handled the contracts for such companies. For example, he had several factories in Czechoslovakia and Slovenia."

"How did Susan know this?"

"David told her. They were close at one point, don't forget. Indeed, David could be very affectionate towards her, showering her with gifts and attention. But he could also turn violent and aggressive. Not to mention insanely jealous."

Arla breathed out. The man sounded like a monster. She couldn't match him with the suave, well-spoken guy she had just seen in the Knightsbridge office. But Arla knew better than anyone else; appearances were deceptive.

Prof Worthington inhaled fragrant smoke, then blew it out the window. "In fact, the more she told me about David, the closer I got to a diagnosis. I might be wrong, but I think he has a condition called narcissistic personality disorder. These people have a very high opinion of themselves, and they like to exert control over everyone they know. That's how they survive."

# CHAPTER 29

*14 years ago*

Carlson walked past the market stalls. He was heading for the clearing where he knew Ronel, Trey, and Nadine worked. He saw Ronel first and hollered at him.

"Hey cousin, how you doing?" Ronel said. They weren't actual cousins, but everyone in their estate greeted each other like this.

"Not bad, Fam," Carlson said. Fam was short for family, another universal term of respect. Carlson rolled his shoulders and bent his lips, trying to look tough. "I need to make some peas."

Ronel grinned. "I thought you were a good little schoolboy."

"Yeah, but it's boring innit?" Carlson pointed to where Nadine and Trey were standing, their eyes watchful and stuffed into their pockets. "Introduce me to them."

Ronel stared at Carlson for a while. They knew each other through Anton. Ronel didn't know Carlson well, but Carlson knew he was a good man. He helped out kids who needed money.

"Are you sure you're up for this, bruv?" Ronel asked. His eyes didn't leave Carlson's.

Carlson gulped and stared at the ground for a few seconds. Then he nodded. "Yes, bruv, I am."

Ronel reached out a hand and grabbed Carlson's shoulder. "If you need some money, I can give you some."

"Yeah, but then I've got to pay you back. I'd rather make my own peas, innit?"

Ronel's silent stare was deep with meaning. He knew the real story. No one had to spell it out, as most of them had suffered through the same life. Homes without fathers, mothers left to fend for themselves, and things got much worse if the single mothers fell into drugs or became sick.

Ronel looked up and considered the sky. Then he turned on his heels. "Come on then."

Carlson was scared of Nadine. She was tall and had a ring on her nose, as well as one on her lower lip. Not to mention the big gangly earrings. Ronel introduce them, and Nadine and Trey looked at each other,

Nadine shifted her focus to Carlson. "Are you sure you can do this?"

Carlson puffed his chest up. "I've sold burgers at school. I've also nicked magazines from the corner shop and sold them at school for a profit."

Nadine and Trey burst out laughing. The girl wiped her eyes. "Sold magazines? Burgers? Bruv, you're having a laugh."

"Hey, I can do this. Trust me." Carlson raised his voice to make himself heard.

The laughter faded from Nadine's face. Her chestnut brown eyes looked into Carlson's with a ferocity that he couldn't tolerate for long. He looked away and shifted on his feet. Then he glanced back up at her. Her jaws were clamped tight as her nostrils flared. Her stare was unrelenting.

Carlson said, "I won't let you down. I promise."

Nadine crinkled her nose like she was smelling something bad. "Won't let me down? What do you think this is, a job interview?" She looked him up and down and cursed loudly. "Get out of my face, man. You are a waste of time. Go back to school and study."

She turned away from him, stuffing her hands back in her black-puffer jacket. Carlson stepped around to face her.

"I can do this. Take me to Kamali."

Nadine raised her eyebrows, staring at him. "What do you want to see Kamali for?"

"I can help him. I've got connections."

Nadine grinned, and so did the others. "Connections? What connections, cousin?"

She stepped closer to him and pointed two fingers at his forehead like the barrel of a gun. She swore at him again. "Listen good, cousin. I'm telling you this for your own good. Stay in school."

She stepped back, then walked away. Ronel shrugged at Carlson and walked off, following them.

Carlson watched them go, determination hardening in his heart. He had never been one to give up easily. Later that evening, he walked round to the corner of the estate where he knew Kamali and his boys hung out. Sure enough, Kamali was there, with two of his cronies. One of them was leaning against an expensive-looking black BMW listening to Kamali as he spoke. They stopped, and one by one, all three men turned to look at Carlson. He stopped a few paces away from Kamali.

"*Wah-gwan*," Carlson said, using the traditional Jamaican slang for what's going on.

Kamali said, "*Everytin' eerie, fam*. What you want?"

"I want to work for you. I can help."

Kamali smiled, and that other two men guffawed with laughter.

"What can you do, Fam?" Kamali asked.

"I can do tricks. Trust me. I got connections."

Kamali laughed, and the other two men were in stitches. Kamali shook his head. "You're a kid, bruv. You should be in school. How's your mother, by the way?"

Most people knew each other in the estate. They met at block parties or in passing.

Carlson shrugged. There was no way he was telling them the truth. "She's okay."

"Yo bruv. Just go home, all right? Take care," one of the others said. Carlson glanced at the man. His head was shaven like Kamali's. They were all younger men, only slightly older than Ronel.

He shook his head. "You don't understand. I can do things that will help you make more money."

Kamali folded his hands across his chest. "Really? How?" One of the men started to object, but Kamali silenced him with a raised hand.

"The pigs know *man dem*," Carlson said, pointing at the three of them. "But they don't know me. I can slip under their radar. I can drop off packets without being questioned. I can go anywhere in the country."

Kamali narrowed his eyes at him. Carlson continued. "Brothers outside London need food too." Food was the commonly accepted term for hard drugs. "You take food in a car, and you could get stopped and searched. But if I carry it in a bag, wearing my school uniform, no one is going to suspect me, are they?"

"Go on."

"I won't look inside the bag, I swear. You make the deal, and I'll drop it off, then come back. But you need to pay me."

Kamali smiled, and his eyes were watchful. "How much do you want?"

"One thousand per trip."

"You're having a laugh, fam."

"Think about it," Carlson urged. "I got more boys who can help. They're all clean skins. We could have a whole team delivering all over London and outside, and the pigs won't have a clue. You could become a big man."

There was silence now. Kamali stood very still, and his eyebrows lowered as he contemplated Carlson.

"Have you told anyone about your plan?"

"No."

Kamali stepped closer. "Then how do you know other boys can help?"

Carlson gulped but didn't step back. "Because I know. They need the money. And they'll listen to me."

One of the guys said, "He's talking about that nerd Anton. Always hangs around with him. Ain't that right, cousin?"

"There's others, trust me."

"Ricky," Kamali addressed the other man, "What's this Anton like?"

"He's a good kid. Straight, tho. Like this bruv here. I can't see them doing it, honest."

Kamali turned to look at Ricky. "Maybe that's the point. No one thinks they can do it, especially not the pigs."

He sucked his teeth, then clamped a hand over Carlson's shoulder. "Let me think about it, cousin. I know where to find you, don't worry."

"Ok."

Kamali raised his eyebrows as Carlson stood there. "Go on then, cous. Fuck off now." He grinned.

Carlson nodded at him, then at the others. Then he walked away slowly, his heart still thumping in his ears.

# CHAPTER 30

Madelyn West peered over her shoulder as she walked down the street. The rain had relented, leaving a glistening pavement and dark clouds hovering overhead. She was wearing her long jacket, with the collars turned up. She had large sunglasses on her face, and the hood of her jacket was pulled low over her face.

She moved swiftly and turned the corner into a side street. She saw the blue Porsche 911 up ahead. The passenger door was open. She got in and slammed the door shut. The driver indicated and moved out on the road. Not until they were moving in traffic did David Braithwaite speak. He cast a long look at his passenger.

"Did anyone see you?"

"As you can see, I'm virtually in disguise."

"That's not what I asked."

Madelyn didn't say anything for a few seconds. Then she decided for the truth. "I didn't check. I can't live like this anymore, do you understand?"

David gripped the steering wheel tighter till his knuckles turned white. His lips were pressed together, also turning white with the pressure on them. He was trying very hard to control his temper. When he spoke, his lips barely moved.

"How many times do I have to tell you to be careful? The police came today. They're not stupid."

"I know," Madelyn said, her voice trembling a little. "They came to see me as well."

A deep frown spasmed across David's features. "When, and why didn't you tell me?"

"This morning. And since when do I have to tell you everything?"

David blinked and looked out the window. They were going past Hyde Park Corner and heading towards Fulham. His nostrils flared, but he managed to keep his voice from rising. "You know what's at stake here. It's going to be fine, but only if we keep our wits about us."

Madelyn stared out the window and shook her head. David continued. "We need to give the police the same story. When they question us, they're looking for gaps in our statements. If you keep telling them the same thing, then this will work out."

Madelyn frowned, then waved her hands in the air. "What will work out? I don't even know exactly what's going on."

She turned her neck to stare at his profile. When she spoke, the trembling in her voice increased. "What happened to Susan?"

David took a lungful of air, then let it out slowly. "What's happened has happened. You don't think I feel bad about Susan?"

A mixture of regret and fury clouded Madelyn's mind. She slammed a fist down on her thigh. "I don't even know what you think anymore," she cried out. "Just look at what's happened. This is all your fault."

David didn't reply and kept driving. They went through Chelsea, then crossed Battersea Bridge. Madelyn asked, "Where are we going?"

"Somewhere we can talk in private," David said. "Are you hungry?"

Madelyn shook her head, shrinking back in her seat and getting closer to the door. David took the exit for Clapham Common and drove down the road that led to the Commons ponds.

Madelyn was mystified as the car bounced along the dirt track. She stared at the dense woodland on both sides, frowning.

"Where are we?"

David didn't reply. He parked on the grass verge close to the bank of the waters. Then he got out. Madelyn followed. She looked at the pond for a while, then the shock of realisation hit her. She walked over to David swiftly. "Is this where Susan…

"Yes, it is," David replied shortly. This is where Susan was found."

He moved further back from the water's edge to the shade of a large oak tree. He made sure the ground was dry, then sat down. He indicated Madelyn to do the same. She hesitated at first, observing him closely. Then she joined him, making sure there was distance between them.

David looked at her, his eyes filled with longing. The frown was gone from his face, and his lips were parted open. "I meant what I said about Susan. I'm sorry it happened. But we also need to move on."

Madelyn stared at the ground, not speaking.

"Move on with us, I mean," David said.

She could feel his eyes on her, but she ignored him. He leaned towards her. "I still feel the same way about you."

She shook her head. "David, I'm not sure it's a good idea anymore. Both of us will get into trouble."

David narrowed his eyes, his heartbeat picking up a notch. "What do you mean?"

"With the police. If word gets out, think about what's going to happen. Not to mention Susan."

David's jaw fell open, and he breathed deeply. A lethal cocktail of anger and frustration was mushrooming like a cloud in his brain. He was approaching the point of no return, but he didn't care.

"What are you trying to say?"

She looked up at him, seemingly not caring about the mottled blood on his face. "I'm saying I don't want to see you anymore. Enough is enough."

David frowned. "What?"

"You heard what I said." He stared at her intently for a few seconds, and she couldn't tolerate his gaze. She looked out towards the pond. Her forehead creased as a thought struck. "Why did you bring me here?"

David responded with another question. "What did you tell the police?"

Madelyn didn't answer. David repeated his question. She shrugged. "I guess they asked me the same questions they asked you."

"Did they ask you about us?"

"No. They don't suspect, so far. And I'd like to keep it that way. Do you understand?"

"Don't talk to me like that," he said. Surprised, she turned to look at him. But maybe she shouldn't be surprised. David's arrogance radiated off him in waves.

He held a finger up in front of the face.

"I tell you what to do. Got that?"

She huffed and tried to get up. He grabbed her hand and pulled her down. She fell with a thump and tried to wriggle free. David's grip was strong, and he held her in place. "Just listen to me," he panted, his face inches from hers.

"What did you tell the cops?"

"Let me go," she cried. "Or I'll scream."

"You can scream," David said, a thin, evil smile appearing on his lips. "No one is going to hear you." He breathed a few times rapidly. "Did you tell them about her psychiatrist?"

Madelyn stopped struggling and stared at David for a few seconds. He read her eyes, and his mouth opened.

"You stupid bitch," he whispered.

# CHAPTER 31

*14 years ago*

Maxine and Ricky, two of the senior members of Kamali's gang, faced Carlson. They leaned against the staircase wall in one of the council estate's labyrinthine hallways. Graffiti adorned the wall, and some beer cans littered the corner.

Maxine handed Carlson a phone. "It's encrypted, bruv. You only call me in an emergency. My code name is Hammer. Got it?"

Carlson took the pay-as-you-go mobile phone from her and nodded. Maxine continued. "There's another number called anvil. When you get to Luton, come out of the station, cross the road and sit in the park. Make sure no one's followed you. No one is watching you. Look out for cops, beggars, and junkies. Undercover drug squad detectives often disguise themselves as beggars. Or, they pay beggars money to act as informers. Be careful. Do you understand?"

Carlson exhaled, trying to quieten the hoofbeat of excitement pulsing through his chest. He was dressed in his school uniform, dark blazer, dark trousers, and black shoes.

Ricky gave the backpack to Carlson. "Don't look inside. Look inside, touch anything-- I'll get the fingerprints later on. Yes, we have fingerprint analysers. They show up in fluorescent light. Everything inside has been handled with gloves and is sterile. No fingerprints. Do you understand?"

Carlson nodded, gulping. He took the offered bag and put it on his shoulder. It wasn't as heavy as expected. It looked like a normal school bag, with stickers and badges on the front.

Maxine said, "The guy who comes to pick you up will be Latino, and his name is Hugo. He will take you to the safe house, where you will exchange this bag for another. Again, don't look inside that bag. Bring it straight back here. You wait till nightfall before getting on the train. You can stay at the safe house. Hugo will drop you off at the station."

Carlson nodded. He put the phone in his pocket and accepted the wad of cash that Maxine offered him with a murmur of thanks. It was £100, for his train journey.

Then he turned and left. The journey to Luton was uneventful. Several times, he looked at the bag. It would be so easy to open the chain and have a look inside. But he remembered what Ricky had said. It wasn't worth the risk.

The ticket inspector did his rounds and checked Carlson's student ticket. No one suspected him in his school uniform. He was just a boy going to school.

Luton train station was busy. There was an airport in Luton as well, and the train station had frequent connections. It was easy for Carlson to melt into the crowd and come out at the main entrance. The park opposite the station was large. Carlson saw two beggars, and he avoided them, choosing a park bench that was isolated. He called the number, and a man answered. Carlson gave the passcode, and after a pause, the man responded.

"Look out for a black Range Rover. It's going to be to your left. Ten minutes." The line went dead.

Carlson guarded the bag with his dear life and kept an eye out. A few people strolled by and mothers with prams. Then he saw the black Range Rover across the road. He crossed the busy road walked up to the car. The driver's seat window came down. A man with a long, pockmarked face looked out. He had tattoos on the sides of his head and his forearm. He looked scary.

"Are you Hugo?"

The man frowned at Carlson, then jerked a hand to the back seat. He swore loudly. "Get in the back, you little pest."

Carlson hunkered down in the back seat, holding the bag tightly on his lap. The car drove through the main streets till they entered the deprived inner-city areas. They stopped outside the back entrance of a butcher shop. The door opened, and a man came out, his white apron splattered with blood, and carrying a butcher's knife. Hugo got out of the car and pulled Carlson out.

"Get inside," he barked, giving him a push. Carlson straightened, put the bag on his back, and walked past the butcher holding the meat cleaver. The man was short and fat, thick at the shoulders. His beady eyes followed Carlson.

He walked through the back of the butcher shop, where stacks of meat were piled up. He was shown into a side room, where two men sat at a desk. They took the bag off him and had a look inside. One of them pulled out a rectangular package entirely covered in black plastic.

Carlson noticed the man wore gloves when he took the packet out. With a knife, the man nicked one corner, and a tiny bit of white powder leaked out. He rubbed it on his gums, then nodded. He zipped up the bag and put it away

Carlson stood there, and the two men completely ignored him. He cleared his throat. No one looked at him. He said, "Where's the bag I'm taking back?"

The two guys looked at each other, then stared at him. These men were the same skin colour as him, and he guessed they were either Mexicans or South Americans. Tattoos covered their faces and arms. He knew the tattoos on the face depicted which gang they were from, but it was a code he didn't recognise. Down in London, gang members didn't have face or neck tattoos.

He shifted on his feet, feeling scared. He couldn't shake off the coldness in his arms and legs. He shivered and tried not to make his teeth chatter.

One of the men rose and came close to Carlson. He was of average height but thickset and wide. He reached out a hand and cupped Carlson's face. He squeezed his cheeks till it hurt. His fingers smelt of grease and sweat—a revolting odour.

The man swore at him. "Sit in that corner and wait. You don't ask questions. We tell you what to do. Got that?"

Carlson nodded, heart hammering against his ribs. He still had his phone and some change from the return ticket. There was an open window close to him, that looked out into the side alley. He could jump out through that, if they tried to kill him. He swallowed hard, and glanced at the men. They were ignoring him, speaking together in hushed tones.

The hours went by, and darkness fell. The guy at the desk rose and approached Carlson with a black bag, which was identical to the previous one. The weight was about the same.

"Don't look inside. Just carry it straight to Kamali. Got that?"

Carlson nodded. Without a word, the man strode out the back entrance, and Carlson followed. He got into the black Range Rover, and drove. Carlson didn't see the man who had picked him up. The man dropped Carlson off at the station and again, without a word, drove off.

It was 7 PM by the time Carlson got off at Battersea station. He heaved a sigh of relief. He had made it. Happiness flooded his veins. He pulled the straps of the bag tightly on his back. His bladder was bursting, and he had to go for a leak.

He walked out of the station and found a deserted old archway by the railway bridge. Stepping across a puddle and making sure there was no one around him, he unzipped his trousers. He had almost finished when he heard a movement behind him.

146

He zipped up, but before he could turn, a strong arm grabbed him by the neck and a hand slammed over his mouth.

# CHAPTER 32

*14 years ago*

Carlson fought, but his assailant wasn't alone. He kicked with his legs, but there were three of them. Two of them held Carlson down while the other took the bag off his back. Then they ran off. Carlson screamed, fear and frustration running riot in his blood.

He chased after the three boys, who were taller than him. He targeted the boy who had the bag. They ran down an alleyway, and Carlson chased, shouting at them to stop. They turned left and right, taking the back alleys, trying to dodge him. But Carlson knew these routes like the back of his hand. They ran through a council estate and through more backstreets. Sweat poured down his face, blinding his eyes, but he didn't care.

The guy he was chasing tried to jump a fence. Carlson dived forward and caught his leg. The guy kicked, but Carlson held on. He managed to drag the guy down and get a hand on the bag. But his two friends attacked Carlson from the rear. The three of them held Carlson down again, and this time, he heard a snapping sound. He didn't know what it was, but it became clear when he saw the glint of a knife. It was a switchblade, and when he felt the sharp tip on his chin, he went still.

"Shank him man," one of them said. Shank was slang for knife.

"Go on, do it," the other and other urged. "We should have done it the first time."

Carlson closed his eyes. He had failed. He was going to die like this. But he wouldn't plead. He had another plan.

"I can make you guys very rich," he said. "Do you know what's inside the bag?"

The three men, whose faces he couldn't see, looked at each other. "What's inside the bag?"

"Let me go, and I'll tell you."

"No. You die here," the knife rose in the air as the hand tightened around his neck.

Carlson gagged, and closed his eyes. He clamped his jaws tight and stiffened, waiting for the blow. They would hit him in the neck, and he would bleed to death. His mother's face flashed before his eyes. Regret suffused his heart. He was sorry. God, he was so sorry.

The grip on his neck and arms relaxed. The boy astride his chest, holding the knife, rose. Carlson blinked his eyes open. Footsteps sounded, walking slowly. Carlson stumbled to his feet. He felt dizzy, his mouth dry. The corner of his mouth was bleeding but he didn't bother wiping it. Warily, he watched the three boys who had chased him. They stood in silence, watching him. Three other figures walked up to them slowly.

"You okay, cousin?" A familiar voice asked. Carlson strained his eyes in the darkness. Then the man stepped forward, right up to his face.

Carlson opened his eyes wide, his jaws dropping. "Kamali!"

Kamali smiled. He clapped a hand on Carlson's shoulder. "You did well, fam. We took the bag. You did well to chase and fight for it."

Carlson looked around at the two other shapes, who were huddled in the darkness. They came forward and recognised Maxine and Ricky.

Kamali said, "You're one of us now, bruv. Let's get back home. You need a drink."

*****

Over the next few months, Carlson made several trips outside London. Like a spider's web, Kamali's drug distribution network spread. Three times a week, Carlson would skip school and make his delivery runs. His school attendance record fell, and several times, Shola was called for a parent-teacher meeting. But she never read the letters, as Carlson got them before her. Shola's health had deteriorated, and she was having chemotherapy.

The Home Office still continued its deportation order, and Carlson used his newfound wealth to finance a legal battle with the Home Office. They got a free lawyer from the citizen's advice bureau, but that lawyer was no good.

Carlson had saved up almost £30,000 by then, all in cash. He kept the money under a loose floorboard in his bedroom. He searched online and found a Queen's Counsel immigration lawyer.

QC lawyers charged more than £500 an hour, and when he met Shola and Carlson for the first time, the surprise was evident on his face, but the eminent lawyer tried hard not to show it.

But his jaws dropped when, on mentioning his fees, Carlson pulled out a wad of notes. Carlson felt Shola's eyes on him, but he ignored her. He pushed the bundle of £50 notes to words the lawyer.

"There's £5000 in there. Please do whatever you can to keep my mother in the country."

The lawyer simply stared at them in silence as Shola and Carlson rose and left.

Six months of legal wrangling continued. Finally, with the help of the local member of Parliament's's letters, Shola was allowed compassionate leave to remain in England. Their case had succeeded.

Carlson continued to rise up the ranks in Kamali's gang. He had recruited Anton and a couple of other carefully selected schoolboys, who used their brains and kept their mouths shut.

150

One evening, he made a delivery to Kamali's flat, where he was relaxing with other gang members. As he got up to leave, Kamali told him to sit back down. Casually, Kamali took out a gun from his pocket and handed it to Carlson. It was the first time he had seen a gun so close-up. He stared at the gun, then at Kamali.

"Take it," Kamali said.

Carlson knew this was a test as well. He could feel his life slipping past him, all senses of normality slowly evaporating. He was now steeped in the ways of the gang, and there would be no going back. And what did he have to go back to?

Would he ever have a job, children, house, and mortgage?

Or could he use his brains and become like Kamali one day? Make a lot of money, and then maybe retire. Or die.

As he continued to stare at the gun, his 16-year-old mind grappled with the consequences. When all was said and done, he was a black kid from one of the worst council estates in the whole of London. Normal life for him wasn't normal for the people outside, the people on TV, the people with 9-to-5 jobs.

At least the drug money had allowed his mother to stay with him.

He took a deep breath, then leaned forward and took the gun from Kamali's hand. The polished butt felt warm and snug in the palm of his hand.

"Put it in your pocket," Kamali said. "We're going on a job tonight. You're coming with us."

# CHAPTER 33

It was eight in the morning, and Arla was at her desk with a steaming cup of coffee. Most of yesterday had been spent taking statements. She didn't have much time after she came back to the station. She briefed the team and submitted a quick report to Johnson, and then left. Luckily, her fantastic team had been working hard to get more evidence.

She opened up the file scene-of-crime had left in her tray.

A used condom had been found under Susan's bed. The condom had semen in it, which had been sent for DNA analysis. Arla knew it was time to get DNA samples from every member of the Remington family, and also David Braithwaite and Madelyn West.

She stopped and stared when she turned the page. There was a photo of a tiny plastic wrapper, and it contained a few white granules. Arla had taken part in drug busts before, and she didn't need the lab to tell her this was cocaine. But what arrested her gaze was the sign on the wrapper.

It was a dollar sign. The similarity with the crude mark carved on Susan's left hand was unmistakable. Breath caught in her chest. There was a significance to the mark, after all. It was clear Susan had been using cocaine - but was she mixed up with the drug gangs as well?

Arla sipped on her coffee and sat back. It was unlikely. Susan wouldn't be the first younger professional to take cocaine recreationally. The use of the drug was rife, and Susan fit the profile of a user, but not a gang member. Then her mind turned to the Afro-Caribbean man in Susan's flat. She flipped open her laptop and went to the film clip. She played it again.

The black-and-white image showed Susan walking in through the main door downstairs and the man next to her. Arla froze the image and zoomed in. The man had short curly hair, and he wore a dark T-shirt that clung to his muscled, athletic frame. He wore a gold chain on his neck, with a cross. Arla frowned and zoomed in for a closer look.

Had Susan not been wearing a similar chain?

Arla scribbled on her notebook and circled the words gold chain. She returned to the film and played it again. Susan went up the stairs, and the man followed behind her. Arla paid attention to the man from the rear, noting any bulge in his pockets for a weapon and any distinguishing features in the exposed parts of his body – he did have some tattoos on his left forearm, just below the bicep. She zoomed in again but couldn't make out a great deal.

She frowned, deep in thought. She hated being judgemental. This man could be a perfectly normal guy, maybe someone Susan was dating. And he had no link with the packet of cocaine with the dollar mark.

But what if there was a link? What if this guy was supplying Susan with those packets, or maybe he was using it with her?

Either way, chances were that he knew about Susan's drug habit. And even if he didn't, Arla knew she needed to question him. She checked the date on the corner of the flickering screen again. 15th of March. Tuesday. No one had seen Susan Remington after that day. Arla reached out a finger and tapped the man's figure on the screen.

This man was the last person to see Susan Remington alive. Arla needed to know who he was. But so far, the image identity software in HOLMES and the national crime databases had turned up a blank. This person clearly didn't have a police record.


Scene-of-crime had also documented another DNA sample from Susan's bathroom sink. It was different from the DNA contained in this semen sample, but they didn't have a match. Arla sht the report, aware the time had come to take swabs from all the suspects. It needed to be done today.


Rob had got hold of the call log from Susan's phone. Arla went through the numbers, circling the ones that had called her more than twice in the last two weeks. She frowned when she saw a number that was a series of crosses. That meant an encrypted phone. It had called her twice in the week of her disappearance and three times the week before.

 In total, the encrypted number had called Susan ten times in March. The next frequent number belonged to Madelyn West and had been flagged up by Rob. About half the calls from the encrypted number had lasted ten minutes, which signified a conversation.

She noticed a similar pattern with Madelyn, but the calls were of longer duration. Arla also saw Sheila Remington's number appear a couple of times in March. Some of the numbers were still unidentified, and they could be work-related.

Arla was still going to the call log when there was a knock on her door. It was Rosslyn, and her face was red, her breathing laboured. Arla looked at her bulging eyes, and a sense of dread fluttered in her chest.

Rosslyn came inside. "Guv, you won't believe what just happened."

"What?" Arla rose from her desk.

"Madelyn West's body was just seen floating in the pond. A couple of joggers saw it. The same pond where Susan Remington was found."

# CHAPTER 34

*Present day*

It was early morning, and the red and gold glimmer was still bright in the sky. The still waters of the pond seem to hold a glow in them as if something shining lay beneath the waters. It passed quickly, and little wavelets appeared on its dark breast as the gentle breeze shimmered across the water.

The breeze sounded like a desperate sigh to Carlson's ears. He stood with his head bent, staring at the water. He wasn't close to the bank, where the blue and white police tape had cordoned off the crime scene. He was more than a hundred yards behind, on the crest of a small slope, behind the shade of an oak tree.

Regret and sadness broke the barriers in his mind and threatened the back of his eyes with tears. He didn't want this. First Susan, and now Madelyn. Both had been nice girls, and he didn't want them to die in this way. He saw the police hovering around the body.

One of his runners had spotted the police activity when they were making a drop. His runners were active in Clapham common, a popular place for young professionals to pick up their bags of crack and cocaine.

When Carlson heard about the body, he knew instantly who it was. He had rushed to the crime scene and observed from a distance.

He shook his head as he stared out over the desolate, dark scene. He was losing his grip on sanity. He had urges he couldn't control, and he had given in to them time and time again. But Susan was different. Susan could have got him on the path to recovery, turned his life around. But his thirst for violence had remained unabated. He was filled with remorse again. With a heavy heart, he slumped down to the ground.

He played with the gold chain on his neck, with the gold cross pendant at the end. His fingertips brushed over the smooth metal.

What had he done?

And was there any way back for him?

His eyes filled with tears as his head hung down.

# CHAPTER 35

The body had been dragged to the bank. Scene-of-crime still hadn't arrived. The blue-and-white tape had been stretched across the plants that lined the pond bank. Arla stood for a while and watched, taking the scene in.

Susan's body had been found further to the left, closer to the dirt path. They had to walk about ten minutes to get to this new location. She stepped forward, noting the wet grass. It was still cloudy, but the rain had stopped. Arla looked behind her at the dense clumps of trees. She walked further away from the water, keeping her eyes on the ground. Harry came up to her.

"What are you looking for?"

She pointed behind him. Harry's boots had left imprints on the wet grass. It was 9:30 in the morning, and moisture still clung to the ground.

Arla walked up to the tree line, stepping carefully, eyes scanning the ground. There was a row of mature oak trees, with huge tree trunks and roots that swelled out of the ground. She came to an abrupt halt in front of an oak tree. Grass became sparse closer to the tree trunk, and brown earth was more prominent. She bent low at the waist and looked carefully. Then she pointed with one hand, and Harry crept forward, then stopped.

"Boot prints. I see them."

As he was closer, he took out his phone and snapped some photos.

"They look big to me," Arla remarked. "Size eleven, right?"

"Maybe." Harry tiptoed forward, then knelt at the margins of the grass.

"What?" Arla said, aware Harry had seen something.

"Smaller shoes. A woman's flats, or pumps, I'd say. We need to get our boot expert up here."

Arla stared at the wet earth for a few minutes, and although she could see the smaller boot print, it wasn't immediately obvious it belonged to a woman. She turned around. She couldn't find any boot prints going down to the water's edge.

With slow steps, she walked back to the body. This time, the face wasn't bloated. The skin had shrunk and tightened and was bone white, almost translucent. Madelyn West's lifeless eyes were open and staring.

Arla crouched by the body. She was wearing gloves and had shoe coverings on. She could see bruise marks on the neck. Small lacerations were present on the knuckles of both hands, along with bruises, signifying a struggle. An iron fist circled her guts when she saw the dollar sign engraved on the left hand. Madelyn was wearing a summer dress with a cardigan on top. Her shoes had been removed. Arla glanced up at one of the uniformed sergeants standing close by.

"Did we find any of her personal belongings?"

"Not as yet go. We are still looking."

Arla re-examined the body without touching anything. Photos of the face were sent to the station, and Rosslyn had identified her. Arla couldn't find any other evidence of a struggle on the body. There was no blood coming out of the ears or nose. She heard a sound behind her and half turned. It was Dr Banerjee, wearing the same crumpled grey suit as two days ago. She straightened, and her knees creaked in protest.

Dr Banerjee shook his head sadly. "This routine is becoming depressingly familiar."

"Tell me about it," Arla stood next to the pathologist, and they stared at the body together.

"Why didn't she drown? Arla asked.

"Because she wasn't in the water for long enough. Which is strange because her mouth is open. Even a few hours of submersion can cause the body to sink."

Banerjee moved past Arla and knelt by the body. He opened his briefcase and took out a pair of forceps with his gloved hands. He opened up the mouth with his forceps on his left hand, and with another pair, he pulled something out from the oral cavity. Arla walked towards the feet to watch the pathologist.

Dr Banerjee was pulling out some white cloth from the victim's mouth. A sense of nausea churned inside Arla's guts, and she looked away.

"Her mouth was stuffed with gauze. That absorbed a lot of water; hence the body floated."

Arla squeezed her eyes shut, disgust and anger swirling in her mind. "Why would someone do that?"

"Quite clearly, they didn't want the body to sink. Perhaps they wanted the body to be found."

Arla's head snapped back, and she locked eyes with Dr Banerjee. Through his glasses, she watched him blink. They both knew the score. It was the same M.O, and this time, the killer was bolder. He was not content with engraving the dollar sign on the hand; he wanted the body to be found without delay.

Dr Banerjee transferred his attention back to the victim. "Good news is I will get more out of the body this time. More DNA and skin samples. There is virtually no bloating, so the gastric and intestine components should also be preserved."

Harry was standing next to Arla, observing. "Time of death, Doc?"

"Early hours of the morning, I'd say. When was the body first noticed?"

"About 7 AM by two members of the public."

Banerjee touched the body, then put a thermometer inside the mouth. He rose and took the water temperature as well. Then he glanced towards Harry and Arla.

"The water is always colder than the ground. The differential is about 2° at the moment. I would say she's been there for 7 to 8 hours. Which means you can put a time of death at close to midnight."

"Let's move this body to the morgue, and I'll get to work on it straight away. Have you got DNA samples from all the suspects?"

"I've already sent a team out to do just that," Arla said. "They will be coming straight back to you."

Her brain churned with possibilities as she considered her next move.

But she didn't have an answer to the question she dreaded the most.

*Who's next?*

# CHAPTER 36

Madelyn West's smiling, attractive face was on the whiteboard in major-incident room one. Her face was right next to a photo of her body. Arla took a few seconds going through recent events as she faced and assembled staff. It seemed incredulous that she had met Madelyn the day before. Since the body was discovered, Arla had gone through Madelyn's statement in her mind. In the end, she had said something that stuck in Arla's mind.

*We all have our secrets, don't we?*

The statement had struck Arla as odd, and she had been in two minds whether to ask Madelyn to elaborate. Now she wished she had.

Madelyn would have been pivotal in cracking this case. And now she was dead. Arla rapped the whiteboard with a knuckle, and silence fell across the room.

"We need to stop this from happening again. The killer is laughing behind our backs. I, for one, intend to teach him a lesson." Her eyes scanned across several faces, and she nodded at each one of them. She wrote number one with a black pen and circled it.

"We need visibility. I want uniform units guarding the pond area 24/7. I will rope in extra units from Balham, Lambeth, and Tooting. We need to do a thorough search of the Woodlands and the surrounding areas of the common. This includes the opposite banks of the ponds. I don't care how long it takes, but we need to be thorough."

"What are we looking for, guv? One of the uniformed sergeants asked.

161

"Apart from the obvious personal items like phones, purse, clutch bag, jewellery, we are also looking for torn pieces of clothes, drops of blood, anything unusual that grabs attention. Look for discarded condoms, lighters, packets of cigarettes, anything and everything. We will end up with a lot of junk, but you never know what will be useful."

Arla wrote number two on the whiteboard. "I need a drone over that area, capable of infrared and thermal imaging. The drone stays up there 24/7 for the next week. I will get clearance from commander Johnson and speak to the tech lab. I need two people to go through the images on a daily basis."

She pointed to the two victims. "These women were innocent. They deserve our help. Let's not leave anything to chance."

She wrote number 3 on the board. "Every car going in and out of the road that leads to the ponds has to be stopped and asked questions. One of the uniformed units will do this."

"And lastly, we need to bring in specialised marine units from Scotland Yard. Divers." She glanced towards Harry and her team. She hadn't spoken to Johnson about this as yet, and she didn't know if he would agree. But in her mind, it was worth it.

A uniform sergeant asked, "How many divers, guv? And will they search every pond?"

"Divers normally come in teams of two. The three ponds, but we focus on the first one where the bodies were found, and which also happens to be the largest."

She wrote the dollar sign on the whiteboard and circled it. "This sign was marked on both the victim's hands. We found a packet of cocaine in Susan Remington's room, with the same sign. Are the two related? I think so."

Arla coughed into a fist, then continued. "I want an intelligence report from the drug squad about any criminal gang who uses this symbol. I want it by this evening," she turned to look at her team. Rob gave her a thumbs up, indicating he would be on the case.

Arla turned to the assembled staff and pointed towards Andy Jackson, the uniformed Inspector.

"If there are any drug dealers in Clapham Common, I want to know about them. I'm sure we had some arrests in the past, right?"

Andy nodded. "Yes, we did. Of late, though, none of the gangs who deal has been seen in the Common. That doesn't mean they've gone away. No one knows what happens after dark in the Common."

Arla shivered inwardly but kept her calm. The spectre of a drug-crazed killer stalking innocent victims at night in the Common gave her bones a chill.

"You know what to do. Let's make sure there's not a third victim."

The meeting broke up, and Arla went back into office. She rang Johnson and told him about the divers.

"I'll have to get approval from one of the assistant commissioners." Johnson's voice was quiet. "But you know they'll want something in return."

Arla knew the score. Diving units weren't cheap, and if she was going to employ them, she had better produce results: a list of suspects, and more importantly, charging one of them.

"We have a lot of evidence now, sir. I'm hoping something will click for us. But if the divers find something important like a phone, that could solve this case."

"I'll see what I can do. No promises." Johnson hung up. There was a sharp knock on the door, and Harry poked his head in. "Libby Alderson, one of Madelyn West's friends and co-workers has arrived. We called her office this morning, and she agreed to come down to give a statement."

"Good work. I'll meet them in interview room one."

*****

The interview room was sparsely decorated. The lime green walls were blank, and to the left of the table, a blacked-out viewing box was carved on the wall. Libby Alderson was seated at the table, which like the chairs, was nailed to the floor. Harry spoke into the recorder and started the tape.

Libby was a plump thirtysomething, dressed in a business suit that bulged at her waist. Her skin had blotches of red, and there was a sheen of sweat on her forehead. She adjusted her glasses and looked nervous. Arla smiled at her reassuringly and spoke in a friendly voice.

"Please introduce yourself for the recorder." Libby did so, and Arla started.

"How long have you known Madelyn West?"

"Almost a year and a half. I joined the firm as an intern, and she was the accountant who showed me around. I was lucky enough to get a job at the firm, and she took me under her wing. We became friends."

Her head dipped as she stared at her lap. The tip of her nose turned red, and Arla could see that she was fighting her emotions.

"I'm very sorry this has happened, Libby. And thank you very much for coming down. If you can help us in any way, you will be helping Madelyn ."

Libby's head remained bent, and she nodded without looking up.

"When did you last see Madelyn?"

"Two days ago." Libby's head lifted to make eye contact with Arla. "It was the day you came to the office. I saw the two of you going into the room with her."

"Did you see her at the office after that as well?"

"No. She was often busy in the evenings. She had a boyfriend."

Arla's ears picked up. "Do you have any details about this boyfriend? Did you ever meet him?"

Libby exhaled. "No. She was very secretive about him. It was a bit weird. That's why I came to talk to you about it."

She wiped her nose with a tissue and continued. "She didn't tell me who he was, but I saw him pick her up after work a few times. Once, I also saw him walk into her apartment."

"And where were you at the time?"

"I was at the bus stop opposite her apartment. I met her after work for a couple of drinks and then was going home."

"Did you get a good look at him?"

Libby nodded in excitement, clutched in Arla's guts. This was a real breakthrough. "Can you please describe him to us?"

"He was tall and thin. He had black hair which was side-parted. He wore glasses. And a grey suit."

"What colour shoes?"

"Black."

"What did he have on his fingers? Did you see any rings? And please think about his face. Did he have any marks anywhere?"

Libby pondered her face a mask of concentration. Then she shook her head. "No."

Harry asked, "what sort of a car did he drive?"

"A blue Porsche 911."

Arla didn't know much about cars, but she knew Porsche 911's were expensive. The description of the man triggered alarm bells inside her. She leaned over to Harry and murmured in his ear. He left the room and returned shortly with an A4 packet. He took out photos of the Remington

165

family and the Braithwaite family. He spread the photos of Susan's brother, Rupert, her father, and David Braithwaite and his family.

Libby observed the photos with interest, then her eyes widened.

Her finger pointed to the photo of David Braithwaite. "That's him. That's the man I saw going into her apartment, and it was his blue Porsche that Madelyn got into."

# CHAPTER 37

Arla and Harry waited by the front door of the Remington residence.

The small door that was waged within the massive portcullis swung open, and an elderly man poked his head through. "Do come in. Lady Remington will see you."

This time, they didn't have to wait in the cathedral-like atrium. They followed the man, who walked with the slow step of someone well past their prime. They went up to the double doors and then were shown to the reception room on their right. They even sat down on the same sofa, facing the green lawns.

Sheila Remington walked in shortly. A man came with her, wearing a tweed jacket, dark trousers, and brogue shoes. His blonde hair was combed sideways, and he regarded Arla and Harry with avid curiosity. Arla returned the frank gaze, looking him up and down.

The wealthy classes prided themselves on their dishevelled appearances, a trait Arla had seen several times. Sheila's husband was no different. His jacket had seen better days. Even the leather patches at the elbow were worn out. His trousers needed ironing, and the tips of his shoes were scuffed. Despite that, he wasn't a bad looking man, Arla mused. He had an ageing Robert Redford air about him.

"This is my husband, John Remington. I believe you wished to see him," Sheila said. They shook hands and sat down.

Arla glanced at Sheila, who was sitting resolutely next to her husband, showing no intention of leaving. Arla cleared her throat.

"It would be easier if we could speak to Mr Remington in private."

"I understand that, Inspector Baker," Sheila said in her prim voice. "But my husband has been rather distraught. I just want to make sure that he is okay during the interview."

"I do not wish to sound insensitive. But by distraught, do you mean anything more than bereavement?"

Husband and wife looked at each other. She opened her mouth to speak, but John raised a hand. "It's okay," he told his wife. She lapsed into silence. She sat facing her husband, her spine straight, hands folded on her lap.

John turned to Arla and Harry. "Like any father, I have found this difficult to come to terms with. To say this is going to change my life is an understatement. I know we speak for all of us when I say we will miss her terribly."

His eyes flickered away, and his lips trembled with emotion.

Arla warmed to the man immediately. He was a decent human being, and he was being himself.

John said, "What would you like to know?"

Arla glanced at Harry. They still hadn't found the reason why John couldn't be left alone. She decided to probe later.

"When did you see your daughter last?"

"At Sunday lunch on 13th March. "

"And before that?"

"Sometime in February. She came for lunch on Sundays at least once a month. She was busy with her work and her life."

"So, after 13th March, you didn't see your daughter?"

"No, but I spoke to her. "

"What did you talk about?"

Arla noticed Sheila was staring intently at her husband, who was not meeting her gaze. She could feel something here, an invisible barrier that stood between them.

"Susan spoke to me every now and then about her problems. You know," he waved his hands in the air.

"Would you like to elaborate? What sort of problems?"

"Stress due to her work. That sort of thing, isn't it dear?" Sheila interjected. John glanced at his wife, then looked away swiftly.

Arla ignored Sheila, who was irritating her. She focused her attention on John and repeated her question. For a few seconds, there was a tense silence. Arla could hear the grandfather clock ticking loudly. Eventually, John spoke.

"She did have stress problems. She was also anxious about her work, and…"

"And?"

"She didn't feel very safe. She felt someone was following her. She felt her phone had been tapped, as well."

Sheila Remington's head sank on her chest. John stared at the carpet and rubbed his hands together. Harry cleared his throat.

"Do you know why Susan felt that way?"

John looked up at Harry. "I'm not entirely sure."

"But you suspected there must be a reason why she felt that way, didn't you? Did she mention names?"

Harry was persistent because he could see in John's eyes an understanding. Men were emotional when it came to their daughters, perhaps more so than sons. Fathers hate it if their daughters are in trouble, a feeling that Harry had never experienced, but he understood it intuitively. He would be the same way if anything happened to Nicole.

John stared at Harry for a while, not speaking. It was Sheila who raised her voice. "I think that's enough for today. As you can see, detectives, my husband is tired. He's just come back from a business trip. Now, if you, please excuse him."

A knot of irritation was gathering at the back of Arla's mind. And with it, a hardening suspicion. Whatever Sheila Remington was trying to hide had implications for this case. She decided to test the waters.

"Did Susan tell you she was scared of her ex-partner?"

John glanced up, and Sheila's head snapped towards Arla. She glared at him, and Arla glared back.

"Whatever do you mean, Inspector?" Sheila said in a frosty voice.

"I asked the question to your husband, not yourself," Arla bit the words out. Her dislike of Sheila was reaching new heights.

"And as I've explained, my husband is not feeling himself. Surely, if you had experienced such a tragedy, you would want to excuse yourself."

"This is a murder investigation, and by not answering the question, you are deliberately impeding the investigation."

A frown increased Sheila Remington's face. "I'm not sure I care about the tone of your voice, Inspector."

Harry intervened. "Mrs Remington, all we wish to know is if your daughter had been pursued by anyone. If she felt someone was watching her, we just want to ensure it wasn't a jealous ex-partner."

Harry's intervention seemed to ease matters a little. He turned his attention to John Remington and asked him pointedly. "Mr Remington, were you aware of anyone?"

Again, John hesitated. He opened his mouth to speak and shut it.

Sheila rose, and so did her husband. It was clear that their interview was over. Arla stood as well, along with Harry, who stood several inches above everyone else.

Arla had wasted enough time. She was out of her patience, and in her experience, people like Sheila Remington needed to be put in place. The wealthy and powerful didn't like being talked down to. However, when they got angry, they made mistakes.

Arla spoke with deliberate slowness. "Was it David Braithwaite? After all, he was her ex-husband, and their divorce was far from amicable."

Sheila Remington squeezed her eyes shut, and a tremor worked its way across John's features. He swallowed hard and then breathed heavily. He held Arla's eyes for a few seconds, and she saw a fractional incline of his head. That was all the answer Arla needed.

"Thank you," she said to John, then cut her eyes to Sheila. If looks could kill, Arla would have been vaporised right now. She locked eyes with Sheila.

"When I asked you about Susan, you didn't mention her eating disorder."

Sheila frowned. "It was a long time ago, Inspector. Susan recovered from it and moved on with her life. Besides, you didn't ask for her medical history, did you?"

"I am now. Is there anything else we need to know?"

Both Sheila and John were silent. Arla asked, "I'm interested about her mental health. She was clearly fragile emotionally. I'm sure you noticed that."

It was John who spoke. "Yes, she was. As my wife mentioned, she recovered well from the eating problems, but it left her with anxiety She had panic attacks often." His eyes flickered to the floor.

Sheila sighed. "Will that be all, Inspector Baker? If you wish for Susan's medical history, I'm sure you can get it from her doctor?"

171

Arla ignored Sheila and turned to Harry, gesturing towards his coat pocket. Harry pulled out a plastic packet containing the DNA swab sticks. He explained what they were for.

Sheila Remington looked mystified. Then she snarled, completely outraged. "We're Susan's parents! And you're treating us as suspects?"

"No, we're not," Arla's voice was calm but firm. "We need the swabs to exclude you from the investigation."

Sheila's eyes flashed, and her jaws ground together. Arla also knew she didn't have a choice. Harry did the needful, and then they asked for Rupert.

"Goodbye Inspectors," John said as he shuffled away, his wife literally pushing him along. Rupert walked in, and Harry explained to him about the swab. He had no problems with his swab being taken. He opened his mouth, and Harry repeated the procedure with his gloved hand.

After Rupert left, they were shown out by the elderly man. As they walked back towards their car, Arla pursed her lips, deep in thought.

"What's wrong with John Remington?"

"I don't know. But what are the chances he also has some mental illness? After all, problems like eating disorders can run in families, right?"

Arla stopped dead in her tracks. "Maybe that's why there was an understanding between father and daughter. They could talk to each other." She looked at Harry, her pulse rising to a drumbeat in her ears. "Let's get in touch with Prof Worthington. And find out John Remington's medical records."

# CHAPTER 38

arry parked the BMW behind the white scene-of-crime van. There was a squad car in front, and one of the uniformed sergeants waved at Arla, and she waved back. She got out of the car, pulling her coat around her.

The gloomy weather continued, the sunny skies of Easter suddenly a distant memory. The green expanse of Hyde Park lay on the other side of the road. Low bellied clouds hung over the horizon, browsing along the green treetops. To her far right, she could see the crenelations of Kensington Palace. It was a wonderful location, but it came with a price tag. Never mind the rent, she knew even the Council taxes would be exorbitant, given the famous Park just opposite.

She turned and followed Harry inside the stucco apartment complex block. Madelyn West had lived on the third floor in a two-bedroom flat facing Hyde Park. The apartment was simply furnished, with a modest reception area and two similarly sized bedrooms.

It was far less glitzy than Susan Remington's place. Blue Scene of Crime tiles had been placed on the floor, and Arla walked along with them carefully, a precarious act that she hated. She was wearing low heels, which were flat, but she still didn't trust these sterile slabs. She stepped off them with a sigh of relief and put the shoe covers on.

One of the blue Tyvek-coated scene-of-crime officers was kneeling beside a bedside table. As Arla watched, he pulled something out with a pair of tweezers from the floor. He held it up to the light, and Arla kneeled to take a better look.

It was a small plastic packet with the dollar sign on it. Inside it, she could see a few crumbs of white powder.

"Bag that. Tell Parmentier here I need it analysed as a priority."

The SOC officer nodded, and held up a thumb. Harry strolled into the room, and Arla showed him the evidence bag. His eyes widened.

"The two friends obviously liked getting high. Evidently, they had the same supplier."

"Yes, Arla frowned. "We need to find out who that person is."

Harry squatted on the floor and looked underneath the bed. With his gloved hand, he pulled out a small suitcase. He opened it, then whistled. Arla stepped to one side to get a better look. It was leggings and small tops made out of red spandex with metal studs on them.

Harry lifted a pair of knickers that had pointed metal studs are going down one corner. Then he picked up what looked like a table tennis racket, but in reality, it was something to slap buttocks with. Her cheeks coloured as Harry held it up to her, smiling lecherously.

"Getting any ideas?" He whispered very softly. Arla glared at him, her eyes falling to the scene-of-crime officer only a few feet away. He didn't pay them any attention.

Harry ducked his head underneath the bed again and rummaged around.

He came out with a discarded condom. He put it in the evidence bag and handed it to the SOC officer.

"That'll be good for DNA analysis," Arla said. "We have the swabs from David Braithwaite now, right?"

"Yes, we do. It's already in the lab."

"Did we find Madelyn's phone or her laptop?"

"No phone, but there was a laptop on her desk. The books on the shelf were a mixture of romance and urban fantasy. Nothing special. No personal diaries."

Arla walked over to the dresser and opened the doors. She looked through the dresses and in the underwear drawers. She poked her hand inside a small slim drawer where she couldn't see very well. Her fingers struck something, and she pulled it out. Her eyes lit up. It was a small Nokia phone, the type that was popular in the late 90s. She had seen these phones used as burner phones.

"Look what I found," she exclaimed, turning it to Harry. He held out an evidence bag.

"Let's take this back to the Tech lab ourselves."

Harry nodded and showed it to the scene-of-crimes officer so he could log the serial number. Then they got back in the BMW, and Arla started making calls as Harry drove.

# CHAPTER 39

B enny walked with his hands stuffed inside his grey Puffer jacket. It was the latest design, and he loved it. He also had his new Converse trainers on, and he couldn't get enough of them. All his friends were jealous.

Benny was eleven years old, and his real name was Benedict Angelo. He liked his nickname, but he would prefer being called Big Ben. He felt the name was justified, given the amount of money he was earning at the moment. There was no other kid in the entire Winstanley estate who could afford the latest phone, laptop, and shoes as he did. He was making almost £one thousand per week, and all he had to do for that was make drop-offs.

He whistled and tried to look nonchalant as he gazed around. It was mid-morning, and Clapham Common had a green Easter tinge around its corners. The rains had relented, and a bright, jovial sun was riding higher in the sky. Benny felt good. He and his mother were still living in the council flat, and he was giving his mother money for shopping. She didn't like it and told him off repeatedly, but he didn't care. Money was money, right?

That's what his leader, Carlson said. Carlson could have gone to university and become a doctor or a lawyer. But he would have earned far less money that way. Instead,

the Battersea Dollar gang (as they were known in the underworld) was shifting huge amounts of cocaine and crack every week. Benny had heard Carlson had houses all over the world. Apparently, he even owned a boat that would sail from Battersea docks in case the Feds came after him.

Benny bounced along the concrete path that went deeper inside the common, his mind filled with visions sitting on a gold throne in mid-air while everyone did his bidding. Carlson was like that now, and maybe one day he would as well. He adjusted the straps of the backpack on his shoulders. He was instructed not to look inside it, but he already knew what he was carrying. He had made so many of these drop-offs, he could now tell by the weight.

A submachine gun was only slightly heavier than a handgun. He had only carried one of those once. Most of the time, it was kilo bags of cocaine. The most he had carried was four, and by today's weight, he could tell it was no more than 2 kg. He had to go and sit on the park bench and wait for 10 minutes while he pretended to look at his phone.

When he got the text message to say the man had arrived, he had to take the bag off and leave it under the park bench. He had strict orders not to look for the man. He simply got up and left. As his confidence had grown, he walked off, then hid behind trees and looked. Last time, he saw a white man come to pick the bag up. He was older than one of his teachers at school. And he was well dressed. Benny wondered what he did with all that cocaine. He knew one kilo was worth one hundred thousand pounds. That seemed like a lot of money.

A movement caught Benny's eyes. Two boys were walking towards him. They were much older, probably seventeen to eighteen. They had a hungry, raw look about them. Their baseball caps were pulled low, their jackets big, and their trainers stylish. Both wore black.

They gave Benny the eye, and his heart froze. They were from the Clapham gang. This was their territory. This was the reason why none of the elders came here on business. Benny was a clean skin, and he had slipped under their radar several times. He looked like a schoolboy.

He averted his face from the close scrutiny, and his heart thumped loudly as he walked past them. He had seen both these guys before, and they had ignored him. He kept walking, hearing their footsteps fade. He breathed a sigh of relief.

177

But it didn't last long. His ears pricked up as fast footsteps approached, and he didn't look back as he had been ordered. He increased his pace, and the footsteps increased, then broke into a run. A heavy hand clamped on his shoulder. He was swung back, and he found the two boys looking down at him. They were men, really, at that age when they were almost adults.

"I've seen you around, bruv. You're from Winstanley, right?"

Benny stood rigid with fear, not knowing what to say.

The other guy spoke up. "Yeah, I've seen you riding with Carlson's boys. Isn't that right, bruv?"

Terrified and not knowing what to say, Benny shook his head in silence.

"What's in your bag?"

Benny knew hesitation was fatal. "Schoolbooks," he replied promptly.

"Don't lie. Let's have a look."

They reached for the straps of his bag, and Benny knew the game was up. He turned and sprinted off the path into the woods. The boys came after him. They were faster, with longer legs. Benny crashed and fell as one of them tackled him. He was held down, and he could feel the bag being ripped from his back. He screamed for help as loud as he could.

A dog barked close by, and the sound got louder. Benny saw four brown legs running towards him, and a big dog appeared, barking and snarling. Benny felt the pressure ease from his back. A white man appeared, calling after his dog. He stared with an open mouth as Benny got to his feet. The bag was still on his back. The two boys were retreating, and the dog was still barking ferociously. Before Benny knew what was happening, two uniformed policemen appeared.

"What's going on here?" One of them shouted.

Benny looked behind him. The two boys had disappeared. He turned and ran for all he was worth. But he was tackled again, this time by one of the policemen. They didn't hurt him as the boys had. He was pulled up by the scruff of the neck, and he found himself staring at the uniformed policeman's face.

*Dammit... I've been nicked by the feds.*

"What's going on, son? What are you running away from?"

"I'm late for school," Benny mumbled.

"Why did those two boys attack you?"

Benny didn't answer. One of the policemen pursed his lips and glanced at the other. "What's in your bag?"

Benny shut his eyes. His dreams of making it big had just come to an abrupt end.

# CHAPTER 40

Harry parked the car in the rear parking lot of the Clapham police station. Arla was still speaking on the phone, and Prof Worthington was on the other line. Arla had warmed to the man. He might be eccentric, but he had a sharp mind, and he had clearly cared a lot about Susan Remington. His help so far had been invaluable.

"So, you don't know anything about John Remington?" Arla asked. She continued speaking as she got out of the car and slammed the door shut. Harry strolled back towards the double doors of the station. She walked slower, listening intently as the professor spoke.

"She mentioned a few times that she liked talking to her dad. Because he understood."

"And did she say why he was so understanding?

"The professor thought for a while. "Not in so many words. I must say I never asked her specifically if her father had a mental health history."

Arla tried her best not to sound disappointed. "But her father could have a history, right?"

"Yes, of course. Mental health issues do run in families. Depression does, and there is a strong link of schizophrenia in first-degree family members."

"What about eating disorders?"

"There can be," the professor said in a guarded tone. "However, eating disorders are rarer in men because men suffer less from body dysmorphia."

He cleared his throat. "However, there are links between eating disorders and other mental health issue issues, such as bipolar and severe or psychotic depression."

Arla had already described her meeting with John and Sheila. She asked the professor what he thought.

"Difficult to say. Don't forget that many people with schizophrenia and psychosis live perfectly normal lives. They are helped by medication and counselling. However, if they stop the medication or go through a stressful event, their symptoms can relapse. Like any other physical disease, such as diabetes. In modern medicine, there is no difference between mental and physical disorders."

"Yes, I get that," Arla said. "But do you think Susan's father might be hiding his mental health issue?"

The elderly doctor sighed. He reminded Arla of Dr Banerjee in the way he spoke. He took his time and was circumspect.

"It's impossible to say, Arla. The biggest clue you've given me is that her father was frank with you about David Braithwaite. Quite clearly, he wanted you to know. And the mother's attitude does bother me. But I'm sorry, I cannot say definitively that her father has a mental illness."

"Well, unless we arrest him, we cannot go through his medical records."

"Then I guess your only option is to ask him directly. Preferably without his wife being present."

Arla tapped her foot on the road, staring at the black asphalt. "Thank you very much, doc. I really appreciate your help."

"No problem."

Arla was still deep in thought. She was wrestling with an idea. Could she tell Prof Worthington about Madelyn West? He didn't know her personally, but Susan had mentioned her to him. She decided to take the risk.

"Prof, as you know, this is an ongoing investigation. Anything I tell you has to be regarded with total confidentiality. And the same obviously goes for anything you tell me."

"I know that," he said mildly.

"I need to tell you about a new complication. Please keep this to yourself." Arla told him about Madelyn, and the professor listened, then was silent for a while.

"Hello?"

He cleared his throat. "Yes, I'm still here. My goodness, I cannot believe this. And you say she was killed in the same way?"

"Yes." Arla's mind was churning away. Everyone was a suspect still. True, David Braithwaite was top of the list now, but Prof Worthington knew a great deal about Susan and the Remington family. Arla knew very well that doctors could be devious, and she had to tread with caution. And yet, her interaction with Prof Worthington so far didn't make her alarm bells ring. Trusting someone was always a fine balancing act.

"I'm not sure if I told you something about Madelyn West," the Prof said.

That got Arla's attention. "What's that?"

"Susan said the closer people are to you, the more they can hurt you. I remember those were her exact words. I was asking her what she meant. After some hesitation, she said Madelyn had betrayed her."

In silence, Arla thought about this. In light of what Libby Anderson had said, it was clear Madelyn was having an affair with David Braithwaite.

"Why didn't you mention this last time?"

182

"I'm sorry, it must've slipped my mind. I remembered because you spoke of Madelyn."

Arla remained silent, her mind spinning dark, complicated loops.

"If you think about anything else, no matter how trivial you think it might be, please let me know. You have my number."

"I certainly will. Take care, and I hope you find who's responsible for these atrocities."

# CHAPTER 41

Arla hung up. She rubbed the tip of the phone across her lower lip. Then she thrust her hands deep into her coat pocket and walked towards the rear entrance of the police station. A couple of uniform sergeants were smoking outside, and she caught a wisp of their cigarette smoke and inhaled. She had given up the dirty habit two years now, but she couldn't lie to herself. At times of stress, she still felt like taking a drag.

Arla waved at Lisa and Rob, who looked up from their desks as she walked in. Along with Harry, they rose and followed her into her office. Harry shut the door and leaned against the door frame while Lisa and Rob sat down in front of her.

"Where's Gita and Rosslyn?" Arla asked as she opened up her laptop. Rob went to look for them and returned. The room was crowded now, and with almost the entire team assembled, Arla could begin.

"Quite clearly, David Braithwaite was sleeping with Madelyn West. Right?"

In response, Lisa stood with a tablet on her hand. She put it in front of Arla, who saw the photos of a blue sports car in front of a smart townhouse. "That's a Porsche 911, in David Braithwaite's driveway. It's definitely his car; I've checked with the DVLA."

Rob said, "The colour and make match the description Libby Alderson had provided. She doesn't remember the registration number but said it was a private one. And this car's registration is DB 22, which is obviously a personal license plate."

Arla thought rapidly. "A good defence lawyer will chuck that out as coincidence. There are lots of blue Porsche 911s in London, and licence plates can be forged. We need something more."

Harry spoke, his voice coming from way above them. "We need a match of the DNA from the semen analysis of the discarded condom we found under Madelyn's bed."

"Yes, exactly."

Harry continued. "And don't forget the boot print by the tree trunk, near the pond. That's clearly a man's shoes, and if we can get a match with David's shoes, we're in business."

Arla stood, clasping her hands behind her back, and paced in front of her table. "David doesn't have an alibi for the week in which Susan went missing. I wonder if he can produce an alibi for yesterday evening and the night."

She held up a hand in the air. "If he cannot, and we get a match with his boot print or the DNA from the condom, then he has a problem."

Rosslyn said, "The Tech lab is going through Madelyn's phone. We should have a call log very soon. Her laptop is also being examined."

Harry voiced the question that was forming in everyone's mind. "Do we have enough to charge David Braithwaite with murder?"

Arla shook her head. "Not as yet, but we definitely can if we get the DNA match."

There was silence for a while. Arla locked eyes with Harry like she often did when she was deep in thought about a case.

"Susan had found out about David and Madelyn. She knew her best friend had betrayed her."

Harry said softly, "So Susan had to be silenced."

Arla sat back down and put her elbows on the desk. She gazed into the distance, thinking aloud.

"So, David killed Susan because he didn't want her knowing about his secret affair with Madelyn."

"Murder is quite an extreme reaction, though, isn't it?" Rosslyn asked.

Arla nodded. "But it's possible that David's affair with Madelyn wasn't the main factor. Susan possibly knew other secrets about the Braithwaite family. That's what Prof Worthington told us."

"David's father, Lord Braithwaite, is basically a spy. He owns factories all over Eastern Europe and gives the MI5 valuable intelligence." Arla smiled. "The Lord who spies around. All very cloak and dagger, this."

Arla turned to her team.

"Do we have all the medical records for Susan?"

Gita raised her hand. "I have it here, guv." She scrolled through the screens of the tablet on her hand. "I have the clinic letters and the GP records. I made a chronology."

"Good work," Arla said approvingly. She asked Rob and Lisa to get some coffee and doughnuts, and they left the room.

Gita said, "She was almost seventeen when she first saw her GP about the problem. She had lost a lot of weight and was suffering academically. Prior to that, she had been a good student. Her GP referred her to a private psychiatric clinic for eating disorders." Gita scrolled through a couple more pages. "She was actually treated as an inpatient and given forced feeding via a nasogastric tube. She had to do this once a month while she was a senior A-level student."

Arla felt sad. She couldn't imagine the mental anguish Susan and her family had gone through.

"There's an interesting section in one of the clinic letters. It's about the family dynamics."

"Please read it out loud," Arla instructed. Gita cleared her throat.

186

*"Susan has poor eye contact. She listened more to her father and seemed to have a better relationship with him. She barely looks at her mother, even when her mother speaks. She does not respond when her mother asks her a question. However, she answers to her father."*

"So, mother and daughter always had a difficult relationship. I wonder why."

Harry asked, "What about the brother? There's a three-year age difference between them, right? So, he would have been fourteen to fifteen years old at the time."

"The clinic letters do not mention him, except in passing. He was not present at the family meetings with the doctor."

"Perhaps he was considered too young," Arla said. There was a knock on the door, and Harry opened it to let Rob and Lisa in. Rob carried a tray with steaming coffee mugs, which was received by everyone with murmurs of thanks. Lisa had a packet of doughnuts, which she opened up. Arla took a sip of her coffee, ignoring the doughnuts.

"One last thing," Gita said, munching and then swallowing. "Her boyfriend is mentioned. She broke up with him while she was doing her A-levels. Apparently, he wasn't happy about it and pursued her. Susan spoke about this issue with her counsellor. Guess what her boyfriend's name was?"

Gita's question hung in the air, and Arla stared at her with a frown on her face. She saw the smirk tugging at the corners of Gita's lips, and her eyebrows rose.

"No way."

"Yes."

"David Braithwaite?" Arla whispered.

Gita nodded vigorously. "The one and the same. Looks like he had a fixation on Susan right from the teenage years."

# CHAPTER 42

There was a knock on the door, and a uniformed sergeant poked his head in.

"Sorry to bother guv, but looks like we found a drug dealer in the common. He was carrying narcotics that had the dollar sign on them."

Arla stood, excitement seizing her limbs. "Excellent! Where is he?"

"In IR 5. But there's one problem."

Arla walked towards the sergeant. "What problem?"

The sergeant, whose name badge said Mark William, looked hesitant. "Uh, he's underage, guv. Eleven, he tells us, and looks like it as well."

Arla frowned. "Really? Are you sure they got the right person?"

"Yes, guv. He had a bag on his back, and the narcotics were in it. Two-kilo bags of cocaine, confirmed by the drug squad."

"Is the drug squad here?"

The sergeant nodded, and Arla strode out with him. Harry followed after a quick chat with the others. They knew their various jobs – mainly chasing down results with SOC and the labs.

Arla and Harry followed Mark to the interview room. He knocked on the door, and a female uniformed sergeant came out.

She smoothed down a few stray strands of her hair as she addressed Arla. "He was arrested and brought here on suspicion of procuring and distributing narcotics. He said his age was nine at the beginning, but we found his young person's Railcard inside his bag. His date of birth was on it. His real age is eleven, so he could be arrested."

Arla nodded. The law in England said children below the age of ten couldn't be arrested unless there were special circumstances.

"Does he have a lawyer?"

"He asked for one."

Arla sighed. If he had already asked for a lawyer, then she couldn't question him without a lawyer being present. "What's his name?"

"Benedict Angelo, according to his ID card. He's refused to give us his name or address. When we ask him about the cocaine in his bag, he says no comment." The female sergeant smiled, and Arla nodded back.

Those responses meant the boy had been told what to say. In turn, that revealed the tentacles of organised crime behind him.

Arla looked behind the female sergeant as a middle-aged woman approached them, dressed in a smart black business suit. She was in her 40s, with straight jet-black hair that fell below her shoulders and searching dark brown eyes. Her skin was the colour of night, and apart from being attractive, she was also in good shape. Arla locked eyes with her, and the woman looked her up and down. Then she extended her hand. "Nadia Husseini. Legal counsel for Benedict Angelo."

They shook hands, and Arla introduced everyone. Nadia said, "Can I please have ten minutes in private with my client?"

They stood to one side, and Nadia went inside.

Arla went to the main deck and met the drug squad inspector who had turned up. He had his back to Arla and was looking at some evidence on the counter with the duty sergeant. His name was Andrew Jamieson, and he turned when Arla said his name. She introduced Harry, and the three of them sat down to talk.

Andrew was a short, podgy man with a tie that seemed too tight at his neck. His black linen suit was also tight, bulging out his round shoulders. In some ways, he reminded Arla of Rob. Andrew had a brown moustache that matched his brown hair. His large, rotund eyes fixed on Arla as he spoke.

"We have had our attention on the Battersea dollar gang for a couple of years now. We believe they originate from the Winstanley estate in Battersea. They supply a large area in southwest London, stretching from Putney and Richmond all the way to Wandsworth, Battersea, and Clapham."

Harry said, "Presumably, the boy who was arrested is a footsoldier. Do we know much about the leadership?"

"The boy wouldn't be the first person who was arrested carrying one of their kilo bags. Last year we apprehended another boy. Unfortunately, he was below the age of ten, so we could not arrest him. However, he was kept in juvenile Custody at a youth correction centre."

Andrew sipped from a glass of water before he continued. "In answer to your question, yes, we had their team under surveillance for the last year. The leader appears to be someone called Carlson Adeyemi. He is a second-generation immigrant from Nigeria. He runs the gang with three sidekicks. Their names are Rick, Bally, and Ali. The four of them are the senior members of the gang, and they have relays who supply for them. But Carlson is the head, and he's the only one who knows their supplier."

"Where does this Carlson and his three sidekicks live? In the Winstanley estate?" Arla asked.

"Carlson lives in the Winstanley estate. That's their nerve centre. I think Rick lives there as well, but Bally and Ali live in council houses outside the state."

"And who is the supplier?"

"We believe they are a Turkish organised criminal gang in north London. They have always had deep connections with mainly heroin supply. But a lot of the cocaine comes from Rotterdam, which is Europe's biggest port. And there is a large Turkish immigrant community there."

Arla raised her hand. "What we are concerned with is the relation of the dollar gang to our victims." She pulled out her phone and showed Andrew the packets of cocaine found in Susan and Madelyn's apartment. Andrew looked at them carefully, zooming in with his fingers. Then he nodded.

"That's definitely from their gang. No one else uses a dollar sign on the packets." He looked at Arla with curiosity. "I heard that your victims had the dollar sign carved into the left hands. Is that correct?"

Arla nodded. "While we have found recreational use in the victims, there's nothing else to suggest they were involved with the gang. Their bank accounts show healthy balances, and all their money has been traced back to their jobs." She shrugged. "Of course, if they had any financial dealings with the gang, it would presumably be in cash and not be revealed."

"That's right. These gangs don't use banks or do any online money transfer. When they save up a lot of cash, they buy and sell assets like houses or expensive cars. And jewellery."

At the mention of the word jewellery, a brief vision of the gold chain on Susan's neck flashed in Arla's mind. Her eyebrows lowered in concentration. "I'm not sure how closely this guy Carlson has been watched, but do you know if he wears a necklace with a gold cross?"

Andrew shook his head. "No, I don't. But we do have numerous photos of him."

Arla smiled and glanced at Harry. He went to his desk and got his tablet. He opened up the CCTV clip that showed the Afro-Caribbean man who had been seen in Susan's apartment.

Andrew watched the clip closely and several times. Then he stabbed a finger at the screen. "Yes, that's him."

191

His eyes shone with excitement. "This is interesting. What is the leader of this dangerous gang doing in your victim's apartment?"

# CHAPTER 43

"Could Carlson Adeyemi have killed the victims because they owed him money? Or something else?" Arla whispered aloud. She was back in her office, and Harry was sitting opposite her.

Harry appeared deep in thought, his fingers stapled in front of his face, elbows resting on his knees as he leaned forward. "Susan and Madelyn don't fit the profile of drug dealers. But, you never know. Maybe they saw this as a business venture."

Arla scribbled in her notebook and circled Carlson's name. "Yes. A very profitable business venture."

She shook her head as doubts sailed across her mind. Something wasn't right here. She could see a vague shape, but it stayed just out of reach.

"But why do it? Especially for Susan, who had no shortage of money. Okay, so she didn't get on with her mother, but surely her family wouldn't leave her out of the inheritance. And she was doing well in her job."

There was a knock on the door, and Lisa poked her head in. "Sorry, Guv." Arla waved her in.

Lisa said, "I looked through HOLMES and the NPD. Turns out Carlson Adeyemi has been nicked a couple of times. He's never been convicted, however. He was arrested on suspicion of the murder of a gang member called Kamali Jacobson."

Lisa crossed her arms and smirked. "That's where it gets interesting. Kamali Jacobson, by all accounts, was the previous leader of the Battersea dollar gang. He's got a rap sheet as long as an arm, and he's been inside twice. Once for armed robbery, and once for possession with the intent to supply."

"Good work, Lisa," Arla beamed. "Can I please have that report on my desk?"

"No problems, guv. And the kid is ready."

Arla thanked Lisa again, and she and Harry walked out, heading for the interview room.

*****

Nadia Husseini and Benedict Angelo were sitting side-by-side. Harry introduced himself and other people in the room, and their recording started. Arla took time. She gazed at Benny for a while, noting his matted, curly black hair and his flawless dark skin. He was a good-looking boy, but he was mixed up with some dangerous people. Benny couldn't hold Arla's gaze. He kept looking away, then shrank back into his chair, looking uncomfortable.

He looked like a naughty schoolboy, and Arla suddenly realised how innocent this little boy was. He was just a child. His innocent mind had been poisoned with promises and false hopes.

For the first time in her career, Arla was caught in two minds. She wouldn't be harsh with Benedict. But at the same time, she couldn't be too soft. He might have information on Carlson that she needed.

Nadia Husseini cleared her throat. "Shall we begin, Inspector Baker?"

Arla flicked her eyes at her, annoyed. "Got somewhere to go, have you? A more important case, perhaps."

Nadia's voice was as frosty as Arla's. "No. But my client has spent a long time here, and as you can see, he needs to attend school."

Arla and Nadia maintained a heated stare for a few seconds, then Arla let it go. She turned to Benny.

"Tell me what happened today, Benedict."

194

Nadia spoke for her client. "He has already explained everything, and there is a detailed statement. He has nothing more to add."

Benny remained silent, but he wouldn't meet Arla's eyes. She said, "Do you know what was in the bag, Benny?"

Benny spoke for the first time. "No comment."

"Who packed your bag this morning?"

"No comment." Benny glanced at Arla and then looked away swiftly, almost as if he was shy. He had a combination of sweetness and sadness, and Arla couldn't believe this child was in such a predicament. She also knew he would never divulge anything if she carried on with her current line of questions.

"How's your mother?"

Interest sparked in Benny's eyes, and then he looked at Nadia. She spoke for him.

"What does that have to do with the case, Inspector Baker?"

"He's an eleven-year-old. Hence it's a natural question about his guardian?"

Lawyer and client had a hushed discussion. Benny kept his face blank. "No comment."

"Does your mother know you're here?"

Benny said nothing. He scratched the back of his neck, glanced at his lawyer, who smiled at him reassuringly.

"Do you want us to get in touch with your mother? We can get her down here in ten minutes."

Benny's eyes became wide as saucers. He shook his head and opened his mouth to speak, but Nadia pressed his hand and leaned forward.

"Inspector Baker, you are harassing my client. This call is being recorded."

Arla shrugged. "His mother should know, as she is his legal guardian. Right, Benedict?"

Benny avoided her eyes again. Arla exchanged a glance with Harry. He took out the tablet he had carried into the room. He opened up photos of Carlson Adeyemi that Andrew Jamieson had forwarded to him. He put the tablet in front of Benny.

The child stiffened immediately and jerked his face away. That reaction was enough for Arla. She kept her voice beguilingly soft but leaned towards Benny.

"We don't want you, Benny. You can go free if you tell us where Carlson is. He's a very dangerous man. Did you know he has killed people?"

Benny squirmed in his seat. Nadia raised her voice. "Inspector Baker, this is ridiculous! I demand an immediate stop to your questions."

Arla ignored her. The temperature was rising, and she could see Benny was hot under the collar. She kept calm, and her voice low, friendly.

"Do you want to go to jail for Carlson, Benny? Do you know what happens to boys in jail?"

"Inspector Baker!"

"And what will your mother say? If you tell us where Carlson is-

"I don't know where Carlson is!" Benny yelled. "Now, leave me alone."

There was silence in the room. By his admission, Benny had made it clear he knew who Carlson was. Nadia pressed her fingers to her forehead, then turned to Benny. She whispered to him, and he fidgeted, keeping a wary eye on Arla.

Arla felt horrible, and she gave Benny what she hoped was a reassuring smile. Silently, she was begging for the boy's forgiveness.

"Let's take a break," she suggested.

She followed Harry to the drinks machine at the rear, not far from the car park's exit. Harry got her a diet coke, which they would share. Once outside, Arla was relieved to find they were alone. She slumped into Harry's chest, and he comforted her with a hug.

"I feel awful," she mumbled, inhaling his scent deeply. He was still the old Harry – wood spice aftershave and the smell of his suit. "That poor kid didn't deserve that."

Harry patted her head, and she felt like crying.

"He's going to be alright," he said soothingly. "Better for him to learn a lesson now than ten years down the road, or worse, in prison."

Arla sniffed, then wiped the corners of her eyes. "We have to charge him with possession, don't we? And intent to supply. God, he's just a child."

"Yes, we do. And it's not your fault. Believe me, I feel for him as well. This is sad, but maybe he will understand that he made a mistake."

"Arla took the can of Diet Coke from Harry. She stared out at the tepid sun peeking out from behind clouds, its rays diffracted by an invisible prism of air and moisture. Her resolve hardened into conviction.

"Let's get Carlson Adeyemi in. I think we have enough on him for an arrest and a statement."

"Okay. I'll get a team ready and head down."

"I'm coming with you."

Harry raised his eyebrows, and his chin tilted upwards as he stared at her. Arla shrugged. "Don't give me that look. I can handle myself."

"That's not the point. These people might have guns. I'll have to take a firearms unit with me."

Arla grimaced and waved a hand in the air. "No, no. We're not going there to start a gunfight."

"Oh yeah? And what will you do if he doesn't come of his own free will?"

197

Arla sucked on her teeth. "Trust me. I've got a plan."

# CHAPTER 44

Carlson lifted the tumbler of dark rum to his lips and took a sip. Ricky was sitting in one corner, counting a stack of twenty pound notes. There was a knock on the door, and they both stiffened. Carlson put a hand on his rear pocket, where he had his Colt revolver. It was old-fashioned, but it did the job. He gestured to Ricky, telling him to stay where he was.

"It can't be the feds. They would have broken down the door."

He looked through the peephole and relaxed immediately. He opened the door, and one of his footsoldiers, a teenage girl, called Latoya, walked in. She was 17 and the girlfriend of a member of the gang.

"What you saying?" Carlson asked as he sat down on the chair opposite Ricky. Latoya remained standing.

"I've just come back from Clapham."

Carlson narrowed his eyes. A snake of apprehension slithered up his spine. The big pond at the common was where he'd last seen Susan, and try as he might, he couldn't get the image out of his head.

"At the common? What did you see?"

"I went by the pond like you asked. It's full of feds. But there's this something else."

Carlson fumed with impatience. "Well, go on then."

"They found another body. Another girl. And..." Latoya stopped when she saw the shocked expression on Carlson's face.

"Come on!" Carlson yelled. "What else?"

"And Benny got nicked."

Ricky put down the stack of notes. Both the men stared at Latoya. Carlson was the first to speak. "How did he get nicked?"

"Two boys from the Clapham gang started on him. He tried to run away, and then the feds nabbed him."

Carlson passed a hand over his face, his jaws flexing. "What about the bag?"

"I think the feds got the bag as well."

Carlson took a gulp of the dark rum, sat the tumbler down, then poured himself another. He drained the glass, then slammed it down on the table. He stood, swore, and kicked at the chair.

"Okay, go," Carlson said, waving his hand to dismiss Latoya.

Ricky leaned back in his chair, shaking his head. "Damn. The boy better keep his mouth shut."

Carlson stared out the window. Velvety blue darkness was falling, and yellow blobs of light were flickering everywhere. He nodded to himself slowly. "I think he will. I told him what to say. But the feds are clever. If they scare him, I don't know what he'll do."

"Yes," Ricky said. "That's what I'm thinking."

Carlson shrugged. "You know what? They got nothing on me. Even if he says my name, your name, what difference does it make? The feds know our names anyway. But they can't charge us with anything."

There was another rap on the door, louder and more urgent this time. Ricky frowned, and the two men exchanged a glance. The wrap was replaced by loud thumping, shaking the door.

Carlson went up to the door, gun in his hand. He looked through the peephole, and his eyes widened. He dropped the gun and kicked it away. He ran back into the room and skidded to a halt. Ricky was trying to climb out the window, but two uniformed policemen were standing outside. He rented this ground-floor apartment, as it was easy to escape. The windows looked out into a playing field, and the road was just behind that, over a low fence. But their escape route had been blocked off.

The thumping came again. "This is the police. Open up or we break down the door."

"Don't stress," Carlson mouthed to Ricky. Then he whispered, so the two policemen outside the window couldn't hear him. "Throw your piece down. Do it now."

Carlson turned and opened the door. To his surprise, the first person he saw was a woman. She was attractive, with dark hair, a sharp nose, and a lean face with jutting cheekbones. Behind him, there was a tall, wide-shouldered man wearing a suit. Surrounding them were three uniformed policemen. The woman held up a warrant card, but Carlson already knew she was a detective.

"Inspector Arla Baker," the woman said. "Can we come in?"

Carlson smiled at her. "Do I have a choice?"

The woman smiled back, and her easy attitude bothered Carlson.

"No, I guess you don't have a choice, as we are here to arrest you."

"Is having a drink inside one's house considered a crime these days?" Carlson smiled wider. He knew the police didn't have any dirt on him. They couldn't tie him to the drug dealing, no matter how hard they tried.

He folded his arms across his chest. "So, tell me, inspector. What are you going to arrest me for?"

"For suspicion of murder, Mr Adeyemi. I am arresting you for the murder of Susan Remington."

Carlson tried hard not to show the shock on his face. He felt like a sledgehammer had hit him, and his heart had turned to ice. Words were frozen in his brain, and his lips parted, but he couldn't speak. Arla read him his rights, and then the three uniformed policemen came forward.

"You've got this all wrong," Carlson mumbled as one of the policemen pushed him against the wall and handcuffed him.

"You can tell us all about it at the station," Arla said.

# CHAPTER 45

Arla spoke on the radio as they drove back. Harry was at the wheels, and Carlson was behind them with a uniformed sergeant on either side of him.

"IC3 male arrested. Keep IR1 ready."

IC or the International Colour Code was how police officers identified people of different races. Arla turned the black knob of the radio anticlockwise and switched it off. She glanced at the specially fitted rear-view mirror on the passenger side that allowed her to glimpse at the backseats. Carlson was staring out the window. He was definitely the man she had seen on CCTV at Susan's apartment. He was wearing a dark-coloured full-length shirt now, with jeans. His skin was darker than hers, but his complexion was lighter than most Afro-Caribbean people she knew.

His curly hair was cut short. His dark eyes were large and liquid, and his nose tapered to a set of full lips and a strong, masculine jaw. He was a handsome man, and he triggered a memory in Arla's mind for some reason.

Had she seen his mugshot somewhere? He had been arrested once before, and maybe that's where she had seen his face. But she couldn't be sure. Arla frowned. The familiarity of his face disturbed her especially when she couldn't remember when or how she had seen him.

She glanced at Harry, and their eyes met. His large hands were gripping the steering wheel lightly as he drove skilfully through traffic. Arla suppressed a yawn. It had been a long day already, it was past 5 PM and past her time to pick up Nicole.

Rita was doing her grandmother's duties again, looking after Nicole. Arla often wondered what they would have done without Rita. A good grandparent, she was starting to realise, was an absolute godsend.

They pulled into the front car park, and the two uniformed officers hold out Carlson, whose hands were cuffed already. Arla and Harry went inside the station while the uniformed sergeant's checked Carlson in at the main gate.

As Arla had expected, Carlson had called for a lawyer immediately. After a ten-minute coffee break, she and Harry strode to IR1, which had a uniformed constable standing guard outside. He nodded to Arla and then opened the door. Carlson was seated next to a black man dressed in a pinstripe suit. The man was older than Carlson, although Arla found, in her experience, coloured men never looked their age. Dark coloured skin didn't suffer from sunlight as much as paler skins did. However, she put the well-dressed, consummately professional-looking lawyer to be in his 50s.

"I am Jeremy Johnson," the lawyer said. "I know you have met my client already." He didn't rise from his chair or offer to shake hands, which was the norm. A police station wasn't the place for pleasantries.

Harry started the tape, and they both sat down with a pile of papers, a laptop, and two tablets. It carried the bulk of evidence gathered so far.

Arla opened up her notebook, then glanced up at Carlson. He was relaxed in his chair, head inclined to the left, regarding her with a slight smile on his face. Both he and Jeremy Johnson said their names for the tape.

Arla started. "Did you know a woman called Susan Remington?"

She watched with satisfaction as the smile faded from Carlson's lips. He didn't move a muscle, nor did he take his eyes off Arla.

Carlson said, "No comment."

"Did you know a woman called Madelyn West?"

"No comment."

Arla asked him about the individual members of the Remington family and Madelyn West's family, who didn't live in London. Madelyn was an only child, and her mother had died. Her father had since remarried and lived up north.

"Do you know an eleven-year-old miner called Benedict Angelo?"

"No comment."

"Have you ever heard of the Battersea dollar gang?"

Arla asked a few more questions about the gang, its members, and where Carlson lived. To each, his answer was the same. Arla had expected this, and it was time to change track. She kept her voice soft and friendly but maintained eye contact.

"Do you did you know a woman called Shola Adeyemi?"

Carlson's jaws relaxed as his expression became more serious. He cleared his throat, and his shoulder is stiff and slightly. The muscles on his forehead contracted as he pursed his lips together. Jeremy Johnson leaned over to him and whispered a few words. Carlson nodded, then locked eyes with Arla again.

"Yes. She was my mother."

"She's no longer alive, is she?"Arla kept her tone low and respectful.

Carlson shook his head. Arla said, "Could you please speak aloud for the tape."

"No."

"When did your mother pass away?"

Carlson flicked his eyes sideways a couple of times. "Five years ago."

Jeremy Johnson leaned sideways and forward, getting into Arla's line of sight. "Excuse me, Inspector Baker, but what does this have to do with the suspicion of murder?"

Arla didn't reply. She scribbled on her notepad, opened up a tablet, then turned the page of her notebook.

"I'm sorry to hear that, Carlson," Arla used his first name intentionally. She watched him blink, and the corners of his eyes softened. "How did your mother die?"

Mr Johnson leaned in again. "I must say this line of questioning is most bizarre."

Arla ignored him, staring at Carlson. He remained silent.

Arla stared at her notebook, then glanced up at him. "She died of metastatic breast cancer, didn't she? And the Home Office was also trying to deport her, weren't they?"

She watched Carlson's chest rise and fall. Johnson whispered a few words in his ear. Carlson's expression didn't change.

"How did all this affect you, Carlson?" Arla folded her hands on the table, leaning forward.

"How would you feel if you'd been told you can't live in the country where you grew up and which was your home?" Carlson's voice was soft, and once again, nothing moved apart from his lips.

"I cannot imagine," Arla said softly. "Did it make you angry?"

For the first time, Carlson's face became animated. He smiled wider, and his head moved sideways a fraction. "Angry black man, taking his revenge on society. Is that the stereotype you think I am?"

Arla pressed her lips together and stared back at him. "Can you please answer the question?"

"No," Carlson replied. Amusement was still written clearly on his face.

"What was your father's name?"

"I don't know my father's name. Are you a sociologist or a detective?"

Arla noted his well-modulated speech and his choice of words. In her experience of dealing with drug dealers and gang members, they weren't like this. Carlson was different from the ordinary organised criminals. Most organised crime leaders were very clever. But none had the suaveness that Carlson possessed. He was clearly intelligent and sounded educated.

"Benedict Angelo was arrested this morning, and he will be charged with possession and intention to deal in narcotics. He mentions your name as the leader of the Battersea dollar gang." It was a statement, but Arla ended it like a question.

"No comment."

"Were you a foot soldier like Benny once?"

Carlson's expression changed, his eyes narrowing a fraction. Arla pressed on. "Did you gain experience as a clean skin, delivering narcotics?"

Jeremy Johnson sighed loudly. "Can this interview please be terminated? This is becoming exasperating. Inspector Baker, can you please explain what you want to do with my client?"

To everyone's surprise, Carlson spoke again. "I am not the disease, inspector. I am merely the symptom."

Arla frowned at him. "Excuse me?"

"A doctor treats the disease, and the symptom goes away. Do you understand?"

Arla understood the gravity of his words but kept her expression carefully neutral. She just wanted to keep him talking. "Could you please elaborate?"

Carlson smiled. "It's very simple. Cure poverty and the symptom of crime goes away. Cure inequality, and again, the symptom of crime vanishes."

He was very much unlike any criminal Arla had met before. She knew he was vicious and cunning. But he was obviously clever as well.

She smiled at him. "Who's being a sociologist now?"

Carlson shrugged. "You started it."

"No. I was merely exploring your background. I want to understand what makes you the leader of the gang and why you employ innocent children like Benny."

She watched as her words hit home. She had penetrated a barrier. Carlson's jaws clamped tight, and his nostrils flared.

Arla went in for the kill. He was unbalanced, and she knew it was time to strike.

"Why do you wear the same gold necklace as Susan Remington?"

Carlson was already disturbed, and the sudden change of topic bothered him even more. A snarl came across his lips, and his eyebrows contracted. He looked away and around the room as if he was searching for a way out. Mr Johnson leaned in towards him and whispered urgently in his ear. Carlson looked askance at Arla.

"No comment."

"What were you doing with Susan Remington in her apartment at 7 PM on Tuesday 15th March?"

Carlson said nothing. But he was breathing heavier now, although his face had returned to its earlier calmness, and he maintained eye contact with Arla.

"You had a relationship with Susan Remington, didn't you?"

Again, Carlson said nothing but didn't look away.

"But something went wrong. Maybe she wanted to break it off. The two of you had an argument. You went down to the Clapham pond, where you drowned her first, then strangled her. Before you let her go, you carved her the dollar signon her hand. Didn't you?"

Arla's voice had risen, and so had the temperature in the room. Carlson's jaws were clamped tight, and he breathed through his nose, his chest rising and falling rapidly.

Arla glared at him, and her tone was harsh. "Carlson Adeyemi, I am charging you with the murder of Susan Remington." She read him his rights. Carlson's eyes were wide open now, alive with rage and hatred. His spine had jerked straight, and the snarl was more pronounced on his lips. Jeremy Johnson was whispering in his ear, and Carlson nodded. He blinked a couple of times.

Johnson said, "My client denies all the charges against him. He denies knowing Susan Remington. In short, he denies all the accusations against him. Can I please have a few minutes with my client in private?"

Arla happily packed up their stuff. Harry spoke into the tape, concluding the interview. They went outside, and Arla sagged against the wall. She massaged her forehead. Harry touched her shoulder.

"You need to go home. Come on."

Arla did exactly that. When she finally got home and opened the front door, Nicole ran into her arms.

"You're late," Nicole said, fixing her mother with her habitual serious look. She had large chestnut brown eyes like her father. Same skin shade as well, and Arla loved her to bits. She kissed Nicole's plump cheeks and squeezed her tight. Rita watched with a smile on her face.

"I'm sorry," Arla said. "And as a prize for waiting, shall we have some hot chocolate?"

"Yay!" Nicole jumped up and down, clapping her hands. She became serious again. "I've had my dinner."

Arla laughed as she walked into the kitchen with her daughter. Rather annoyingly, her phone buzzed. She thought of ignoring it, but with a murder suspect in custody, she had to answer.

"Hello?" It was the gravelly voice of Commander Johnson.

"Sir," Arla responded, her heart sinking a touch. Getting a call from her boss at this time was never a good thing.

"Well done on charging the suspect, Arla. The case looks good."

"We still have a lot to prove, sir."

"Oh, nonsense," Johnson's voice was jovial. He sounded relieved, in fact. "He was seen on CCTV with the victim, and two days later, she's reported missing. He probably killed her that night he was seen with her, and due to the drowning, no one can tell the exact date of the murder."

"You did stellar work here, Arla. Commendations," Johnson enthused.

Arla narrowed her eyes. Something was not right. Johnson sounded too eager. Yes, they did have a good case against Carlson, but it wasn't over yet.

"We still have the DNA results to come back, sir. And I'm not sure if Carlson has any connection with the second victim."

"Don't worry," Johnson cut her off. "The CPS cannot fault us on this. I'm looking forward to the conviction. Tomorrow, shall we make a press statement?"

Arla's eyebrows rose, along with her sense of unease. "That's a bit premature, isn't' it, sir?"

"Oh, nonsense. It's an open and shut case now. I'll see you tomorrow."

He hung up. Arla put the phone down slowly, her mind running loops.

# CHAPTER 46

Arla was at the office by 8 AM the next day. A steaming mug of coffee raised tendrils of fragrant fumes as she poured over Madelyn West's mobile phone's call log.

She noticed with interest an encrypted number, with its digits crossed out. An encrypted number had also called Susan Remington, and she wondered if they were the same. The number had already been circled by Rosslyn, who had left them in her intro.

Susan's number was already highlighted, and Arla noticed that Susan had called Madelyn on 17th of March, Thursday. The call was not answered. It was at 7 PM, and although Madelyn called back immediately, Susan did not answer either. Madelyn had reported Susan as missing on Friday 18th March. Just the day after. Arla paused to think.

Susan had tried to call Madelyn. This surely had to be Susan's last known attempted contact with Madelyn. However, Madelyn had not reported this when Arla spoke to her. It wasn't on her statement. But she did call Susan back, who didn't answer. Perhaps it had slipped Madelyn's mind.

Another thought occurred to Arla. What if the killer had called Madelyn, using Susan's phone? She shook her head. There wouldn't be a point to it. It didn't make sense that the killer would be calling up Susan's friends after the murder.

Banerjee had also left Madelyn's autopsy report on Arla's desk. The time of death was, as he had suspected, around midnight. From the wound, Banerjee thought the same knife was used to carve out the dollar mark, and Arla agreed.

A toxicology report showed a low concentration of cocaine and alcohol. There was some evidence of bruising on her forearms and on the face, which showed there had been a struggle. Madelyn had been hit on the face a couple of times. Two of her nails were broken due to resistance.

Banerjee concluded there had been a struggle, Madelyn was subdued, and the cause of death was asphyxiation due to strangling. And then the body was left in the pond. Arla touched her forehead, her disbelief rising as she read the report.

Why would the killer stuff Madelyn's mouth and throat with gauze to prevent the body from sinking? The gauze was also found up her nostrils.

Arla picked up the phone and rang scene-of-crime. Derek Parmentier, Arla's long-time ally, and head of the Department picked up the phone.

"Well, well, it's the doyen of the Metropolitan police force," Parmentier said jovially. His Yorkshire accent was pronounced, and he never missed the chance to have a dig at Arla.

"The early bird gets the worm," Arla said dryly. "You'd know all about that, wouldn't you?"

"Guess I can't *worm* my way out of that one, seeing that I'm in the office the same time as you. It might interest you to know that I'm here this early because of you."

"What do you want, a medal?" Arla grinned. She knew Parmentier wouldn't take it the wrong way. If anything, their jokes were in danger of becoming predictable.

"Have the DNA matches all come back?" Arla asked.

"Funny you should ask that because I've just heard from the lab. Yes, I believe they are all back. The results are interesting. Shall I send you a report?"

Arla became excited. This was the breakthrough she had been waiting for. "Yes, please, but do tell me the reports now."

"Okay, let's deal with the first victim. The swabs from her bed reveal her own DNA, but also David Braithwaite."

Arla's jaw dropped open. David Braithwaite was still sleeping with Susan? Her mind grappled with the enormity of the revelation. What had possessed Susan to go back to an evil, possessive man like David?

She knew Susan had also been a tragic, broken person. Her feelings of deep insecurity and anxiety probably played a part. Arla knew the stains on Susan's bed were fresh. Even if the stains were a month old, it meant David had been in the same bed as Susan the month before she disappeared. Arla shuddered.

"Are you still there?"

"Yes," Arla said quickly. "What else?"

"David's DNA is also found in the bathroom."

"What about the cigarette butts on her balcony. Any DNA from their skin fragments?"

"I was just getting to that. The cigarette butts show Susan's DNA, and also that of Carlson Adeyemi."

"Okay," Arla said slowly. So Carlson had definitely been in Susan's flat and had smoked with her outside, at least. But was he not sleeping with her?

"Did you not find Carlson's DNA on Susan's clothes or her bed?"

"We only checked the clothes that she had left outside. The answer is no, and nothing on the bed either. Carlson's DNA was only found on the cigarette butts."

Arla digested this in silence.

"Anything else?"

"The toothbrush and her shaving razor only showed her own DNA. Nothing else to add about Susan Remington." Parmentier paused.

"Regarding Madelyn West, the condom underneath her bed bears the DNA of David Braithwaite. We also found David's DNA on her bed, clothes and on a spare toothbrush in the bathroom."

Arla's cursed under her breath and cradled her head in her palm. David had been sleeping with both women at the same time, she figured.

"Doesn't look good for old David, does it? I mean Lord Braithwaite," Parmentier said.

"No, it doesn't." Thank you, please send me the report, and keep this confidential."

"Your wish is my command, as always."

# CHAPTER 47

Arla faced Harry and her four trusted detective sergeants in her office. She informed them of the latest findings.

Rosslyn said, "As Gita found out, David Braithwaite had a long-term fixation with Susan Remington, starting in the teenage years. Maybe he never gave up on her, even after the divorce. She became his obsession."

Gita said, "And he liked to control people, right? He tried to control Susan. Maybe sleeping with both Susan and Madelyn at the same time was the ultimate form of control for him."

Arla nodded solemnly at her sergeants. The thought had already occurred to her. She felt bad for both women, and she wondered again if Susan had known about David and Madelyn.

Harry asked, "So he murders Susan because she found out about Madelyn, and they had an argument? Or some other reason?"

Arla had a chance to look at Susan's phone log again. She was sure by now the encrypted number belonged to David Braithwaite. That number had called Susan several times on the 16th and 17th of March. Susan tried to get in touch with Madelyn that day and then vanished. Arla was growing more convinced that 17th March was Susan's last day on earth.

"Susan was David's obsession," Arla said, "and if she wanted to break up with him, or she learnt about Madelyn and wanted to break up, then David would see that as a huge loss. He might not be able to take it, and in a fit of rage, he kills Susan. Maybe the same thing happens with Madelyn. She had enough of him, and instead of losing her and seeing her with another man, he decides to kill her."

Harry was rubbing his cheeks thoughtfully. "I looked up narcissistic personality disorder, by the way. People who have it do suffer from insane jealousy. David used to lock Susan up in her room so she couldn't socialise. Maybe he did the same with Madelyn."

Arla said, "So we have a motive and obvious opportunity. He had the means as well, as he could take the women wherever he wanted to." Arla leaned her elbow on the table and massaged her temple. "Right, we need to arrest him."

Rob spoke up, "where does that leave us with Carlson Adeyemi?"

Arla squeezed her eyes shut and tapped her forehead with one finger. "From the DNA evidence, it doesn't seem as if he was having a relationship with Susan. And apart from the packet of cocaine, we have no connection between him and Madelyn. Unless I'm missing something?" Arla looked pointedly at her sergeants and then to Harry.

Harry said, "I don't think so. It will be difficult to show a motive, means, or opportunity for Carlson to kill Madelyn. He might have met her through Susan, but that's just a guess. There is no evidence."

Lisa added, "There are no emails or social media contacts between Madelyn and Carlson. However, Carlson's phone number does pop up on Susan's call log."

Arla nodded. "Yes, I saw that. But only a few times. Well, we knew that anyway. He's obviously been to her apartment and spent time with her."

"Right," Arla said, rising from the desk. "Get a uniform squad car ready." She addressed Gita. "Did you get in touch with David Braithwaite's secretary?"

"Yes, guv. He is working from home today, apparently."

Arla fixed her eyes on Harry. "Then let's go and arrest him."

\*\*\*\*

Finding David Braithwaite's home address was easy enough from the land registry. The townhouse in Knightsbridge, not far from his office overlooking Hyde Park, was bought in the 1970s by Benjamin Braithwaite, whom Arla assumed to be his father. Harry was driving as usual, following the squad car ahead of them.

Blue lights flashed atop the car ahead, and its loud siren pierced the air, trying to cut through the knot of traffic. Harry had his lights on as well and weaved in and out.

He wiped a sheen of sweat off his forehead as he focused on the road ahead. Luckily, they had an open stretch now, but there were traffic lights at regular intervals. His heart was in his mouth, and with one ear, he listened to Arla.

Harry pressed their radio key on the dashboard. "Inspector Mehta speaking. Cut the sirens when we are half a click out."

Static buzzed, and the voice of Inspector Andy Jackson came through the radio. "Roger that. Over and out."

Knightsbridge was one of the most expensive residential locations in the world. Since Victorian times, England's wealthy families had built houses there. So had plenty of rich Americans, and now it was the turn of Arabs and Russians, looking for a place to invest their oil and gas wealth.

As the beautiful mansions flashed by, Arla's brain was ticking over time. She hadn't spoken to Johnson. She had tried once, and his phone was engaged. There was no time, especially as she suspected Johnson would try and stop her.

At the back of her mind was the nagging suspicion that David Braithwaite would use every trick in the book to escape justice. Arla knew very well even the CPS would have difficulty in treating him as a suspect. He was the justice minister's nephew, after all. If nothing else, his case could be thwarted by expensive defence lawyers for a long time.

Justice wouldn't be served for Susan and Madelyn. She suspected David was the killer, and she shivered when she thought of how many victims he could have had in the past. The divers would be descending into Clapham pond later on today. The thought of what lay in those deep, dark depths was frightening.

She needed to do that and build a watertight case against David. She was hoping that catching him unawares would force him to make a mistake.

Harry Parked the black BMW at the top of the street, but the squad car was now behind him. With its bright white and blue striped appearance, the squad car was easily visible. It parked discreetly five or six cars behind Harry. The uniformed officers got out of the car but stayed put as Harry and Arla strode towards David Braithwaite's home.

The street was a line of terraced townhouses, each incredibly handsome and well maintained. Most were of redbrick, with sandstone yellow eaves and corniches, the typical Knightsbridge 'look' that had remained constant for hundreds of years. They went up the stairs of the house, and Arla rang the doorbell of the glistening black mahogany door. She took a few steps down the stairs and looked at the long Georgian windows again.

Heavy drapes were drawn across the floor to ceiling windows.

Below ground level, she could see a basement. Harry joined her, turning his back to the house. He turned the knob of his radio. "Send two men to the rear of the property. Maintain radio contact."

They turned as there was a sound, and the door opened. An elderly man, with a shock of white hair, and wearing an expensive-looking Paisley bath robe, stood with an inquisitive look on his face. He was tall, his spine erect as his forehead creased in a frown. Arla showed her warrant card, and so did Harry.

"We need to speak to David Braithwaite please," Arla didn't care who this man was, and she tried to peer down the hallway, but the man moved, blocking her vision. Annoyance was now written plainly over his expression.

218

"I am Jeremy Braithwaite, David's father. May I know what this is about?"

"I'm afraid I'm not at liberty to discuss this with you, Mr Braithwaite. This concerns an ongoing police investigation, and we have to ask your son some questions."

Arla stepped closer and put a hand on the door. She could feel Harry tense beside her. Jeremy Braithwaite glanced at Harry, then to her.

"I'm not sure where my son is at the moment. Could you please come back later?"

"No, we cannot," Arla snapped. Harry got closer and placed a foot close to the door, afraid Mr Braithwaite might try to slam it shut.

"This is about a murder investigation, and we need to see your son now." Harry's voice was like steel, and from his body language, it was clear he wouldn't hesitate to barge past the elderly man. "By not allowing us in, you are obstructing the police, Mr Braithwaite," Harry got to closer the man, stepping in front of Arla.

Mr Braithwaite opened his mouth to say something but then thought the better of it. He stepped back, and Arla pushed the door open and strode inside quickly.


She paid no attention to the ornamental frescoes on the walls and the lovely oil paintings. Harry and herself took turns to dive into the two lounges that opened up on either side. Each was tastefully decorated with brown bookshelves and Persian rugs on the floor. But apart from the expensive period furniture, the rooms were empty.

Harry ran up the staircase while Arla checked out the rest of the ground floor. The kitchen was huge, modernised, and open-planned, and the long sliding glass door looked out towards the garden. The garden was almost a hundred feet, she guessed, with mature trees lining the sides and rear.

She came out, almost barging into Mr Braithwaite. Arla apologised and ran past the man, going upstairs. Her feet sank on the nice carpet on the wide staircase. Before she could reach the top floor, she heard a shout and the sound of breaking glass. Adrenaline surged through her veins as she ran towards the rear of the upper floor hallway. She could hear sounds coming from a bedroom on the right. She went in to find Harry staring out one of the long windows.

There was broken glass on the floor, and Harry took off his coat, wrapped it around his right elbow, then punched at the window, breaking the remainder of the glass.

# CHAPTER 48

Fragments of glass flew in the air as Harry grimaced, averted his face, and continued smashing through the glass to give himself enough space to get out of the window. Arla stood back, her own hands raised to protect her face from the glass.

Harry ducked his head through the opening and stepped out on the ledge. Right below, there was a drop of about 5 metres to a flat roof. Ahead of him, streaking through the grass, he could see the figure of David Braithwaite, running for his life.

Arla screamed, "What are you doing?"

Harry didn't reply. The ledge outside the window was broad enough for him to plant both feet. He took a deep breath and jumped. He landed on the flat roof pillow and rolled over, his back striking the raised dome of a skylight. The roof formed the extension of the kitchen below, and through the glass, he caught a glimpse of Mr Braithwaite staring up.

Harry ran to the edge of the roof. The drop was less now, no more than a couple of metres. He landed on the patio, and rolled over on the grass. His ears pricked up at the barking of a dog. His head jerked left and right, but he couldn't see a dog anywhere. However, the barking was loud and ferocious.

Harry had no time to waste. Ahead of him, David was disappearing into the line of trees at the rear of the property. Harry set off in hot pursuit, pumping his legs. The barking continued, and he looked back. To the left, he saw a garden door at the side entrance and a big German Shepherd locked behind it. The dog was up on its hindlegs, its front paws scratching the garden gate. Harry blessed his lucky stars that the door was shut.

David had broken through the trees and was scrambling up a fence. With a burst of energy, Harry ran forward. With raised hands, he brushed away the foliage from the trees as it struck on the face. He was too late to stop David from jumping over the fence. Harry panted on his radio.

"Suspect escaped through the rear of the property. Send units to surround."

The radio squawked as he placed both hands on top of the fence and heaved himself upwards. Sweat blinded his eyes.

He landed on the other side, and instead of a garden, found himself on a path. There was a gap between the houses. On both sides, the path opened out to the streets. He couldn't see David anywhere. For a few seconds, he wondered if David had simply gone into the garden of the house ahead. Harry ran up to the fence and heaved himself upwards, his feet scrambling for purchase. He could just about raise his head, and his eyes saw a well-maintained green lawn, but no sign of David.

"Got him," a voice yelled down the radio. "Blue Porsche 911 just went past us. We are chasing."

Harry cursed and turned right, running out into the street. He heard Arla's voice on the radio.

"Meet me at the car." Harry ran up the pavement, and at the corner of the street, he saw Arla rushing to the black BMW. He caught the flashing blue lights of the squad car as it zoomed down the road, obviously in pursuit of David.

He got into the driver's seat, and Arla was already inside.

Harry wrenched at the steering wheel savagely, his sirens and lights on. He did a U-turn and then floored the gas pedal, propelling the car forward with a screech of tyres. Arla held onto the handle above the door as the car careened through traffic and bounced out onto the main road.

"The father was burning paper in the kitchen, "Arla shouted. "He stopped when he saw me. I think he was destroying evidence."

Harry didn't reply. His eyes were fixed on the road, and his knuckles were white, clutching the steering wheel.

"Send two more units to assist. Suspect heading south-west from Kensington High Street." Arla twirled the knob of her radio and spoke quickly

"Request received already. Two units are being dispatched. Standby." The voice of the switchboard operator crackled on the radio.

Arla's head banged against the window as Harry jerked the steering wheel viciously to avoid an oncoming car. "Sorry," he mumbled without taking his eyes off the road.

"Don't worry," Arla replied as she got back on the radio. "Switchboard, patch me through to Detective Sgt Lisa Moran."

"Hello guv," Lise said.

"Go to David Braithwaite's house, and ask his father to attend the station. We need to interview him."

There was a pause, then Lisa spoke. "What if he refuses, guv?."

"Then arrest him," Arla responded. She had no time for games anymore. As far as she was concerned, if the father was destroying evidence pertaining to the case, he was as guilty as the son.

"Okay, guv."

The cars were all pulling up on the pavement as Harry raced through, sirens blaring. It was busy, with the trendy boutiques and fashionable restaurants of Kensington open. It was a nice day too, the sun peeking out after a few days of cloudiness. As a result, the pavements were packed with people, many of them tourists. They stopped to gape at the police cars as they sped past. It wasn't a common sight in this genteel, upmarket borough.

223

"Suspect heading towards the river. I repeat, heading towards the river." Andy Jackson's voice was high-pitched. Arla got the urgency. If their suspect fled on a boat, there was nothing they could do.

"Got that. Stay on him." Arla plucked her radio out and, with her thumb, turned the dial on the side of the radio. She located the frequency of the marine support unit, the London Metropolitan police force division responsible for policing the Thames as it flowed through London. She got through the switchboard, gave her name and ID, and asked for their chief inspector. Soon enough, a male voice came in through the radio.

"Inspector Bell speaking. Is that DCI Baker?"

Speaking quickly, Arla filled him in.

"Okay, we have a station at Waterloo. I will ask one of our petrol boats to be on standby. Is the suspect on water yet?"

"Last I heard, he's heading for the river." She glanced at Harry, who shook his head. "We will give you an update as soon as we hear."

And she did hear, as soon as she changed frequency. Andrew Jackson's voice was loaded with frustration. "He got away, guv. I can't believe it. He left the car on the roadside, crossed the road, and jumped into a jetty. There was a mood book boat waiting for him. As far as we could see, he was the only person driving the boat."

"Can you describe the boat to me?" Arla shouted. Harry was driving dangerously fast now, at risk of hitting something. She closed her eyes as he squeezed through a gap between two converging lorries. When she opened her eyes, they had made it. But they still had to go through the remaining traffic. Cars kept pulling over to give them passage, but the traffic was a nightmare.

"A white and black motorboat, guv. About 20 to 30 feet, I'd say. Goes fast, lifts its nose straight out of the water."

Harry raised his voice. "Which way is it headed?"

To the east, towards Dartford."

"He's heading for Kent and out into the North Sea," Arla said. "Straight across to Amsterdam."

She could see the flashing blue lights ahead. Harry screeched to a stop, and they got out and ran over to Andy and his team, who had gone down the steps to the river, and was standing at the jetty. The wind whipped Arla's hair around, and a humid, putrid stench rose from the muddy river banks. Andy lifted a hand and pointed to the east.

"That way, guv. He is a small speck now, and we actually just lost him. He's gone round the bend."

Arla grabbed her radio. "We are in Battersea, right?" Across the river, she could see the four white towers of the Battersea Power Station.

"Yes," Harry said. Arla spoke into her radio, relating the news to Inspector Bell of the Marine Support Unit.

"Don't worry, our headquarters is actually in Wapping, further down East, and near Dartford. We can still get hold of him."

"Great. Can you please send a unit to pick us up from the Battersea harbour?" She could sense Inspector Bell's hesitation, and spoke quickly. "I am the SIO in this case, and the suspect is a high-value target. Please send us a unit."

"Okay, please send us a location pin on the GPS. We are on the lookout for the speedboat. Over and out."

# CHAPTER 49

The thirty-one feet rigid inflatable boat, or an RIB, came to a stop outside the Battersea harbour and bobbed up and down on the water. The pilot engaged the back propellers and reversed the boat close to the jetty. Two of the marine support unit officers, dressed in the dark blue uniforms, jumped out and held the boat by its hooks as Harry and Arla boarded. Arla had already issued instructions on what to do with Carlson. He was still charged with the crime, and under no circumstances could he secure bail. Arla knew it took time for a bail appeal court hearing, but she didn't want to take any chances.

The RIB took off at high speed, its nose lifting straight out of the water. The boat's hull was deep, and Harry and Arla crouched down with the other three officers, to protect themselves from the wind. The pilot was shielded by a glass windshield. They flew under London Bridge, and Dartford Bridge appeared in the distance, its steel pylons gleaming in the sunlight. Arla turned to the officer next to her and pointed to the radio hooked to his chest. He understood, and spoke briefly on the radio, then tap the microphone in his ear. Then he leaned close to Arla and cupped a hand over her left ear.

"No sight as yet. Did you have the name of the boat, by any chance?

"No."

"That's a shame. With the name, we can search for the serial number. The boat must be registered to be on the river."

They zoomed down the muddy waters, and Arla looked behind her briefly to watch the white foam surging like a gigantic fountain behind them. Harry grabbed her arm and shouted in her ear.

"Triple 2000 L engines powering those propellers. More than 6000 brake horsepower units." He was grinning like a schoolboy, excitement dancing in his eyes.

She shouted back in his ears. "This isn't a joyride, Harry. You better hope David doesn't escape."

Harry pointed to the sky. "We should call a helicopter unit."

Arla nodded, mentally slapping herself for not thinking about it sooner. She spoke quickly on the radio, and switchboard patched her through to the air service. As a DCI, Arla could request a helicopter to be dispatched. She gave them the location and hung up.

She looked out at the water, and the barges and boats were slipping past at breakneck speed. Her hopes were sinking. If David could make it past the Isle of dogs, he was into Kent. A few miles down the river, and he was in the great wash of the North Sea.

If David had a seaworthy boat, and she had no reason to doubt that he did, then it would be difficult to catch him. International manhunts were beyond her expertise.

Harry gave Arla's hand a squeeze and rose. She pulled on his hand, and he looked down at her and winked reassuringly. He steadied himself by spreading his legs wider, then moved up to join the pilot.

The boat was going around the curve of the Isle of dogs. The Thames river went round a U-shaped bend here, and they were fast approaching the eastern limits of the city. Beyond that, the river widened and would soon be flowing past the Kentish towns of Gravesend and Rainham.

Harry saw a pair of binoculars on the dashboard and picked it up. He leaned against the windshield to steady himself, then looked through the binoculars. The boat shuddered and shook as the pilot cranked up the revs, pushing the engines to their maximum capacity.

Harry could hear the reverberations travelling up from his feet, making his teeth chatter. He used his strong legs to stay in position and moved the binoculars slowly in an arc from left to right. He wasn't paying attention to the slower pleasure boats or, the longer passenger craft.

A blur of movement to his extreme right caught his eye. He whipped the binoculars back and found what he was looking for. It was a white shape, leaving a plume of foam in its wake as it sped down the river.

"There he is," Harry screamed, grabbing the pilot's shoulder. The man followed the line of Harry's hand, his neck creaking to the right. Then he nodded. The boat swerved, banking to the right.

Harry held the rims of the windshield tightly as he watched the boat get closer. Excitement mounted in his body as he realised they were gaining ground. He used the binoculars again and read the name of the boat as they got closer.

Seabird was the name, and Harry could make out the direct figure of a man at the wheel. The man turned around, and it was definitely David. There didn't seem to be anyone else aboard, but Harry couldn't rule out someone crouching in the hull.

"Get me closer," Harry urged the pilot. The engine screamed as the pilot shifted gears, and then the boat vibrated as it hit choppy waters. The river was broader now, the muddy waters coalescing with the colder streams from the North Sea. From the countryside around him, Harry knew they were flying past Kent. If they kept going much longer, the sea wouldn't be far away.

The Seabird was a couple of hundred yards away when Harry stepped out from the pilot's cockpit into the gun whale. He heard the pilot shout something and looked back. They couldn't hear what they were saying.

He also heard a scream from behind and briefly looked to see Arla being restrained by two of the officers. She was shouting at him to get back. He held her eyes for a brief second and shook his head. He had made his mind up. There was no way David was escaping.

As the distance diminished to less than 100 yards, the pilot eased back on the throttles. The boat slowed but moved more in the choppy waves.

Harry was on his hands and knees, holding on to the landing hoax as he crawled out to the front of the boat. Water splashed in his face, and the wind was so strong he could barely open his eyes.

# CHAPTER 50

The boat dropped into the trough of a wave a few feet deep, and Harry was hurled forward. He almost toppled over the edge, the weight of his body not helping. His feet snagged into a coil of rope, and it lashed out, fastened to a hook. That saved him from going overboard. He thanked his lucky stars and stayed prone on the gun whale. They were less than 50 yards out now, and the pilot had speeded up again as the Seabird was getting away.

Harry stayed prone, peering out over the water, the rushing foam only a couple of feet beneath his face. He could sense they were gaining on the Seabird again. David kept looking back, and Harry knew he was panicking. There were fifty yards out, then thirty. Harry felt the boat slow, and he raised himself on all fours again. The Seabird was suddenly much bigger, and it was a sleek, thirty feet pleasure boat.

By the large size of the twin engines at the back, Harry knew this boat was built for speed. It had a canopy over the top and also a deck below. He hoped there wasn't someone hiding there. He also hoped David didn't have a weapon.

He turned his head and waved with his left hand, urging the pilot to get close to the Seabird. They were within ten yards. It was clear that the Seabird couldn't compete, but it had now changed direction. It was heading for the shores, and Harry could see a harbour and the buildings of a town. His heart sank. David could get lost in the harbour, and he could steal a car and make his escape.

Harry bit down on his jaws and steeled himself as the RIB inched closer to the trail of foam the Seabird was leaving in its wake. He rose to his feet. The force of the wind almost knocked him over, but he hunched his shoulders and bowed down at the waist.

He bent his knees and waited for the right moment. Water was splashing all over Harry's jacket now, soaking him. The boat was jerking around alarmingly, and Harry knew it wasn't safe at these speeds.

The last thing he wanted was the pilot to lose control, and the boat hitting the Seabird. He sprung off his back feet, using all the strength in his thighs. He propelled himself forward, diving across the boat. His dive was big enough to land him inside the Seabird, and his shoulders hit the wooden seats, breath knocking out of his chest.

He rolled over and tried to stand but the deck was slick with water. He slipped and rolled down the deck. He stood, and again fell to his knees. His clothes were sticking to him like a second skin, and water dripped down his face, blurring his view.

David was still at the wheel, but he kept looking back. He saw Harry approaching and did something at the controls. The boat kept moving forward at the same speed. David turned round, a mad glint in his eye. He had picked up a baseball bat and brandished it in front of him. Harry's boots were squeaking wet on the slippery deck. He was trying his best to stay on his two feet as David advanced, swinging the bat.

When he was close enough to hit, David swung the bat up and slammed it down. It would have hit Harry, but the water turbulence helped. Harry slipped, the baseball passed harmlessly over his head.

Harry knew he didn't have much time. Sooner or later, David would connect, and he didn't quite feel like having a broken jaw today. David advanced again, snarling, hatred pouring from his eyes. He took a short jab with the bat, poking Harry in the chest. It was meant for Harry's face, but he managed to raise himself up.

He grabbed the bat and pulled it to him. David lost balance, and Harry punched him in the face with all his might. Harry's fist made solid contact

231

with the side of David's face, snapping it back. David fell on the deck, and Harry jumped on top of him, his knees pinning down David's arms. Another blow to the face and David went limp. Harry picked up the baseball bat and chucked it overboard.

He rose, his legs wobbling like jelly. He grabbed onto a chair and pulled himself forward. He got to the cockpit, and his eyes skimmed the dashboard. He had some experience of driving boats. When he was younger, his father took them on boating holidays in the Norfolk waters. He didn't recognise much on the dashboard, but the red power button was easily visible.

He didn't want to press it as it might mean a sudden deceleration that could launch both of them into the water. He saw the black throttle handle and pulled down on it, sighing in relief as the boat slowed. He looked behind him, and David was still flat on the deck, but he was moving his head. The boat slowed further and eventually came to a standstill.

Harry heard the drone of the marine support unit boat to his left, and it came alongside. The first thing he saw was Arla's scared, drawn face, standing next to the pilot. He smiled weakly and gave her a wave.

# CHAPTER 51

Harry got changed at the Marine support units headquarters in Wapping. Wapping was in east London, close to the financial district. One of the officers was kind enough to lend Harry a spare change of clothes. Apparently, all of them came to work with that because they never knew when they'd get soaking wet.

David Braithwaite was arrested and delivered back to Clapham police station in a squad car. Arla thanked Inspector Bell profusely, and they shook hands. Harry got a round of back slaps and good-natured shoulder punches and fist bumps from the officers who had watched his heroics from close quarters. Inspector Bell even announced that if Harry wanted to work for the Marine support unit, he would be welcome.

Arla stood to one side, feeling proud. Her heart had been in her mouth when she watched Harry hanging off the corner of the boat, then leaping across. She was just glad he was all right.

She was famished, and so was Harry. They had lunch in the canteen, and then one of the officers drove Harry back to the Battersea harbour, where he'd left his car. When the doors slammed shut, Arla grabbed hold of Harry's hand.

"Are you okay?" They hadn't had a chance to talk since the event. Not by themselves, anyway.

Harry's chestnut brown eyes blinked, and the smile danced on his lips. He leaned forward, and she kissed him lightly on the lips, then grabbed the back of his head and dragged him forward. She was so glad nothing had happened to him.

They kissed hungrily, and Arla felt desire untangle itself low in her belly. Harry moved his hand to her waist, and it slipped down to her buttocks, needing the soft flesh. Arla whimpered and opened her mouth to let his tongue flick inside her mouth.

Then she remembered where she was. They came up for air, but she still kept her hand on his face, their foreheads touching. They kissed again lightly, and then Harry settled back in the driver's seat. They still held hands across the gearbox, and Harry lifted her hand to brush it across his lips. She liked that sensation. It left tingles of desire travelling up her arm.

"We need to finish this later," Harry looked at her and grinned.

She smiled coyly, then glanced away. He started the engine, and they took off. It took them about half an hour to get back to the station. Word had spread already. As they walked in through the rear car park entrance, a couple of the uniformed sergeants stopped to congratulate Harry.

One of them called him a daredevil, and Arla could see Harry really liked that. He threw his head back and laughed, then bumped fists with the sergeant. Arla knew it would be a talking point later on at the pub, and everyone would be buying Harry drinks. She frowned at the thought. She didn't want him coming back home drunk, then snoring in bed.

Harry got plenty of waves and whistles as they walked into the open plan detective's office.

"You trying to be an action hero, Inspector Mehta?" Justin, one of the detective inspectors, called out.

"Yes, speak to my agent. I've got an offer from Hollywood," Harry shot back. Everyone laughed, and it was good for morale, Arla thought. She didn't want Harry getting a big head, though. He loved to brag about things, and she had no doubt he would be mentioning this for weeks. Arla summoned her team inside. Rob and Lisa were the only ones present. Rosslyn and Gita were out for lunch.

"Braithwaite is in custody," Lisa said as soon as they walked in. "He's got himself a lawyer. Do you want to interview him now?"

Arla glanced at Harry, who nodded. "What about his father?"

"He's here as well."

"Their house is now a crime scene. Please send scene-of-crime there to start the investigation. I also want the street cordoned off with squad cars on both sides."

Rob and Lisa looked at each other, and then Rob scratched the back of his neck. Lisa looked at her shoes. Arla frowned. "What?"

Lisa looked at her and grimaced, and Arla had a dreadful feeling. She knew what Lisa was going to say.

"The top brass is here, guv. They want to see you and inspector Harry upstairs in commander Johnson's room."

Arla's shoulder sagged, and she cradled her head in her hands. Not again. She was so close to cracking this case, and now these idiots would put new obstacles in her way.

Rob said, "The boot print analyst has also reported some interesting results."

Lisa flipped open the notebook in her hand. "I've sent you the emails already. But in summary, the boot print by the tree trunk near the pond matches Madelyn West's. She was wearing size 8 flats, and she's left a clear trail from the dirt track to the tree trunk. For the larger male boot print, we still don't have a result. "

Arla said, "You need David's shoes for that."

"Yes, guv. We have already tried Carlson's shoes, and the boot print doesn't match, neither does their gait analysis, according to Mary." Mary Atkins was their forensic boot print and gait analyst.

Arla pursed her lips together. "So Madelyn was there with another man, and it doesn't seem like it was Carlson. Does he have an alibi for that evening?"

Rob nodded. "He was with, as he puts it, one of his several girlfriends. We've spoken to this woman already, and she's given him an alibi."

Lisa glanced at Rob and raised her eyebrows. Rob said, "Oh sorry. We got him on CCTV that night as well, outside the woman's house. Looks like Carlson was speaking the truth."

Arla leaned back in her armchair and exhaled. She caught Harry's eyes, which were hooded, and gazing at her meditatively. She knew what was on his mind. Harry said, "I guess that rules Carlson out of murdering Madelyn West. But he remains a suspect in Susan's case."

Arla nodded, but she was losing confidence in Carlson's guilt. True, the man was a criminal. But did he kill Susan?

She glanced at Lisa and Rob. "Get David's boot prints immediately. Send them to Mary. If there is a match, I want to know as soon as possible."

"It's already been done, guv," Lisa said, with a smile on her face "We're waiting to hear from Mary."

"Good work. Make sure you get all the shoes from David's house and use all the prints."

Arla placed both her palms on the desk and lifted herself wearily. So did Harry, and his facial expression matched the dejection on her face. "Might as well get this over and done with."

They took the elevator, as both of them were exhausted after the car and boat chase. Harry was leaning against the elevator wall, his eyes closed. She grabbed his hands and gave him a hug. They stayed like that for a few precious seconds before the elevator doors opened.

Johnson asked them to enter as soon as Arla knocked.

She felt a cold fist of fear sink in her stomach when she saw who was present. Nick Deakins, the deputy assistant commissioner, was seated next to Johnson. Arla swallowed hard and said hello to both men. They took their seat opposite, and there was silence for a few seconds.

It was Nick Deakins who spoke first. He had his usual box frame glasses on, and his sunken cheeks, small chin, and thin nose always gave Arla the creeps. He even had paper-thin lips, and she had never seen a man who looked like Mr Deakins. It didn't help that they had sparred in previous cases, and loathed each other.

"What happened today, DCI Baker? Deakins asked.

Arla glanced from him to Johnson. Her boss merely raised his eyebrows in silence. Arla shrugged and gave them both a sit rep. Deakins was shaking his head about halfway through her report, and she stopped.

"DCI Baker, you have a suspect in custody already. Why did you have to go after Lord Braithwaite?"

"Because his DNA was found in both the semen samples in the victim's homes. He had relations with both of them, and I have evidence that David Braithwaite had a dangerous obsession with Susan Remington from her teenage years."

Deakins gave Arla a long, hard stare. "Assuming the role of a psychiatrist isn't going to help your cause."

Arla felt her temper rise. She bit down on her back teeth and choked her reply. Deakins continued.

"The Crown Prosecution Service will dismiss this as conjecture and hearsay. I have read the reports you have submitted already. So what if David was in love with Susan? And he became very attached to her. It's not a crime, is it?"

Arla's jaw fell open. She was exhausted, and a sense of incredulity washed over her. She couldn't help but suddenly laugh out loud.

237

She saw both Johnson and Deakins frown, but she ignored it. Harry leaned forward slightly, glancing at her to get attention. She ignored him as well.

"Love? Attraction? Since when do you lock someone up and threaten to beat them up if you love them? And what about appointing a detective to watch Susan's every move and sending her hate mail? These are dangerous obsessional traits, and David Braithwaite wouldn't be the first person to be convicted for such crimes."

Deakins folded his bone-white hands on the table. "Really? Then why did Susan go back to him?"

"Because she was a fragile, damaged individual. She suffered with an eating disorder when younger, and it left her with anxiety and insecurity."

Rage blossomed inside Arla, consuming her soul. Her eyes poured vitriol on Deakins.

"If I didn't know any better, sir, I would be saying you are speaking in a sexist way about the victim. This wasn't Susan's fault, was it? David Braithwaite killed her, and all the evidence points to it."

Deakins's mouth opened in shock. Johnson slammed the table with his fist, and it seemed everything in the room shook, including the windowpanes and the chair Arla sat on.

"Enough!" Johnson roared. "DCI Baker, you will not speak in that way to a senior officer again. Do you hear me?"

Arla turned to Johnson. "I hear you perfectly well, sir. But did you hear what Commander Deakins just said?"

Deakins put up a palm, trying to defuse the situation. "I'm afraid you took my words the wrong way, DCI Baker. Of course, everything we do is focused on getting justice for the victims. What I meant was if David Braithwaite was such a bad person, then why did Susan rekindle their romance?"

Arla shrugged. "Because she had issues, sir. Besides, David was two-timing her. He was also having a relationship with her best friend."

There was a pause, and Johnson took over. "I did warn you to take permission from me before you went to see the Braithwaite family. Didn't I?"

Arla was tired, and she didn't have time for this. She decided to shoot straight from the hip. "Because they're related to Justice Minister Braithwaite?"

Johnson gnashed his jaws together and breathed heavily. Both men were silent, glaring at Arla.

Harry spoke up. "The fact that David Braithwaite tried to escape makes his guilt clear."

Deakins looked at Harry for the first time, it seemed. "Guilty of what exactly? Being obsessed with Susan and sleeping with her best friend does not mean he's a double murderer."

"Did you have a suspect in mind, sir?" Arla asked, her voice intentionally innocent.

Deakins gave her a shit-eating grin in return.

"You have one of London's most notorious drug dealers in custody. And yet, you go traipsing round London in a movie chase sequence to bring back Lord Braithwaite?"

"Look at the evidence, Sir, and not the name. David might be a Lord, but the evidence against him is worthy of a criminal."

Neither man opposite Arla said anything. She pressed her point. "And the evidence points to him being a murderer."

Her phone beeped twice. She excused herself and took the phone out. She read off the screen, and her heart surged. She smiled at her commanding officers.

"The boot print analysis just came back. Next to Madelyn West's shoe prints, the number ten shoes belonged to David Braithwaite. There's a match on both the boot print as well as the gait."

She smiled at Harry and then looked at the two men opposite triumphantly.

"David doesn't have an alibi for the night Susan was murdered. I have yet to ask him about the evening of 27th March, about Madelyn. But we have his DNA at both crime scenes, his boot print, a history of a frankly obsessional disorder, and I can bet you any money the encrypted phone that kept calling both women belonged to David as well."

Deakins leaned back in his chair. He stared at the desk, and he rotated a pen. Like a dog trying to chase its own tail, Arla thought. The slimy bastard was looking for a way out. For a way to help his friend, the Lord justice minister. No doubt that would put Deakins in a good light when he came for the top job in the London Met.

"I grant you he was sleeping with both women. And he has his faults. Maybe he met up with Madelyn on the 27th, but does that make him a murderer? David has no prior convictions. He has a history of minor violence against Susan, but nothing of this sort. And there is no explanation why the dollar signs were engraved on both the victim's hands."

The smile faded from Arla's lips. What Deakins said was true, but they were ignoring that mountain of evidence accumulated against him.

"Sir, I'm not the type of investigator who charges a man for murder without good cause."

Deakins said nothing for a while. Then he spoke quietly. "We need more evidence against him that directly ties him to the murders."

Johnson cleared his throat. "And do not visit the Braithwaite or Remington family again, DCI Baker. That's an order."

Arla ground her teeth in irritation and fumed in silence. She wanted to tell Johnson exactly what he could do with his bloody order.

# CHAPTER 52

David's lawyer was a tall, angular man with a long neck. He distinctly reminded Arla of a stork with his hooked, beaky nose. His name was James Lampard, and he rose to shake Arla's hand. It surprised Arla, as defence lawyers were often combative to the police.

David sat with his hands folded on his lap, his dark hair neatly combed sideways, and his round thin-rimmed glasses in place. Only his clothes had changed – instead of the expensive suit, he now wore a simple blue T-shirt and jeans. His face bore no expression. He glanced at Arla and looked away. He seemed very casual, Arla thought, considering they'd just been in a massive chase which could've ended badly.

David paid more attention to Harry. His eyes glinted with interest as he looked Harry up and down, then settled on his face. He kept staring at Harry, Arla noted, even as Harry spoke into the tape, introducing everyone.

For some reason, Arla found it difficult to compare the man she'd seen in the Knightsbridge office to the man in front of her now. It was hard to imagine the same person had just escaped from his house and led them halfway across London. She had no doubt he intended to escape into the North Sea and to Holland.

That spoke of a long-term plan, and although his calmness now seemed incongruous to his previous actions, Arla knew very well the most violent of criminals often were calm and quiet people in normal life. That was precisely the reason they were so dangerous.

"As you know, your DNA was found on Susan Remington's bed and also on Madelyn West's bed," Arla started. "Could you please confirm when you last saw each of them, starting with Susan Remington first?"

The answer had clearly been rehearsed. David didn't waste any time. He spoke in a calm and detached voice. "On Wednesday 16th March. She came to my office."

"What for?"

"To ask my professional opinion about a client of hers."

"Could you please elaborate?"

David glanced at Mr Lampard, who inclined his head. "The investment management firm I run has corporate clients. I look after their pension funds. One of those clients had asked Clifford and Sons to become their auditor. Hence Susan spoke to me."

"I see. And that's the last time you saw her?"

"Yes."

"Susan made her last phone call on 17th March. In the preceding four weeks, and even before that, she was called several times by an encrypted phone number. Do you have an encrypted phone, Mr Braithwaite?"

"No comment."

Arla smiled. "We will certainly have a look at the phone we found you with. Do you have any other phones?"

"No comment."

Arla delved into Susan Remington's past life and David and Susan's teenage romance. When he asked David if he had an obsession with Susan, she noticed a change in his appearance. He glared at her, his eyes flashing. Mr Lampard got Arla's attention.

"Can you please keep your questions pertinent to the case? Susan Remington's and my client's previous life has no bearing to it."

"On the contrary, I think it has every bearing." She turned back to David. "Could you please answer the question?"

"No," David replied with a stony face.

"Did you target her with revenge porn?"

"No."

"Did you leave the remnants of tortured, dead animals outside her door?"

David frowned, his expression bewildered. He glanced to his lawyer, who raised his eyebrows. "Inspector Baker, these questions have nothing to do with the case."

"I'll explain their relevance" Arla watched David as she spoke. His facial muscles were tensed.

"These past events are not connected to the current case," the lawyer insisted. "My client has no reason to answer them."

David raised a hand, not taking his eyes off Arla. "It's okay, I'll answer. I did nothing of the sort."

"You locked her in the bedroom once and also slapped her. She didn't press any charges, however. Is that true?"

Again, David answered quickly, and Arla knew he was expecting the question. He obviously spent some time with his lawyer and gone through this. "We had arguments like any couple does."

"But did you hit her? Did you lock her in her room?"

"I did not."

Arla knew she couldn't prove anything. It was in the past, and she had no witnesses or any video evidence. It was her word against David's.

"Did you know that Susan Remington suffered from an eating disorder?"

David nodded. "Did she show any evidence of it while she was married to you?"

David shrugged. "She never ate a great deal of food. I encouraged her to have a healthy diet, but I suspected she didn't manage her condition very well."

"Are you saying her eating disorder persisted while she was in the marriage?"

"Yes."


Harry cleared his throat and leant forwards. "When did you start seeing Susan Remington again?"

"A few months ago. I met her at an industry meeting of finance professionals. We had a few drinks and got talking." He shrugged.

"So, you were able to rekindle your obsession with her. In the meantime, you were also having sexual relations with her best friend, Madelyn West. Correct?"

Mr Lampard raised a hand. "My client does not have to answer these questions."

Harry carried on unperturbed. "The truth is you never let Susan be. You blamed her for the loss of your child after the abortion. Then you started sending her hate mail. When the chance came to be with her again, you capitalised on her loneliness and insecurity."

Harry stared at David, whose face was mottling with crimson.

"You wanted to exact revenge because she didn't have the baby. You thought she was your chattel, and you could do with her as you pleased. Now you had your chance. You took her down to the common and made sure she had alcohol and cocaine. Then you strangled her and…"

Mr Lampard raised a hand, interrupting Harry. "Didn't you hear what I said, Inspector Mehta?"

Harry's volume increased, rising to a crescendo.

"Then you strangled her, carved the dollar sign on her hand to mislead us because you knew she was taking cocaine. Then you discarded her body in the pond." He stabbed a finger towards David. "Isn't that the truth?"

David's teeth were bared, his lips turning white. His nostrils flared, eyes wide with hate. His shoulders shook with rage, and Mr Lampard spoke into his ear. David didn't pay any attention to his lawyer.

"That is not the truth," David seethed. "You have no idea what you're talking about."

Harry paid no heed to his words. "And you did the same thing to Madelyn. She became angry when you told her you had started sleeping with Susan again. She was tired of your devious, controlling ways. So you callously killed her and made sure you drew the dollar sign on her hand as well to plant false evidence. Then you discarded her body in the pond."

"No, I did not," David shouted, his cheeks burning red, sweat appearing on his forehead.

Harry smirked. "Then why did you try to escape?"

"Because I didn't want to give you the satisfaction of catching me, Inspector." David slid his eyes to Arla, his lips bending down, jaws grinding. "With your two-bit brains, you think you can drag me down here like a common criminal?"

He grimaced. "What do you think would happen to my reputation if I was caught? To my family's reputation? I would have to live with that."

"And now," Arla said, "You have to live with it anyway." In her own mind, she marvelled at the man's megalomania. Two women were dead, and he was worried about his family's reputation?

"At least I tried."

Harry raised his eyebrows. "Do you think you are above the law?"

David sneered at Harry. "The law is intended to serve justice. You have no idea of what that is, Inspector. Which is ironic, considering you're a law enforcement professional."

Arla raised her voice. "Then why don't you tell us what happened to Susan and Madelyn? If you're so clever, then help us seek justice for these two women."

David looked at both of them for a few seconds, his composure slowly returning. He took a deep lungful of air, then shook his head. "If I told you, you'd never believe me."

# CHAPTER 53

Arla frowned at him. It was a strange statement to make, given the circumstances. "What do you mean?"

David had lapsed into silence. He looked away from Arla, then slouched back on his chair. Arla repeated her question, and he ignored her.

"I think my client has answered enough questions," Mr Lampard said.

A headache was beginning to throb in Arla's forehead. She was exhausted after a long day, and she still had a mountain of paperwork to complete, not to mention a meeting with Carlson's lawyer. She had to decide what to do with Carlson right after this.

"I'm afraid your client has left many issues unresolved," Harry said. "He needs to provide an alibi for 27th March." Harry stared pointedly at David.

David glanced at his lawyer, then leaned over to him. The two had a hushed conversation.

David said, "I was at my private club, Annabel's in Mayfair. The receptionists there and a couple of my friends were witnesses. "

"I see," Harry said. "Then why was your boot print next to Madelyn West's shoes in the Common, just by the pond?"

David's head snapped up, and he stared at Harry.

"The banks of the pond begin just a few metres down from where your boot prints were found. Is it not true that on the evening of 27th March, you took Madelyn down to the pond? Then you killed her the same way you did, Susan."

Mr Lampard frowned. "My client could have been there at any time. Why do you think he was there on the evening of the 27th?"

"Because the boot prints were fresh, no more than a day old. Unluckily for your client, it hadn't rained the night before, and the prints were well preserved."

Both Mr Lampard and David were silent. Arla took over. She folded her hands on the desk and leaned towards David. "Boot prints and gait analysis are effective forensic markers, Mr Braithwaite. The shoes you are wearing now match those boot prints. You know all about the rest of the evidence."

David stared at her in silence. Arla continued. Her voice was low. "We know you were there with Madelyn on 27th March. What did you do to her?"

To Arla's surprise, David nodded. Mr Lampard sat stock still, and Arla wondered if this was another rehearsed move.

"Yes, I was there. I needed to speak to her. But I didn't kill her. We had our discussion, then I left."

"You left her there?"

"Yes. She said she wanted some time on her own. She would walk to Clapham Common station or get a cab back to her place. She needed time to think."

"At what time did you leave her?"

"Between 7:30 and 8 PM. I finished the gym session at my club at 6 pm, then picked her up. We drove down to the Common and stayed there for about half an hour. Then I left," he said with emphasis. "I don't know what happened after that."

Arla wrote the times down in her diary, then circled them. She could check CCTV images, which would not show the road that led to the pond, but it might show David's blue Porsche going in and out of that road at the specified times.

His private member's club had CCTV; Rosslyn had already checked. David's arrival and departure times would be logged in reception.

"I believe that's enough of the questions," Mr Lampard said. "I know he will be charged with resisting arrest. Do you have any other charges against him?"

Arla looked at Harry, and he blinked twice. Arla said, "Yes. He is charged with the murder of Susan Remington and Madelyn West."

David's shoulders slumped. He leaned forward with his elbows on his knees and cradled his head.

Mr Lampard had a smug look on his face. He opened his briefcase and produced a paper. "I have a bail release statement prepared for my client. You can charge him for murder, but he has no previous convictions for such offences, grievous bodily harm, or any violent crime. Therefore, bail will be granted by the court."

Arla frowned at him. "But I've only just charged him. You have to apply to the courts to get bail."

"My client has an extenuating circumstance. He suffers from a medical disorder, and he needs to be treated at home." Mr Lampard's face creased into a little smile before he corrected himself.

Arla stared at him, bewildered. "What medical condition?"

"Epilepsy. My client is on medication for it."

Harry's jaw had also dropped open. "Is that true?"

"You can check his medical records if you wish to. According to the duty medical officer, if he has an epileptic fit in custody, then it will be the responsibility of the London Met. Hence he is to be set bail."

Mr Lampard forwarded a sheaf of papers to Arla. She snatched them from his hand and looked through them. The infernal lawyer was correct. David Braithwaite indeed had bail secured, set at one hundred thousand pounds. Without a word, she handed the papers to Harry.

*****

"I can't believe it," Arla said, slamming her office door shut. She kicked a chair, and it hit the edge of the table. She put both hands on her waist and leaned against the windowsill, staring at the darkening sky over the parking lot. The late afternoon sun was losing its battle to stay afloat on the horizon.

"We had him, and now we lost him," Arla said. "Ridiculous. I bet you his uncle orchestrated the whole bail thing."

It was only Harry and herself in the room. "Yes, more than likely. But we have his passport, and he cannot leave the country. In fact, for this medical reason, he has to stay at home, and he will be examined by the doctor there. Plus, we'll have him on surveillance. So, he can't run."

"Unless he kills again. I wouldn't put it past him," Arla squeezed her eyes shut, then massaged her temples. Her headache was getting worse. "What about Carlson?"

"He was denied bail. Given his previous conviction for possession of class A drugs, this murder charge was enough grounds for bail to be denied."

"Well, that's something, I guess."

Harry stepped closer and massaged her shoulders. Arla glanced behind him.

"Don't worry," he smiled reassuringly. "I locked the door. I think you should go home." He kissed her forehead, and she sagged against his spacious chest, loving the warm, comfortable feeling as his arm held her in place.

"What about you?" she whispered.

"I'll be alright. See you in a couple of hours."

Arla sighed. She was looking forward to going home. But in the back of her mind, a nagging, persistent doubt started to nibble away furtively.

David Braithwaite was a cruel, narcissistic bastard.

But was he also speaking the truth?

\*\*\*\*\*

On her way out, she bumped into Carlson and his lawyer, coming upstairs from the custody chambers. He glared at her, and his lawyer touched his arm. That didn't stop him. He deliberately stepped in Arla's way.

"What you're doing is wrong, Inspector," he whispered, his eyes blazing.

Arla lifted her chin. "And who are you to be claiming wrong and right, Mr Adeyemi?"

The lawyer was now gripping Carlson's arm, trying to pull him back, but he resisted. His nostrils flared as he leaned forward, his voice dropping to a whisper.

"No one. Like I told you – I am the symptom, not the disease. But when it comes to Susan, you've got this wrong."

"How so?"

"Because I didn't kill her." A sudden spasm of bitterness and pain shot through his expression. His face crumpled. He sank against the wall, his shoulders sagging. Arla narrowed her eyes.

Carlson stared at his feet, his chest heaving. Arla noted his gold chain was out, and he touched the cross once before he raised his eyes to Arla again.

"But when you do find who killed her, you let me know, alright?" He came off the wall and stood in front of Arla. His teeth bared as hate replaced the regret on his features.

"You tell me, Inspector, yeah? I want to know," he whispered menacingly. His lawyer stepped in front of him now, presenting his back to Arla. She moved back.

The lawyer shoved Carlson ahead of him, literally pushing him down the corridor. Carlson turned and met Arla's eyes one more time.

Her mind was whirring and clicking, like a million camera lenses taking photos simultaneously. The multifarious picture that emerged was still a jigsaw with missing pieces, but in bright splashes of colour, a pattern was emerging.

# CHAPTER 54

Arla didn't sleep properly that night.

She had a nightmare that Harry and herself had gone scuba diving, but the boat was sinking. A shark circled the water, and apart from them, everyone on the boat was dead. The captain lay by her feet, drenched in blood, with a dollar sign marked on his forehead. So did another scuba diver.

Then the shark jumped out of the water, and strangely, it bore the face of David Braithwaite. Then Harry ran past her and jumped into the water. I can catch him, he screamed.

"No," Arla shouted and jerked bolt upright. Her breath came in gasps. Tendrils of hair stuck to her sweaty forehead. It was dark in the room, and she could only make out shadows. For a few seconds, she felt strange and dislocated, like she'd lost her memory and ended up somewhere new. Then she recognised the dresser opposite her bed. Harry was lying next to her. She touched his shoulder, then kissed it. Harry kept on sleeping.

Her body felt damp and sticky with sweat. She carried herself off for a shower. The burst of hot water was cleansing and welcoming. Rob and Lisa should have finished combing through the CCTV images with the help of the tech lab's image recognition software. The key image being David Braithwaite blue Porsche 911.

She washed her hair as well, as she had time. There was something about David's interview that bothered her. Harry got him riled up; that was the plan. But there was honesty in his emotions. Arla couldn't find cold, calculating deviousness in his speech, and he wouldn't have got so angry unless he was genuinely upset.

Killers who had malignant narcissistic personalities couldn't understand human emotions. They were detached and cold-blooded. So far, David didn't seem like that, and that was a concern.

Because without David, or Carlson as suspects, Arla didn't have a case anymore. She knew exactly what Johnson would have to say about that, and she wasn't looking forward to hearing it.

She got dressed quickly. As she clipped the warrant badge to her waistline, she gazed fondly at Harry and her sleeping beauty, Nicole. Harry was still asleep. She gave them both a light kiss, and Harry stirred.

"See you at work," she whispered and left.

Rob was already at his desk and looking exhausted. He had dark circles under his eyes, which were red-rimmed. He waved to her.

"You look like how I feel, Rob. Tired?"

Rob yawned in response. "Got all the CCTV images analysed with the tech lab last night, guv. Stayed back till ten."

It was 8 am now, which meant Rob was up early to make his half-hour commute to work.

"Coffee and breakfast?" Arla suggested. Rob grinned.

"Come to the canteen with me," Arla said. "Full English for you, my treat." She knew the canteen would be empty now, and they would have some privacy.

Rob's eyes lit up. He grabbed his laptop, and Arla put her coat and bag in the office.

"Got all the images back from Annabel's club and also in front of DB's house. His statement matches up, guv. I'm sorry," Rob said, as he added a ladle of baked beans to his plate of bacon, eggs, two sausages, and black pudding.

Arla's heart sank at the news, but she was also suddenly starving, looking at Rob's plate. When was the last time she had full English? Pre-pregnancy. She took a deep breath and added one slice of bacon and one egg with a tiny bit of baked beans. At least she was skimping on carbs. The coffee would keep her full. It's what she lived on these days, now that she didn't smoke anymore.

As Rob chomped on his food, Arla watched the CCTV image loops. The grainy images showed the blue Porsche emerging from Clapham's south-westerly end, where the ponds were situated. The solitary road led to the dirt track that ran to the pond banks. While the road didn't contain CCTV cameras, the cameras were situated on the main artery of the A3, and it was easy to spot the distinctive car coming off the bend at 20.00 on 27th March.

Almost exactly the time David had mentioned. Arla zoomed into the private registration plate, just to be sure.

DB 22.

She saw the same car parked outside David's house in Kensington. And outside his office opposite Hyde Park. The times on the top right corner matched David's statement. Arla spun the tape back and watched again to be double sure.

Swallowing the bitter taste of disappointment with the coffee, she pondered her next move. Rob wiped his mouth with a tissue and gave a sigh of happiness. He had colour back in his cheeks now and a satisfied expression on his face.

"Happy?" Arla grinned.

The smile on Rob's face was self-explanatory. It vanished swiftly, mirroring Arla's expression.

"What do you think, guv?"

Arla stared at the fumes rising from her coffee mug. "On 27/3, he could have killed Madelyn, then left the common," she reflected. "And from 13-18th March, just because we have him on CCTV driving from his

255

office to the club, and then club to home, doesn't mean he didn't have the time to kill Susan. He could've taken public transport after he got back home."

Arla forcked a piece of bacon to her mouth. "We have him under surveillance, right?"

"Yes, guv. Would you like a refill of your coffee?"

"Thanks, Rob."

Rob returned with the coffee, and Lisa, who'd just walked in. Rob filled her in and showed her the images.

"What about Carlson, guv?" Lisa asked. "His lawyer wants to appeal the bail refusal. He's not had a prior murder charge, so he might win the appeal."

"Then both our suspects are gone."

Arla sat back in her chair and looked upwards. The dirty white ceiling met her eyes. Lisa's words got her attention.

"I forgot to tell you something, guv. I went through David's call log last night. One number stood out because it matched a number Susan Remington used to call. It's her mother, Sheila."

Arla frowned. "So David was calling Sheila Remington?"

"Twice, I think, the week before Susan disappeared."

"How long did the calls last for?"

"She didn't answer once, so for a few seconds. The second time they spoke for eleven minutes."

Arla wondered, pressing her lips together. "I wonder why."

She lapsed into silence, turbulence raging in her mind. She had never trusted Sheila, and this new information put fuel to her flames of suspicion.

"I'm going to pay the Remington's another visit. Let me know if David 's surveillance team report anything."

Arla paid at the till then left.

# CHAPTER 55

rla drove down herself in a grey BMW that she signed off for at the carpool. She parked inside the wide, multiple-car driveway of the Remington household. She had rung Johnson to let him know she was visiting, but he didn't pick up. She left a message.

At the house, the elderly man opened the door and looked at Arla quizzically. She hadn't announced her arrival, but she knew Sheila was at home, as there was a Conservative Party conference going on in London. Sheila was speaking later in the evening.

Arla asked to see Sheila and followed the elderly man inside. She waited in the same lounge as before. After a few minutes, Rupert, the son, arrived. His hands were stuffed in his pockets. He wore black jeans that were faded, and his dark hair was tousled like he'd been running his hand through it. He was surprised to see Arla. He adjusted his glasses and peered at her.

"I'm here to see your mother," Arla said. "Is she here?"

"No, I don't think so. But my father is. Would you like to speak to him?"

This was a splendid opportunity to speak to John Remington on his own, Arla realised.

"Yes, certainly."

"Okay," the young man shrugged. "Would you like to come upstairs?"

Arla hid her astonishment. She didn't want to be rude. She should decline, but her sixth sense also told her John would be more comfortable in his own element. It gave her a chance to look at Susan's old room, as well. She asked Rupert if she could.

"I can't see why not," Rupert said. "The room hasn't been used for several years, but it's got some of her old stuff. So I guess you could."

"As long as your parents don't mind. But as it is an ongoing police investigation, I also think we have the right to look through her old room. When did she last use it?"

"Two years ago, I think. Yeah, pretty sure. That's when she got her apartment."

Rupert smiled at her, and she noticed he had a nice, engaging smile. His cheeks dimpled, and he was a handsome man. Although his nerdiness was present, he was tall, and his shyness was kind of cute. Now that she was seeing him closer, she thought he looked familiar for some reason. But she couldn't remember exactly why. Rupert took his glasses off and wiped his glasses on the corner of his shirt. He looked up at Arla.

She stared back at him for a few seconds, hiding the frown on her face. She was now convinced she had seen Rupert recently. But where? He smiled at her, and she grinned back. Maybe he had one of those faces that are common in men, and hence he looked familiar, she thought to herself.

Arla followed him out into the main hallway. The marble tiled floor had been polished, and it glistened as they walked across to the sweeping staircase. It was broad enough for an elephant to walk through. The first-floor landing was similarly wide, and Arla's feet sunk in the carpet as she walked.

"This is Susan's old room," Rupert said, stopping in front of a white door. He turned the handle and stepped inside. The room had cream-coloured walls, with patterned wallpaper over the double bed in the corner. It was a spacious room overlooking the large garden. The bookshelves were almost empty, as was the top of the desk next to the window. The room looked unused, as Rupert had mentioned.

"Is it okay to leave me here?" Arla asked. "I wish to have a quick look then will join you."

"Sure," Rupert smiled. "Shall I knock back again in ten minutes?"

"Thank you," Arla said, grateful he didn't object. She was certain his mother would have, and not for the first time she was glad Sheila wasn't here. However, she did need to ask Sheila about David calling her last week.

Rupert closed the door softly and went out. Arla took out the purple gloves from her pocket. The tabletop had a few centimetres of dust on it. The drawers were sturdy, made of solid oak, and all empty.

She took photos, then lay down to observe the bottom of the desk. No hidden compartments. Nothing stuck to the underside. She got out, then ran her hand down the sides.

Satisfied, she went to the bookshelf and went through the books. Then she approached the bed. Moving the red and yellow floral print covers revealed a dark bedsheet that hadn't been used for a long time. She took photos anyway.

The pillows and bedposts revealed nothing either. She looked under the bed, wishing Harry was here. A couple of old shoe boxes gathered dust. She pulled them out. Inside, she found some old photos. They showed Susan in her younger days, out with friends, and on holidays. She saw some old letters, and one of them was from David. It was a love letter, and he had even written a poem. Arla pulled out an evidence bag and collected the letter and some of the photos, all in separate bags.

A further inspection under the bed showed nothing but dust and old cobwebs. Arla checked along the rear bedposts but again found nothing. Her hopes of getting a breakthrough were fading. It wasn't that surprising. Susan had moved her life out of here and into her new apartment. Arla sighed. Well, it had been worth a try.

She collected the bags and pulled off her gloves. She pushed the chair back into the table. Her ankle twisted slightly, and she stumbled to the wall. She straightened, flexing her ankle with a frown. She really needed to start running again; it had been weeks.

Arla was about to turn around when something caught her eye. Behind the table, in the corner a portion of the carpet was raised.

It was easy to miss as the table effectively covered that corner. She wouldn't have seen it unless she leaned against the wall and deliberately examined the space.

Arla frowned and moved forward.

# CHAPTER 56

She pulled a new pair of gloves on and had to go down on all fours. Even then, the end of the table was flush with the wall, and her hand wouldn't reach. She crept under the table again and had to lie spread eagled on the carpet. Now she could see the area. Clearly, someone had lifted the carpet and then not hammered it down properly.

She stretched out her hand and pulled the carpet. It needed a few hard tugs to come apart. With a puff of dust and a tearing sound, the carpet rose. Arla couldn't see under the carpet.

Space was so constricted that her nose was literally touching the wall and skirting board. She could make out the carpet girders at the corner and floorboards beneath. Her gloved hand brushed the floorboards, but her vision was still restricted.

Cursing and sweating, dust covering her face, Arla backed out on all fours, feeling a little undignified in that position. She went to the rear leg of the table. Kneeling, she put all her weight behind the sturdy leg and pushed. It gave way a little. Inch by inch, she moved the table from the wall corner. She stopped when she had enough space to squeeze between the wall and the table. She was covered in sweat, saline buds of moisture on her forehead, blinding her eyes.

She managed to crouch down in the corner. The floorboard under the carpet was loose. She pulled it, but it didn't budge. She pushed, and her heart skipped a beat when it slid back. Underneath, there was a cavity.

With her face squashed against the rear of the table, she rummaged inside blindly. She felt the rectangular contours of an object. Her fingers gripped the edge, and she pulled. It was a box, and it made a dragging sound as it lifted. Arla was able to pull the box out, then she moved back, gasping, and then collapsed with her back to the wall.

The box was made of hard black cardboard and it was dusty. There was a silver monogram on the  dusty surface, which was ornamental, and circled around the letter R.

She lifted the lid. She found a scroll inside, yellow with age. She unfurled it, laying it flat on the ground. It was a birth certificate. Her eyes widened when she read the name of the new-born.

*Carlson Remington.*

Mother's name – Sheila Remington.

Curiously, the father's name was absent.

The time and date of birth were noted. 9th June, 1984. 0600 hours.

A weight blossomed in Arla's head, and then it burst. Lighting flashed across her mind like over a desert night sky. The flash revealed faces, words, blips, and bits of information, all suddenly coalescing in her mind into a gigantic, shocking realisation.

She knew why Rupert looked so familiar. And why Carlson looked like she had seen him before. Because the two men looked like each other. True, Carlson was black, but his skin colour was light because, she realised now, he was mixed race.

Arla's pulse rate was surging, knocking loudly against her eardrums. She put the birth certificate aside and looked at the box. She found photos. A shockingly young Sheila Remington, sitting in a hospital bed with a baby on her lap. She was smiling for the camera, like a proud new mother. Who took the photo? The father? Or a midwife?

Arla looked at the other photos. Sheila in the sunshine, holding a small baby. The baby had curly black hair, dark caramel skin, and big eyes. The close-ups were unbelievably cute, and Sheila and baby both looked radiant. These were taken in a bedroom, inside an apartment. Behind

Sheila, Arla could see a window and blocks of flats. They looked like London's ubiquitous council buildings.

The photos were yellow and blackened with age, curling and ripping at the corners—a miasma of memories, wisps of a forgotten, forsaken life.

She found a photo where the family posed. A black man with his arm around Sheila as she held the baby. They were sitting on a sofa in a living room that looked plain and simple. She turned the photo around and found nothing.

She heard the sound and glanced up swiftly, dropping the photos. Rupert had come back into the room. He shut the door, then locked it. For a few seconds, he stood there, his back to Arla, facing the door. Then he turned and walked over to her slowly.

He stood over her, looking down at the box's contents and the photos on the carpet. His face was blank, but his eyes large.

"You found it," he whispered. "Where was it?"

# CHAPTER 57

Arla stared at Rupert uncomprehendingly. The shockwaves were still jostling in her mind, making her disorientated, dizzy. She forced herself to focus on his words.

"Found...you were looking for this?"

Rupert licked his lip and nodded. He knelt, folding both knees, bringing himself level with Arla.

"I'm so glad you found it," he whispered.

Arla stared at him, her mind still doing backflips, synapses triggering, firing in her brain.

"But how...how did you know...

"Oh, that. I thought you knew. You see, Susan and Mummy were never close. Susan was into drugs, and that's how she met Carlson. She saw his necklace, and it was the same as hers. They got talking. That's how she found out Carlson was Mummy's son."

He held a finger in the air as Arla listened spellbound. Rupert grimaced, then his shoulders rose briefly.

"Susan was silly. Very silly. She tried to blackmail mummy. Told mummy she would tell her Party that Carlson was her son, and now he was a drug dealer. Silly Susan."

Rupert's voice suddenly became higher pitched, and his head bobbed up and down. He had a strange, childish inflection in his voice – an adult pretending to be infantile.

"Mummy said Carlson wasn't her son anymore, and Susan called her a bitch. That's a bad word. Bad word. Silly Susan," Rupert shook his head, his voice still thin and high, but a vortex of anger clouding his features. His eyes bulged, and his teeth clamped tight.

"Susan said she could also tell the papers about Carlson unless mummy took him back. Susan wanted Carlson to be our brother again. Mummy said no. But Susan wouldn't listen."

Rupert suddenly smiled, and all traces of anger vanished. "Mummy could be the next prime minister. Do you know that? She will be on TV. Like, all the time."

Rupert clapped his hands. Then his face fell. "But Susan wouldn't let that happen. She would tell everyone about Carlson. Then Mummy couldn't be the prime minister because her Party wouldn't support her. Mummy told me, and she cried."

The rage returned, mottling his face. A vein stood in his forehead, throbbing. "So, I told Susan to shut up. But she wouldn't listen to me either."

Arla's mouth was open. A numbness had claimed her body, and she was frozen like a glacier. She tried to move her tongue, but it took several seconds. Her voice croaked.

"What did you do?"

"I took her to the pond," Rupert said, his hand moving inside his pocket. He pulled out a spray can. It was short and squat, and it was covered in black tape, so Arla couldn't see what the label said.

He spoke softly "You know what happened after that?"

Arla swallowed hard, her heart thudding so loudly she thought her ribs would crack.

"You? You did this? You killed Susan? And Madelyn?" Nausea was rising in her throat, her brain still grappling with the revelations.

266

Rupert shrugged like he was discussing the weather. "Yeah, of course. Susan told Madelyn as well because she was her closest friend. So, I had to kill Madelyn, too."

Waves of fear were rolling through Arla, making her vision swim. She felt dazed, unreal, like she was inhabiting someone else's body.

She noticed that when Rupert didn't speak of Sheila, his voice was normal and controlled. She shrank back towards the wall. Rupert watched her closely.

Arla felt inside her pocket, and her fingers gripped her phone. She had to speed dial Harry, and her fingers moved frantically, trying to press the green button from memory, without taking the phone out.

Rupert frowned, and he leaned towards her. Arla folded her knees and rose to her feet, but Rupert was too quick. He lunged forward, his hand closing on her neck. Arla slapped his hand away but couldn't stop him from pinning her against the wall. For a thin guy, he was strong as an ox. His hand found her neck, and she gagged. He slammed her head against the wall, and a red-hot ball of pain exploded in her skull.

She kicked his shin, and he hissed in anger, then hit her in the face. Arla moved towards the bed, but he pulled her back. She heard the spray, then the sickly-sweet smell of a chemical hit her nose. It smeared all over her face, drowning her nose. She recognised the stench of chloroform as her senses succumbed to blackness.

Then she didn't remember anything.

# CHAPTER 58

Harry glanced at his watch and his eyebrows lowered. It was almost eleven am and still no word from Arla. His phone had no messages or missed calls from her. He had called her twice and also left a message. He knew she wouldn't reply if she was taking a statement. But she left the station early, around 8:30 am. She wouldn't be taking a statement for two and a half hours now, would she?

He asked switchboard to call her, and they came back with the same response. Worried now, he got up from his desk and approached Rob.

"You sure she said she was going to the Remington household?"

"Yes, guv." Rob looked at his watch. "She drove down there in a squad car. Should be back here soon. Or maybe she decided to go somewhere else after she finished at the Remington house?"

"Like where?" Harry frowned. "No, this is unlike her. Do me a favour. Call traffic and see if you can pick up her car on CCTV or on the tracker."

All police cars were fitted with GPS and radio trackers. "On it now, guv," Rob said, realising the urgency.

Harry tapped his shiny shoe on the threadbare carpet, wondering what to do. Experience had taught him not to ignore the tingling of his sixth sense. Besides, Arla could be impulsive. If she got a bee in her bonnet, she would pursue it without regard to her own safety.

He made up his mind. He called Johnson and incurred his wrath when he learnt Arla was at the Remington residence.

"I'm worried that she's not back yet. It's been almost three hours, and she's not answering her calls."

That gave Johnson pause. Harry said, "I need to visit the Remington's, sir. Find out what's happening."

"She's probably gone somewhere else," Johnson grumbled, but Harry sensed the hesitation in his voice. Johnson also knew this was unusual. "Okay, check it out. Keep me posted."

Harry ran to the black BMW and drove fast, sirens on full blast. He called Arla a couple more times with the same lack of response. His uneasiness was now nibbling away, making his skin prickly and uncomfortable.

The elderly man opened the door and was startled when Harry literally shoved past him. Harry had already seen Arla's car outside and knew she was here.

"Where is Inspector Baker?" he asked the older man, raising his voice.

The man swallowed and wiped his hands on his dark corduroy trousers. "I must say, Inspector, this behaviour is most unbecoming of you. My mistress...."

Harry grabbed the man's collar and dragged him to within an inch of his face.

"Where is she?" Harry snarled. Blood suffused his face, and he was past caring. If this man wanted to complain about him, he could go right ahead.

"Upstairs," the man croaked. "She went upstairs with Master Rupert."

Harry let go of the man and bounded up the massive staircase. The man rushed after him, shouting. "Sir, you can't go up there! Sir...."

Harry paused at the spacious landing. Several rooms lay on either side, and he wondered which one to tackle first. The first room to his right had a white door that was open.

Inside, he found a solid oak table in the corner by the window. The chair was upturned on the floor, and the table had been moved. In the corner, the carpet was lifted, and a gap in the floorboards was visible. The bedsheet cover was crumpled. Harry knew the signs of a struggle when he saw one, and the hole in the floorboards intrigued him.

A cloying smell accosted his olfactory senses, and he inhaled deeply. His eyes widened. He couldn't be sure, but was that chloroform?

The caretaker was standing by the door, wheezing from the effort of climbing up so rapidly.

"Whose room is this?" Harry demanded.

"Miss Susan's old room," the man said.

Harry looked past the man into the hallway. "Where is Rupert? And the rest of the family?"

"Mrs Remington is away. Mr Remington is in his room, I believe."

Harry stepped forward, balling his fists. "Where is Rupert?"

The man retreated. "I don't know."

Harry brushed past him and into the wide hallway. He shouted Arla's name, but as expected, heard nothing back. He went to every door, wrenching the handles.

They were bedrooms of different sizes, apart from the last door on his right. It opened to reveal a dark, cold space.

It took a few seconds for his eyes to adjust to the darkness, and he was confused by the dusty, dank air that rushed to his face. He switched on his flashlight. Ahead of him, the light beam illuminated a concrete landing, followed by steps going down.

Harry switched on his radio. "DI Mehta speaking. Request two units to the Remington residence." He gave them the address, then ran down the stairs.

# CHAPTER 59

Damp air hit his face, with a musty humid smell typical of basements. Harry descended at a fast pace, taking two steps at a time. There was no light apart from his flashlight. He hoped the batteries were fully charged.

The stairs spiralled down, bending to the left. It wasn't easy going, and several times he almost slipped. There was no banister to hold on to. The stairs were chipped and had mould growing on them. The darkness convoluted around him, dragging him down deeper into its invisible breast.

Harry was forced to slow down. The last thing he wanted was a badly twisted ankle that would stop him. The torch beam picked up flat ground, and he exhaled in relief. It was damp, soft, earth. He heard a sound, and listened to it closely. It sounded like water. To his left, the torch beam revealed a brick wall, decayed by moisture and age. He could only turn right.

Harry set off, running now. It was far easier than the stairs, even with his shoes sinking in the earth. His light beam showed footprints on the ground. He knelt by one and shone his light. It was a size ten- or eleven-man's foot. The prints were deep, like the man was carrying a weight. There was no other reason for the indentation to be deeper than Harry's – and he was taller than most men.

Was the suspect carrying Arla?

Harry suspected it was Rupert. Only he was young and fit enough to carry Arla unless there was another man in the house he didn't know about.

It couldn't be John Remington. And Harry doubted Rupert had any help because there was only one set of footprints.

Harry took some photos, then set off at a faster clip. He had one advantage. Arla would slow down the suspect. She was tall and would weigh him down. His heart lurched in his chest as ominous visions rose up like a nightmare. If Arla was a burden, the suspect would also want to get rid of her.

His torch beam flashed against something on the ground, and he stopped. It was a phone, and when he picked it up, his heart hammered faster. It was Arla's phone. It was out of power, and he couldn't turn it on. Harry pocketed the phone and ran along, faster now, but making sure he didn't lose sight of anything on the floor. The tunnel stretched in a long, thin line into the distance. His beam was swallowed up in the darkness, a trail of light that went nowhere.

The dampness increased, as did the cold. Although he was running, he could feel his hands freezing. The sound of running water was louder, above his head, to the left. Was he under the river? It was possible, as Kensington wasn't far from the Chelsea docks.

He saw the light ahead. It was faint, literally at the end of the tunnel, he hoped, but it was enough to guide him. The light grew brighter. It came through a gate in the distance. Harry increased his pace.

The grill of the gate was as obsolete as the rest of the tunnel, rusty and broken in places. Harry paused, panting. Through the grill, he could see a wider opening, with water rushing through it. The water was shallow, and rubbish clung to the walls of this broader tunnel. The floor was below the gate, and the drop was a couple of metres, at least. Harry realised what he was looking at. It was a sewer, and the tunnel connected to London's famous network of Victorian sewers.

But where was Arla?

He heard a sound behind him and whirled around. But he was too late. A heavy object smashed into his midriff, driving the air from his lungs, forcing him to his knees. Another blow followed to his face, and his head snapped backwards. He could see his assailant in the light, a tall young man holding what looked like a baseball bat. Harry couldn't focus, and he fell, splashing into the water.

# CHAPTER 60

Harry was down, and pain consumed his body. He could barely move his head, and his vision was hazy, rocking around like someone was shaking him. He could make out the silhouette of his attacker standing over him. He stood still observing Harry like he was an interesting specimen in a biology lab.

Harry could still move his limbs, but he felt weak. He twisted his right leg, then folded his knee. Bending sideways, his hands slipped on the water and moved to his ankle. He was searching for the leather scabbard of the knife he always kept strapped to the ankle.

His attacker shifted, following Harry's movements. Harry had to distract him. "Rupert," he whispered. His voice felt like it was coming from a distance. His body was freezing cold and wet, clothes sticking to his skin.

"You won't escape Rupert. My team is on their way. Let us go, and I can make this easier for you."

Rupert knelt on the floor, his face coming closer. "Are you in pain," he whispered.

"Yes. Can't you see ? Where is Arla?"

Rupert paused for a while; his face impassive. The glasses were in place, making his eyes invisible.

"You care about her, don't you? I saw that the first time you came."

"Where is she?"

"Somewhere safe."

"Tell me, Rupert. Please, tell me."

"Wow," Rupert smiled. "You really do care." His face suddenly became serious. He rose to his feet. "It's not good to care about people. That way, you get hurt." Rupert moved to his right, and the object appeared in his hand. It was a long piece of timber, a potent weapon.

"It's time for you to die," Rupert said. "Like the others." He spread his legs, making himself stable. He lifted the weapon up slowly.

Harry grimaced as he twisted his ankle, and his fingers brushed the knife's leather holster. He gripped the butt and pulled, and the knife came free in his hand. In the same movement, Harry jerked sideways, lifting himself on one elbow. The movement was agonising, and he shouted in pain.

But the knife sliced through the air and plunged into Rupert's thigh. Harry leaned on the knife, driving the blow home.

Rupert screamed, and the weapon fell from his hand. He tumbled backwards, his back smashing into the wall. Harry didn't let go of the knife. It remained plunged in the flesh, and Harry used it as leverage to haul himself towards Rupert. He grabbed Rupert's head and banged it against the wall as hard as he could. After two loud thuds, Rupert went limp, but his hands still clawed at Harry's face. Harry brushed them away, but he was so exhausted, he collapsed on top of Rupert.

He breathed heavily, wet clothes and the stench of sewage filling his nostrils. He shoved off Rupert's unconscious body and fell to the floor. His elbows splashed on cold water. He screamed Arla's name. There was no reply. His voice echoed desolately in the tunnel. Pain and regret were storming in his heart. Somehow, he made his legs take his weight, and shakily, he stood. He shouted Arla's name again, only to be answered by an empty echo.

Tears filled his eyes as he realised Arla might not be alive.

# CHAPTER 61

The darkness was inscrutable. A heavy, enclosing weight that obliterated Arla's senses. She couldn't feel or think. But around the edges of the blackness, a tremor started. The tremor spread, compressing inward. It sharpened to a tip, and she felt it strongly now, a pain at the back of her head. Her vision lurched, still almost black, but with photons of circulating light. Photons that coalesced, merged, and grew, dilating into a whiter space. Her eyelids were made of iron. Lifting them took effort. The headache was worse, and it made her feel dizzy, sick.

She forced her eyes open. She couldn't see much, but suddenly, in a nauseating wave, memories of what happened resurfaced in her mind.

*Rupert.*

*Carlson.*

She was fully awake now. She was lying on a wet, hard surface. It was made of bricks, and when she tried to lift herself, she succumbed to a wave of nausea. She placed the flat of her palms on the floor and heaved herself upright. She collapsed against the wall. Her eyes were used to the darkness now. Where was Rupert? He had tried to strangle her, then knocked her out with chloroform. That much she remembered, but she couldn't recall anything after that.

Holding on to the sides of the slimy bricks, she raised herself. In the distance, she heard running water. She was in an alcove, a man-sized hole in the wall. She stumbled out into the main passage. Her vision rocked around, then stabilised. She was in a tunnel. The walls dripped with water, and the ground was slimy. To her right, in the distance, she

276

could see a glow of light. It was faint, but it also allowed her to see. To her left, darkness swallowed up the tunnel. Which way had she come?

She knelt and squinted at the ground. She could see two sets of prints, both about the same size. Two men had walked down here. The prints continued on both sides, and she was still confused about which direction she had come from. Her instinct told her to retrace her steps, and maybe she could get back where she had come from.

Right or left?

She decided to move towards the light. At least she could see better, and if there was a light source, it could also be an exit to outside. But it also exposed her to Rupert. He couldn't be far, she surmised. He would come back to kill her. He wouldn't leave her alive, that she was sure of.

Arla clenched her fists. Her hands patted her clothes. Her phone was gone, and so were her keys and warrant card. She started to move, crouched at the waist. The light was getting brighter. It hurt her eyes, making the splitting headache even worse. Her back and shoulders ached like she had been hit there. But she had to keep moving. Her socks were soaking wet and made a squelching sound on the damp ground.

She came to an abrupt halt when she saw the figure of a man. Yes, it was a man. He was walking rapidly, silhouetted by the light behind him.

Fear blossomed inside her. That was Rupert, coming to finish her off. She didn't have any weapons to fight him with, but he might well be armed.

Had he seen her already? Heart hammering like a piston, mouth dry with adrenaline, Arla spun around, running the other way.

She could hear the man shouting. She didn't care what he was saying, only the fact that his shouts were getting louder. He had spotted her because she could hear his footsteps now, splashing on the ground.

Panic gave Arla wings. Fear propelled her legs to move, and she ran like the wind, her pains forgotten. She didn't know where she was going. The light reduced till she could barely see. But she didn't care. She was looking for a turn or a gap in the wall, somewhere she could hide and attack him.

Her heart almost exploded as she heard his footsteps get closer. She could hear him panting now. He was too fast for her. She tried to run faster, but she was out of breath. She was done. Then she heard his voice again.

She knew that voice. Only one person said her name like that. She stopped and shrank back against the wall, holding hands up to her face. She peered out, and yes, it was true. It was Harry. She burst into tears. Harry's right eye was swollen, and his shirt was ripped. He came forward, and she sank into his arms, sobs shaking her body.

# CHAPTER 62

A rla sat inside the lounge room of the Remington household. Through the glass doors opposite her, she could see the beautifully manicured lawn and the topiaries patterned across it. At the far end, the mature trees were beginning to grow foliage. She had come alone, requesting a visit with Sheila. Arla glanced up as the lady of the house entered.

Sheila was dressed for business as usual, with a graphite coloured business suit, skirt up to her knees, legs bare. But she couldn't hide the bags under her eyes and the bloated nests of her face, which Arla knew was due to the trio of insomnia, alcohol, and sleeping pills. The glitter had gone from Sheila's eyes. She looked dull and vacant, like someone had switched off a light inside.

"How can I help you Inspector Baker?" Sheila's eyebrows rose a fraction.

 Arla had spoken to Sheila at length about the investigation, and the older woman had apologised to Arla for what Rupert had done. Of course, no apology was necessary. Rupert would be in prison for the rest of his life, and a psychiatrist was already assigned to him.

Arla studied her for a few seconds. "You didn't want the family liaison officer." The FLO provided important support to bereaved families, but Sheila had dispensed them.

"I didn't see the need. Your investigation is completed."

"Yes, it is indeed," Arla said reassuringly.

Arla decided to get to the point. "I know you've suffered a terrible tragedy." She held Sheila's eyes, which narrowed a fraction. "But I lost my sister when I was young. To some extent, I know how it feels."

Both of them sat motionless for a few seconds, then Sheila nodded. Words were not necessary. Her grief was more than palpable.

"It's my fault." Sheila wouldn't meet Arla's eyes. She was staring at the carpet, and her mind was a million miles away. "I didn't look after Susan the way I should have. And I gave Rupert too much attention. But I never knew it would come to this."

Sheila's mask had slipped. Arla could see the frail woman inside, shivering and cold in her loneliness. But she also knew Sheila had made choices in her life which had tragic consequences. And she had paid for them.

"We cannot change the past," Arla remarked. How well she knew the meaning of those words. "But we can influence the future."

Sheila looked up at her.

"I know you've lost a son and daughter, but you do have another son."

Sheila exhaled, and a spark returned to her eyes. Her breathing rate increased.

Arla said, "Susan and Carlson had become friends. You know that Carlson is your son. I'm not here to be a counsellor. Or a preacher. I just wanted to say; we only get one chance at this life. I know you have lived your life in the way you think you should. You did the things that were important to you. Everyone does, don't they? But sometimes we have to think of the people around us as well. We should think about what effect our actions have on them."

Arla stood. Sheila was staring at her, her mouth open, her eyes bulging. She didn't speak, and she didn't have to. Arla knew how hard her words had hit home. She didn't care whether anyone had spoken like that to Sheila Remington.

"I'll see myself out." Arla turned on her heels and left.

*****

Harry accosted her as soon as she walked into the open-plan detective's office. Arla was aware that several heads were raised, staring at her. Harry and herself had become heroes in the department after their ordeal. But she knew something else was up. No one would meet her eyes, and she knew that it wasn't good news by the consternation on their faces. Harry got close to her and lowered his voice.

"The top brass are here. In Johnson's office. They want you and me there, sharpish."

Arla swallowed, feeling her prickly discomfort shoot down her spine. After Rupert's arrest, there still hadn't been a media storm. Rupert was in custody, but the Remington family had succeeded in keeping the reporters at bay so far. Only one squad car had turned up to help Harry and Arla. Even the ambulance was refused entry inside the Remington residence. Rob and Lisa helped Arla and Harry walk down the street to get into the ambulance.

Arla ground her teeth together. Enough was enough. If Johnson and his cronies wanted to give her a bashing, they had a surprise in store for them.

"Who's there?"

Harry grimaced. "Johnson and assistant commissioner Deakins, as far as I know. Apparently, there is a third person, but no one seems to know who he or she is."

"That sounds ominous," Arla muttered. She glanced sideways and saw others looking at them.

"Give me five minutes, then let's go up. Best to get it over and done with."

She went to the loo and checked herself in the mirror before coming out. Hair tied back in a ponytail; much more make-up. Her face looked drawn and haggard, and since Rupert's arrest three days ago, she hadn't slept well. She had submitted reports and worked with the media liaison team to do a press release about the capture of a suspect for the murders of Susan and Madelyn. To be fair to Sheila Remington, she had been the only person to get in contact with Arla. There wasn't as much as a peep from the Braithwaite family. Arla straightened her jacket and patted her cheeks to get some blood flowing in them. Then she joined Harry, who was standing outside, leaning against the wall.

"Come in," Johnson's heavy voice sounded across his office door. Arla walked in first, and her step faltered when she saw the third person in the room. It was a stranger. He was seated, and it had seemed curiously large for the rest of his body. He wore thin-rimmed glasses, and his dark, sharp eyes stared at Arla with curiosity. He wore a suit with a dark tie, and he sat easily, hands invisible below the table. His face was lined with age, shaven cheeks. Nick Deakins sat next to the stranger, consulting some papers on his desk. He didn't bother to look up when Arla walked in

"Sir." Arla took a seat opposite the men, followed by Harry.

Johnson didn't waste time. "This is Lord Justice Minister Jeremy Braithwaite."

Arla's breath caught in her chest as she stared at the man. Their eyes locked, and Arla felt a knot of apprehension tightening in her guts. However, she didn't find any hostility in the man's stare. If anything, he seemed relaxed, and there was even a hint of amusement in his eyes.

Johnson continued. "I understand what you've been through, DCI Baker," he said in his pompous, official voice. His eyelids fluttered, and they both knew it was an act. "The Commissioner joins me in congratulating you for solving the case."

"Thank you, sir." She cut her eyes towards Deakins, who was still lost in the paper at hand. She muttered a curse under her breath. Her attention snapped to Lord Braithwaite as he cleared his throat.

"I'd like to echo Commander Johnson's sentiments, obviously." He smiled at Arla. It seemed genuine. "I appreciate it was difficult getting access to the suspects and witnesses, in this case, DCI Baker. And by that, I mean members of my family."

The smile disappeared from his face, but there was still no hostility in his eyes. "Look, as much as I like my nephew, David, I also know he had problems." Lord Braithwaite raised a hand. "I cannot condone his actions, of course. But he is a troubled man, and at least now he's getting the help he needs."

There was silence in the room. Nick Deakins finally looked up from his papers and stared directly at Arla. His thin lips parted in a smile. Or was it a sneer? Arla nodded and didn't look away. "Sir."

Deakins nodded. "DCI Baker." He dropped the papers on the desk and then tapped them with a finger. "Five pages of complaints from the families involved about your conduct, DCI Baker. These papers are from the IPCC. You need to respond to them."

The Independent Police Complaints Commission was a bane of many police officer's lives. Arla had dealt with them in the past.

She wanted to get up, walk over and slap Deakins across the face. Pen pushing, box-ticking, smoothly smiling bureaucrat. Deakins had long forgotten what police work was really like. Every part of his brain moved in a robotic fashion. But something didn't add up. Deakins was still smiling at her, making Arla frown. A deep sense of unease was sprouting inside her like a cactus in a desert.

Lord Braithwaite spoke again. "I have seen the complaints to the IPCC. The majority actually came from my brother, Brian. As you can imagine, I will speak to Brian about this." He looked at Arla and smiled. "You don't have to worry about the IPCC or the complaints."

Arla exhaled, and she could feel Harry do the same. Lord Braithwaite moved his chair back and crossed his legs. Authority sat easily on his shoulders. He was mild-mannered, and his voice gentle, but the power in his words was unmistakable.

"You ruffled a lot of feathers, but the golden birds you are dealing with had a lot at stake."

Arla was amazed at his words. Finally, here was a man saying it like it was.

"Susan, God bless her departed soul, had her own issues, as you know. She had a difficult relationship with Sheila, and I believe Sheila and David spoke to each other about it. This happened after David got involved with Susan again. As Sheila was going for the general secretary role in the party, it was imperative she came across as squeaky-clean."

Arla found her voice. "And having a drug-dealing criminal son wouldn't exactly do any favours for that squeaky-clean image."

Lord Braithwaite looked thoughtful. "Certainly not. But you must understand, they were only doing what was expedient. There was no foul play."

Arla merely nodded, keeping her thoughts to herself. The only foul play had been with Carlson's life. And Susan and Madelyn had paid for it with their own. But at least, the real culprit was now behind bars.

"I hope this matter is now concluded, DCI Baker," Lord Braithwaite said. Arla narrowed her eyes, trying to discern the meaning of his words. Then she understood. Lord Braithwaite was asking her to leave his family alone.

She nodded, feeling relief more than anything else. "Yes, sir, it is."

Lord Braithwaite smiled wider this time. "It's a pleasure meeting you."

# CHAPTER 63

*One week later*

The windswept sky was startlingly blue, and the lazy sailboat of white clouds moved across it as if on parade. Spring had indeed arrived, bringing with it a mellowness that seeped into the earth. Sunbeams pierced the new green boughs and illuminated the cemetery.

Arla, Harry, and Wayne Johnson stood at the rear of the service. It was Susan Remington's funeral, and Arla had been surprised when they were invited.

Harry and herself had arrived early, and they stood below the shade of a tree, watching the procession of cabinet members and other VIPs whose faces were recognisable. The cemetery was under lockdown, the branch of the Met that looked after the security of important people was in operation. Despite showing their warrant cards at the gate, both Arla and Harry had been searched before they were allowed in.

The vicar read from the book, and in the still spring air, Arla could hear little sniffs and choked sobs. They punctuated the vicar's speech. The Remington's extended family was large, and by the number of uncles, aunts, and cousins who had gathered, it was evident Susan had been a popular family member. Her friends were also here, as were Madelyn West's parents.

Arla had been introduced to them by Sheila Remington. Sheila was still her usual prim self, but her face was gaunt, cheeks sunken with a fractured, lost look in her eyes. She had now lost both son and daughter, and despite her brief front, Arla could see she was crumbling inside. For the first time, she felt pity for the woman. She also knew Sheila wouldn't hear of it. Women like her believed they could rise above anything.

But Arla knew better. When she had leaned close, she got the smell of alcohol from Sheila's breath. Maybe she had taken a few sleeping pills as well. Nights without sleep, tortured by guilt and remorse, were pure hell, and Arla knew it because she had lived through it. She had given Sheila her card and asked her to call if she needed any help.

"... And dust we are, and to dust return. Amen."

The congregation murmured the last word, and fresh flowers were thrown into the grave. Arla didn't get the opportunity, just as she never had the opportunity to know Susan in real life. A knot of emotion gathered in her throat. Such was her duty. Her days were spent wandering about the dead, imagining their final days on earth. The best she could do was get closure for her near and dear ones. And she had done that for both Susan and Madelyn.

That gave her professional satisfaction, but on a personal level, she also felt the family's pain.

Harry's long arm came around her shoulders and pulled her into him. When she glanced up, he was looking straight ahead, his face impassive. He knew what she was thinking, and she was glad he was here.

Arla blinked, her mind wandering to the fall out from the case.

David Braithwaite's career and reputation were in ruins, but he was a free man. He needed a psychiatrist and a lot of treatment to get rid of his controlling behaviour and violent impulses. He was truly remorseful, and Arla hoped he would rectify his personality.

She hadn't heard from Carlson, and that wasn't surprising. Given the murky world he inhabited for a living, he would like to keep his distance from Arla. But Susan had been his half-sister. Carlson had genuinely cared for her, hence his anger when she was taken from him.

The service came to an end, and they would now attend the church ceremony. Sheila had prepared a statement, and so had a couple of

Susan's cousins. As they walked off, Arla saw a figure standing on his own. He was dressed in a black suit, and he was conspicuous for being the only black man in the cemetery. She recognised Carlson's features as she came closer. He straightened when he saw Harry and Arla.

"Yes, I was invited," Carlson said, reading the question in their eyes. Before Arla could let out a flustered reply, Harry spoke.

"How did Sheila get your number?"

Carlson shrugged. "I guess she had it from Susan. I got a text, as she didn't know my address."

Arla wanted to ask why he was standing so far at the back, but she knew the answer. People like Carlson stayed in the shadows. It was sad because his life should have been so different. However, it was encouraging that Sheila had made contact with him. After all, it was long overdue.

A sad smile played on Carlson's lips.

"The woman who raised me felt like my real mother, but she wasn't. When she died, she told me the truth. This cross I wear," he lifted the heavy pendant which Arla now knew was worn by every member of the Remington family. "This was left to me by my biological mother. Sheila. That's pretty much all I got from her, till she called me last week."

Harry said, " You knew nothing about your extended family until you met Susan."

"Correct. It was pure chance. She saw the cross on my neck, and I guess my whole life changed that day."

"Did your mother not tell you who your biological mother was?"

Carlson shrugged. "It was just a name. There's lots of Sheila Remington's out there. I never looked, as I never cared." He smiled again. "No one cares about me; that's why I'm standing here, at the back."

# CHAPTER 64

Arla was at work the next day when there was a knock on her door. She had the pleasure of looking forward to being duty SIO for the next week. Like a hole in the head, she muttered to herself. She felt she deserved a break after the stress of the last ten days.

Rosslyn poked her head in. "There's a gentleman at the desk to see you." Rosslyn couldn't hide the surprise in her voice. "From the Conservative party office."

"What?" Arla frowned.

Rosslyn held the door open for her, Arla thanked her and walked down to the main reception. A middle-aged man, wearing a suit, and looking uncomfortable as he sat facing a couple of Rastafarians getting booked in, rose hastily to his feet when he saw Arla.

"DCI Baker?" He asked, hopefully.

"Yes. How can I help you?"

Rather mysteriously, the man pulled an envelope from his breast pocket and handed it to Arla without a word. She opened it to find thick white paper with Sheila Remington's name embossed on it. She wanted to see Arla. She apologised for it being late notice and promised not to take too much of Arla's time.

"The car is waiting outside," the man, whose name Arla still didn't know, said courteously.

Arla looked him over carefully. He was wearing a working suit, nothing too flash. But still, she had to be careful.

"Can I please see your ID?" Arla asked casually.

"Of course," the man produced his photo ID card. This was from the Conservative party office, and his name was James Grisham. He was Sheila Remington's secretary, no less.

Arla knew the card wasn't a forgery. She spoke to the duty sergeant at the desk to inform Harry and her team about where she was going. The duty sergeant's face became alarmed at the prospect of Arla going back to the Remington household. Arla grinned at him.

"Don't worry, Dan. There's no danger there anymore."

The car turned out to be a Rolls-Royce. Arla had never been in one before. Mr Grisham held the door open for her. Twice in one day, Arla thought with a smile. She must be going up in the world. The red leather seats were firm and comfortable, and there was enough space for her to put her feet up. The 4.5 L, V8 engine purred to life, then with a growl, zoomed down the street. It took them 20 minutes, and Arla used that time to exchange a few texts with Harry. Both of them wondered what could be so important. Harry was worried and said he was on standby, by which Arla knew he would be waiting outside when her meeting with Sheila was over.

The usual elderly man opened the door and took Arla to the same lounge. She stopped short at the entrance. Sheila Remington was sitting there, but Arla didn't expect to see Carlson there too. They both stood when they saw Arla.

"Please come in," Sheila said.

Arla sat down, returning the smile that Carlson flashed at her.

Sheila said, "I thought about our discussion. You're right; we only get one chance at this life." She turned to look at Carlson, and the two of them exchanged a glance. Then Sheila's head dropped, and she took a deep breath.

"When I was young, I did things that all young people do. I went out partying, took drugs. Much like my daughter, I suppose." She smiled ruefully.

"It's weird how strong the demand for narcotics is in middle-class households."

Arla nodded. "The drug squad is always raiding posh homes in nice neighbourhoods like yours. Sounds surprising, but true."

"Anyway," Sheila continued. "I met Carlson's dad in the same way that Susan met Carlson. It's strange how life sometimes comes full circle."

She closed her eyes and clasped her hands firmly on her lap. She held them till her knuckles turned white. Carlson was staring at her intently, and Arla knew this was difficult for Sheila. She gave her time.

"When I got pregnant with Carlson, I was up and coming in the party. My family was supporting me. I was the next big thing. At the same time, I had just become a mother. But I couldn't disclose it to anyone. I was living a double life."

Her voice broke into a whisper. "And God forgive me, but I chose my job over my son. What I did was wrong. So wrong. And now, I've paid for it."

She covered her face with her palms and broke down. Her shoulders shook as she sobbed. Carlson reached out and touched Sheila's arm. It warmed Arla's heart to see Sheila reach down and entwine her fingers with Carlson's.

Arla felt a familiar pressure behind her eyes. Sheila was getting a second chance at life. Not everyone got that opportunity; Arla knew from experience.

As she watched mother and son reunited after all these years, she felt a loosening in the strands of her being, a surrender to the simple but enduring bonds of love.

Sheila would never get back what she lost, but just like Arla had discovered with Nicole's arrival, the hope of a new life would nourish her heart again.

*THE END*

Made in the USA
Columbia, SC
09 December 2022

73258692R00178